MYSTERY

ANGEL EYES

Alanna Knight

Chivers Press • Thorndike Press
Bath, England   Thorndike, Maine USA

This Large Print edition is published by Chivers Press, England, and by Thorndike Press, USA.

Published in 1998 in the U.K. by arrangement with Severn House Publishers Ltd.

Published in 1998 in the U.S. by arrangement with Chivers Press Ltd.

U.K. Hardcover ISBN 0–7540–3371–6 (Chivers Large Print)
U.K. Softcover   ISBN 0–7540–3372–4 (Camden Large Print)
U.S. Softcover   ISBN 0–7862–1480–5 (General Series Edition)

The text of this Large Print edition is unabridged.
Other aspects of the book may vary from the original edition.

Set in 16 pt. New Times Roman.

Printed in Great Britain on acid-free paper.

British Library Cataloguing in Publication Data available

Library of Congress Cataloging-in-Publication Data

Knight, Alanna.
      Angel eyes / Alanna Knight.
         p. cm.
      ISBN 0–7862–1480–5 (lg. print : sc : alk. paper)
      1. Large type books.   I. Title.
    [PR6061.N45A84   1998]
    823'.914—dc21   98-6682

*For Elizabeth and Dick Warfel, Sedona,
Arizona; Barbara and George Wood, Riverside,
California for their loving friendship and warm
hospitality.*

Author's Note

I have long been fascinated by the American Southwest and among numerous books read over many years and on many visits, the following have played their part in creating this book: L P Bailey *The Long Walk* (1988); Dee Brown *Bury my Heart at Wounded Knee* (1970); J Lee Correll *Through White Man's Eyes* (1979); Natalie Curtis *Songs and Legends of the American Indian* (1907); Hiram C Hodge *Arizona As it Was* (1965); Clyde Kluckhohn *Navajo Witchcraft* (1989); Frank McNitt *Anasazi* (1957); T C McLuhan *Touch the Earth* (1971) (quotes on pp 135 & 209); Se Tewa *Indian Love Letters* (1972); Dick Sutphen *Sedona: Psychic Energy Vortexes* (1985); A E Thompson *Story of Sedona* (1975); Ruth M Underhill *The Navajo* (1956). Last but not least Douglas Preston's superb *Talking to the Ground* (1995).

I am also indebted to my good friend Barbara Wood for permission to quote from her novel *The Prophetess* (Little, Brown 1996) and to Patricia Harrington, Librarian, Scottsdale.

Finally, the idea of this story evolved from family speculations concerning the origins and identity of my sea captain great-grandfather's mysterious 'Spanish' bride (brought back from

a voyage to America in the 1880s). The rest is
fiction . . .

CHAPTER ONE

PROLOGUE: 1880

*I fled Him, down the nights and down the
  days;*
I fled Him, down the arches of the years;

FRANCIS THOMPSON,
The Hound of Heaven

Save my Ma, please save my Ma.

They were the last words the Child ever spoke as Sacramento's most notorious whorehouse dissolved into flames and toppled like a house of cards. The Child's mother had thrown her down to the waiting firemen before making a last valiant attempt to reach one of the girls still trapped screaming in the bedroom.

As the flames spread and gobbled up the more respectable prim-faced frame houses, the whole street disintegrated—a blazing torch against the night.

The local preacher's wife on her way home from a prayer meeting saw the Child wandering about alone and bewildered, occasionally rushing towards the sparking timbers, everyone too busy to pay her the slightest attention. Who was she? Heads were shaken and, picking her up, the preacher's wife carried her to safety. Kind hands soothed, placed her in a bed alongside other small children who woke up screaming that she smelt of sulphur, crying for Papa to come and cast the devil out.

As for the Child, exhausted by pain and weeping, she pretended this was just another of the bad dreams that had haunted her life since babyhood. She closed her eyes. Soon she would wake up in Ma's soft arms with her anxious face smiling, reassuring.

She had inherited Ma's nervous fears that everywhere they were being followed by 'Them'. Them; a faceless word for that band of dedicated savages who would kill Ma and take her away. That was all she knew of Them, a word that filled her waking hours with terror and which as far back as she could remember, had been part of their nightmare flight from one town to the next. Any place where they could hide, exhausted, hungry and cold at night, until Ma gathered strength to look for work.

First of all it had been teaching, then sewing, then working in saloons. Ma would take anything, however degrading, to keep them alive, to keep her child safe, always hopefully putting a few dollars aside to buy them passage on a ship from California, to take them far away across the sea into another world.

We'll be safe then, child. Safe from Them.

Never free from anxiety, always glancing

nervously over her shoulder; anyone who stared at Ma in the street or smiled, might be one of Them.

On the morning after the disastrous fire, the Child found waking up was worse than any dream. She tried to call out for Ma. Over and over. But although the words sounded clear in her head and tears of frustration poured from her eyes, not one sound could she make. Memory was all she had now. She had never been to school, for in those early days of their flight when Ma was teaching she was still a baby. Besides, even when they stayed in one place long enough, Ma was terrified to let her out of her sight. It seemed to the Child that, day and night, Ma kept a tight and painful grip on her hand.

The Schwarz family, new German immigrants with a farm four miles out of Sacramento, had been visiting the local preacher on the night of the fire. Gratefully he and his wife had accepted their offer to care for this child whose presence so upset their own little brood.

Herr and Frau Schwarz were kind but mystified. Their command of English being somewhat hazy they thought she didn't understand their questions. Who was she? Where did she come from?

You must have a name, liebchen.

The Child just stared at them blankly.

There was a name, a strange, long name, but

3

she had never seen it written down and couldn't remember it. It wasn't until she fell in the yard and hurt her hand and couldn't cry out that Frau Schwarz realised there was more than shock or cussedness involved. But whether she had been dumb from birth, no survivors from the whorehouse remained to tell her story.

So they wisely decided it was the good Lord's will that such associations should be forgotten and they prayed earnestly that she might never remember any of it.

They called her Trudy, after their last baby who had died. Their surviving daughter, Constance, hated her, jealous of all the attention diverted from her; the spoilt only child. She vented her fury on this intruder. Constance was sly, all sweetness and caring cuddles when her parents were present but the Child learned to dread the times when they were alone and she could neither protest nor scream at being cruelly punched and beaten.

Tortured, tormented, heartbroken over the loss of her mother, the day came when she resolved to make her way back to the place where she was born.

The place of the red rocks.

The red rocks had been calling to her ever since she could remember. A voice inside her head that eternally whispered, like some unseen force driving her. But the Child had always known that some day she must obey that

4

voice, that she was powerless to resist, despite Ma's attempts to escape from the savage Them and their relentless pursuit. Now that she was helpless to speak, the voice seemed to get stronger, and on bad days, it cut out all other sounds, the gentle whisper became an angry bullying, insistent that she obey.

She made her plans carefully with an ingenuity and inspiration that came to her as if some much older, wiser person inside her was giving precise instructions and directions. Perhaps it was Ma's spirit, she thought wistfully, staring into the night, as if by looking long enough at those bright stars she could penetrate the thin veil of death that separated them. Often sick with loneliness, smarting under Constance's cruel blows, she would sob, tears streaming down her face in a terrible noiseless cry that echoed in the depths of her soul.

It was the sound of trains, the 'whoo-hoo' as they thundered by to San Francisco that gave her the idea. She had no money for a ticket but a sudden clear picture came into her mind of how, travelling so often with Ma in their flight, she had observed lots of other children accompanied by grown-ups. No questions were ever asked of them, nor tickets demanded, only an indulgent smile from the collector, a pat on the head. Putting on the hand-me-down cape and bonnet donated by one of the parishioners and rejected by Constance, she slipped out of

5

the frame house and went down to the railroad depot where the train grunted and snorted like a resting animal for a while each night.

She imagined that she had slipped out unobserved, but Constance had heard her get up and dress and now watched her from the window. Guessing that she had succeeded in driving her hated rival away, she was jubilant. Tomorrow morning, she would feign shocked surprise, perhaps manage to squeeze out a tear or two. But never, never would she tell her parents what she had seen in case they resolved to go in search of the runaway and bring her back.

The Child stepped aboard the train following closely on the heels of a family with a brood of five and a tiny babe in arms. Once inside, she slipped away to join the less affluent passengers in the overcrowded carriages where she was safe—one of many children who ran about, playing and shouting. So far she had managed to stay one step ahead of the ticket collector who might demand to know where her parents were. She looked out of the window, trying to penetrate the darkness, imagining that daylight would reveal the train heading towards a horizon of red hills, the red rocks that called to her.

At last, tired and hungry, the train's motion threatened to lull her to sleep. But sleep would be dangerous. Already her presence was being commented upon by the woman whose family group she had joined. The woman had taken pity on her anguished expression as she passed a basket of food around and had given her bread and cheese. Never had food tasted so good.

Watching her devour it so ravenously, the woman asked, 'Where are your ma and pa, honey?'

The Child smiled and pointed towards the next carriage. The woman nodded indulgently, satisfied that she had only come looking for a seat, for little companions to play with.

'Rest comfy then.'

She hadn't realised that stowing away could be accomplished so easily. With darkness came the sounds of the night. Inside the train the passengers' snores became one with the throb of the engine, to be overtaken by the insistent throbbing of ancient drums that stirred her blood.

She was home at last. Her inheritance was waiting.

Stirring happily, expecting to see the red rocks, beckoning, welcoming, as they did in dreams, she opened her eyes to a completely different sight: the bustle of a huge, echoing train station.

Porters were yelling, 'San Francisco, folks. All change. San Francisco . . .'

She climbed onto the seat. She had come too far west, taken the wrong train. Panic seized her. Jumping down she attached herself to the family with young children heading towards the barrier on the now almost empty platform.

The woman turned, pointed. 'Go find your folks, little girl. You'll get lost,' she warned sternly.

She watched them go and stood shivering in the early morning light, looking for yet another family who would get her past the ticket collector at the barrier. To her horror she saw only couples or single travellers, not one with children.

A tall man breezed by wearing a bright waistcoat. A gentleman like the ones who patronised the Desert Flower. He saw her tearful expression and smiled, tipping back his silk hat. 'Well, what have we here. You lost, little girl? Where's your folks?'

She couldn't tell him, she just stared, shook her head. He seemed to understand.

'Hungry?'

She nodded vigorously this time.

'We'll soon settle that. Come along.'

Gratefully she took his hand and followed him into a saloon outside the station. Afraid at first, she drew back as he opened the door. Then she took comfort from the familiar smells of beer, cigars and stale perfume that brought bad nostalgic memories of Ma and the girls of the Desert Flower.

As she ate, the man watched her, the kind, smiling expression in his eyes held something shrewd and calculating, the way she'd seen men

8

look at Ma and the girls. It made her feel uncomfortable although she didn't know why.

The next moment it was gone and the gentleman asked, 'How old are you, honey?'

She shrugged, held out both hands, fingers outstretched.

'Ten?' He laughed. 'You look mighty pretty and ladylike for ten.'

Her rescuer was a gambler, Mike O'Hara, and she stayed with him for two years.

She learned not to mind the things he did to her in bed at night because he was kind to her, kinder than anyone she had ever met. He never lost his temper, she had lots to eat and, for the first time in her life, pretty gowns to wear. Besides she soon got used to his behaviour, long accustomed to witnessing the extraordinary things men and women did with each other for pleasure and in Ma's case, although she often wept afterwards, for money.

As for Mike, he recognised the inborn grace of this little dumb child whom his saloon girls christened Orphan Annie. He noticed how she loved to dance to the piano player's tunes with a natural sense of rhythm. He decided to invest in some proper dancing lessons and put her in Indian dress. She was either part Indian or Mex and she would be perfect in the role she assumed, as if she had been Indian dancing all her life.

The other girls, much older, scantily and seductively dressed, were intrigued by her

9

novelty. They petted and tolerated her since she was as yet no threat to them, belonging exclusively to Mike.

The atmosphere of the Lucky Shamrock made her feel at home. Sometimes, closing her eyes, she could pretend to be back with Ma but without the nagging terror of being pursued by the mysterious Them. As for that voice from the red rocks inside her head, she told it firmly, yes, when she was older and had saved enough money for the fare she would return.

'I promise. One day—I promise.'

Growing into womanhood, the voices grew fainter and no longer troubled her. Her dancing improved, bolder now and more sexual. Her clothes, scantier and more seductive, dismayed the saloon girls. Alarmed that men now wanted her, yesterday's 'little pet' became today's potential rival.

Worse was to happen. Mike, who had been her protector, her lover and friend, was shot dead in a bar-room brawl. She knew then her own danger. The veiled glances among the sisterhood of whores said plainly that they planned to get rid of her. There would be no more dancing, only a return to that, now distant, memory of childhood pinching and punching. She would become their slave to torment, with only the fading older whores no longer eagerly sought by the men, to protect her.

One of the older women, Milly, had a

terrible row over stealing money from one of the new girls. The sheriff was called in and she left in a hurry. Annie, long billed as Girl Dancing Bear (a pun devised by Mike), went with her.

They found a place on the outskirts of town where they would be safe from the law, but it was soon evident that Milly was a sick woman and the cough that kept them both awake at night wasn't going to get any better. Annie decided that she would dance to earn enough money to buy medicines for her sick friend. But the idea scared Milly. She might be followed. And what would become of Annie if Milly went to jail? Who would look after her until she found a decent man to protect her?

Annie listened to her arguments and decided there was only one alternative, but she didn't like sleeping with men for money. Mike had been different, special. But strange men could be cruel, might hurt her. So, on the day after Milly died, she found another saloon on the town's Tenderloin and tried not to think of the future of a dancer in a whorehouse as she did her wild Indian dance on the table, to tumultuous applause and the drunken lunges of lust-crazed men.

She was young, beautiful—or so her mirror and the men who desired her told her—but she had seen what happened to other saloon girls, how quickly they aged and their looks faded. Such were her thoughts as her feet moved

11

faster, ever faster, inventing new steps, new provocative movements. The knowledge came from somewhere deep inside her being, and she remembered Ma telling her that she had inherited her looks and her grace from her Indian father who had died in a gunfight before she was born.

One night there was a handsome sea captain with yellow hair drinking alone at the bar. He looked sad and she smiled at him. When she took him up to her room she discovered that he was kind and gentle with her, like Mike had been. She guessed that he was lonely too, seeking only the gratification of a woman to hold close in his arms, even if it was only pretend love bought by the hour.

After it was finished, he lay back on the pillows and talked to her about his family who lived far away in that same wild country across the oceans of the world where Ma had been born. The safe place that had been Ma's goal for herself and her child.

The sea captain had one advantage over other men: she could talk to him. He had traded with Indians and also understood sign language. It didn't bother him that she was dumb, for she was the most beautiful creature he had ever beheld as well as the first woman he had made love to, or even wanted, since his wife died three years ago.

When, a week later, he indicated that he must return to his ship, she cried tearfully but soundlessly. They would never meet again, and this was harder to bear than losing Ma or Mike.

He stood at the bottom of the bed, his hands gripping the brass rail, watching her. He couldn't leave her, not to this kind of life, for he guessed she was still little more than a child.

He was a man of sudden decisions. Often his life had depended on it. He made one now. He would take her back with him to Scotland and invent some story about a Spanish girl captured by Indians for his young family and shocked relatives.

He took off his wedding ring and put it on her thumb. They were married in San Francisco that afternoon, two hours before his ship sailed.

*   *   *

The savages, the murderers Ma called 'Them', arrived just as the ship left harbour. They watched helplessly, then one of them pointed. Yes, there was their quarry. The Child, now a woman, was standing on the deck beside the yellow-haired Anglo. Perhaps she saw them too for it seemed that, shading her eyes, she looked straight at them.

The riders had come so far, trailed her so long only to be thwarted now. Hundreds of miles they had travelled, mostly on stolen horses, riding one lot to death and then stealing another. It was the simplest and fastest way to travel, the only one they knew.

They first found the trail in Phoenix where the woman had borne the child. Then both had vanished. Countless shack towns from Arizona to California had followed, all with evidence of a white woman and the sacred child who bore the Talisman of the Anasazi, the lost tribe of the Atalos.

It came naturally to them to track anything, anyone, in desert or canyon. However, they were unprepared for the detritus of the white man's town where trails disappeared completely, confusion everywhere. Soon they were lost, bewildered, deprived of the simple elements of their existence. Tracks vanished under houses and rutted roads. The noises and noxious stenches of the white man's civilisation sickened them, making them feel perpetually unclean. But still they refused to acknowledge defeat and by the merest of chances picked up the trail again in Sacramento. Knowing they were near, they searched street by street, finally house by house, watching who came and went, only to learn that once again they were too late. Disaster had struck, the white woman had died in a fire. Her fate did not concern them. She would have been killed anyway when their quest ended.

That quest was by no means over for although the Sacred Child had disappeared she still lived. The Talisman still existed. It called, beckoned to them, ever onward, onward.

Painstakingly they sought out other Indians who might be sympathetic or could be made to fear the power of the medicine men of the Anasazi. By cajoling or threats, information had been received, new trails followed.

Many moons had come and gone and if they could have measured time by the white man's calendar, it would have run into several years. Now at last their quest was nearing its end.

The Child was within their grasp. Drunk on success, they had thrown wide the doors of the Lucky Shamrock dance hall, determined to kill the white man who held her. Even if she were a willing prisoner, the feelings of a woman who had given herself to a white man made no difference.

Again they were too late. The man was dead. They saw a poster of an Indian dancer. Told it was Girl Dancing Bear and furious at this blasphemy, they tore it down and carried it with them into every whorehouse to brandish before the frightened occupants.

At last the words, 'Yes, we know her. She was here—she'll be upstairs—'

But she wasn't. She had left hours before to marry a rich white man, a sea captain sailing on the afternoon tide. They rode like the wind to the harbour, in time to see the ship heading off the edge of the world.

Silently they watched until the full-masted ship disappeared into the sea, off the face of the earth which they knew ended at the

15

horizons where water and sky meet. Beyond that faint line all things vanished from the Indian world. The Talisman was powerless now, lost to them for ever.

So be it. The Great Spirit had so willed. They were courageous men, not easily defeated. They had given their lives to the quest; more moons had passed than they could count and of the twelve medicine men who started now only five remained. Seven had died, claimed by old age, sickness or fallen to the white man's bullets.

Huddled in their blankets, they turned the heads of their stolen horses once more towards the south-west and the long journey that lay before them back to the red rocks they called home.

*   *   *

When the Captain and his new bride arrived in Scotland, the stunned faces of his children were hard to bear. They were older than their stepmother and he was too embarrassed to try to explain to his eighteen-year-old son his own needs as a man. That, dammit, he was only just past forty and still vigorous in every way. But they thought of him as an old man.

The village added shock to curiosity when he escorted her to the kirk that first Sunday. The minister felt that the sight of a woman so exotically pagan in their midst was vaguely

16

improper and blasphemous. Especially as his carefully prepared sermon from the book of Jeremiah was lost on the congregation whose heads turned constantly in eager curiosity towards the Captain's new bride.

The minister also suspected that the enchanting face with the unnerving eyes of a savage idol was probably in urgent need of Christian teaching. He decided then and there that it was his duty to further God's work by greeting her in his loudest and heartiest voice, dating from his youthful days as a missionary in darkest Africa.

As for the congregation, they wanted to know, 'Why d'ye ken she didna' sing the psalms? Probably doesna' speak the language, puir heathen woman.'

The Captain never discussed with anyone the fact that his beautiful wife was dumb. He had great hopes that one day happiness and security would bring her voice back. Already a dreamer of dreams, by the end of the year he hoped for another son. In the meantime, he could not bear to be parted from her and in anticipation of the birth, he sent his beloved ship away under a temporary command. Sometimes he thought that once the child was born he wouldn't want to leave either of them and even toyed with the mad idea of having his wife go to sea with him once the boy was older.

Their days and nights were happy together, brief in time but in the measure of love, everlasting. They walked in the nearby glen and saw the golden eagle who had his eyrie up on the crag. The Captain's wife was enchanted and clapped her hands. A good omen? They walked a little way hand-in-hand, she rushed forward, picked up a feather, and he anchored it in her thick black hair. A gift from the eagle. What did it mean?

He saw fear furrow her brow as she told him that this was a sign. A sign from her own people. They were calling to her, willing her to return to them.

'What nonsense,' he said, holding her tightly to him. 'You belong to me now. To my world— this world.'

Blinking back the tears, fully aware that she could never be that she shook her head.

'Someday,' he said softly stroking her hair and misunderstanding her distress. 'Someday, the folk here will accept you. Just you wait and see.'

But mostly the Captain didn't look ahead. The future seemed vague and veiled and he wanted only this blissful present of being with her every moment, begrudging even the hours of sleep that took her from him in spirit. Sitting by the stream with her head resting on his shoulder, her lips upturned to his, her eyes, so beautiful, of a strange and luminous amber— this was true happiness.

He knew he was very lucky with every man's dream of a good wife, loving and obedient. Only once had she defied him, he would tell his drinking friends when loneliness and an excess of rum overcame his normal reticence. And he would produce that wedding photograph. Taken in Glasgow on their way home, he would recall that she had been terrified rather than angry, tears rolling, hands trembling, as in sign language she warned him that the image would steal her soul, take her from him for ever.

He had laughed. 'It is only a photograph. Everyone has photographs these days, even the Queen of England.'

But obstinately she had shaken her head. No good would come of it.

'Listen, you are so beautiful,' he had said. 'So beautiful that I want to keep the image of you at this one moment for ever. Do it for me, to make me happy. I will see that no one steals you from me. I am big and strong, a good husband. I will protect you.'

She had smiled through her tears and did as she was bid. But the evidence of her fear remained, to look down the years and haunt the generations who were to know her as Donna Anna, the 'Spanish bride'.

The time of the birth drew nearer. Confident that all would be well, the Captain discovered that his beloved young wife was dying.

He kissed her, sobbing. 'Don't leave me, don't leave me!' He turned helplessly, yelling at the doctor who was trying to get his new daughter to breathe, 'Save the mother, damn you, save the mother.'

They laid the now crying babe at her side, and her eyes opened briefly for she knew it would live, this child who had cost so much and who carried the Talisman.

But her mission was over and, as the Captain clasped her to his heart for the last time, she looked towards the eagle's feather in a vase at the bedside. As the brightness of her eyes slowly faded he remembered that to her people the placing of an eagle feather in the hands of the dead guided them safely into the presence of the Great Sprit.

Gently he lifted her fingers and placed the feather between them. But she had gone from him, her eyes already focussed on a far distant future where a great gleaming iron bird came roaring out of the blue skies to land at the place of the red rocks.

A young boy stepped out of its belly.

His name was Luke Fenner.

CHAPTER TWO

And so it came to me the true meaning of The Way—for it is not the way forward, but the way back to the beginning.

BARBARA WOOD, The Prophetess

Chay Bowman watched the plane's slow

descent towards the airport of Red Rock. He had been delayed by road works and a long line of traffic on the narrow highway. The passengers were already walking across the airstrip as he parked the car.

There was no one answering the description of the drug pusher. His informant had been wrong, his journey a waste of time. He continued to scan the arrivals as they vanished inside waiting cabs or private limousines, priding himself that he could guess their occupations from how they dressed, their luggage, and how they walked. It was easy to tell the well-seasoned commuters who could afford expensive houses in Blackhawk Creek from first-time tourists—like that girl with the young boy at her side, last across the tarmac.

No. Not a girl. His first glance had been wrong. This was a woman, thirty maybe, the boy about twelve, probably her son. Good-looking, he thought, surveying her through narrowed eyes, even if she was an Anglo. Long ripe corn hair, tall, slim, but her manner distinctly apprehensive. Now, what the hell was she afraid of?

Yep, this was her first visit, perhaps even her first long-distance flight. Obviously her fears were concerned with someone she expected to see in the car park, and she passed so close by him, that he smelt her perfume, soft, floral. Pretty nice.

'He isn't here,' he heard her say to the boy;

she sounded annoyed rather than scared as she looked around. 'If he doesn't turn up, we'll have to take a cab. Yes, dear, I know you're tired . . .'

They moved out of earshot. Her accent had been English. Only the rich Brits came by Red Rock en route to the gaming tables at Vegas or to escape cold winters in Sun City.

Golden Hair didn't look rich, jeans and a shirt, no jewellery or make-up. Definitely not the affluent kind showing off with designer-labelled suitcases. She and the boy had a backpack and a modest holdall each and were toting Duty Free carriers.

The boy's hair was pale enough for an albino, Chay thought, watching them as they anxiously surveyed every vehicle that came into the car park.

Curious to see what happened to them, who they might be meeting, Bowman lingered. Curiosity was his job, the satisfaction of solving any mystery however trivial, or was it just because this was a good-looking woman, desirable, the kind he'd enjoy being around. The kind his Indian forebears had taken prisoner from the pioneering wagons crossing the desert, selling the best-looking women and female children to the Mexicans in return for rifles to carry on the war against the white soldiers. Men, old women and babies were speedily despatched as useless for bargaining purposes, but blonde women were valuable

22

barter, worth keeping alive. Some of the warriors even mated with them.

A woman with pale golden hair like this one would be regarded as a prize indeed, because of the old legend that pale hair was a gift from the Ancient Ones, the lost gods.

A car stopped right in his line of vision and by the time it moved on, they had drifted out of sight. He might as well drift too, after a final look around for the drug pusher. There were too many for the law in Arizona to get excited about but this particular one was of importance to Chay who suspected that he had been connected with the death of a couple of young Navajo boys with a remote relationship to his own clan.

Their mother had been Chay's girl from high school days. While he had been making up his mind to ask her to marry him, Lora steamed into his life, the result was Jake and a quick wedding. He'd heard that Dot had married into the Atalos–Anasazi clan, the two boys orphaned when she and her wild biker husband ran into a bus on the highway. Left in the care of an aged uncle, Gerry and Joe were ripe for bad teenage company, already a thorn in the flesh of the local sheriff by exhibiting anti-social tendencies, such as housebreaking and drug pushing.

Give Blackhawk Creek its due though. The entire police reserve had turned out on a joyous animal hunt looking for that cougar, allegedly the boys' killer. Everyone who could handle a rifle set out, armed to the teeth, telling each other that it was a damn shame, two youngsters found dead in the canyon, one with his chest ripped open, the other horribly mauled.

There had been animal tracks, but they never saw any mountain lion. They wished Chay Bowman had been with them, believing that, like in the movies, all Indians were born great trackers and this particular one was also a sure shot with a rifle.

Bowman had been in Los Angeles on a long-running fraud case involving a rich client when it happened. Now he couldn't get Dot's sons out of his mind or shake off the feeling that there was something chillingly coincidental and unnatural about their deaths.

The open and closed verdict, 'Death by misadventure', bothered him as much as their hastily arranged funerals. Red Rock law was known to take its time and this sudden burst of efficiency struck him as suspicious. As if behind the scenes there was more than an accidental killing being laid to rest.

His probing questions were regarded with some mirth.

Gee, what's all the fuss about, they told him, two fuckin' no-good street kids, villains in the making. But Chay thought of their mother, of his own son Jake, and what might have been.

His grandfather Redfeather was equally

unmoved by this burst of sensitivity. 'You're only a volunteer cop. You should stick to what the Anglos pay good money for. The important things in life, like searching for evidence that a married man has been unfaithful, or has run off with the holiday funds,' he added scathingly.

Scorning the white man's ways, Redfeather regarded such activities as beneath the dignity of his grandson who had been a cop in San Francisco until five years ago when a madman sprayed a supermarket with bullets. Tackling him single-handed Chay was hit several times. By a miracle he had survived and returned to Red Rock where nothing important ever happened.

But Chay couldn't give in that easily. He was only slightly lame. No one ever noticed it unless he was in one hell of a hurry. He wasn't likely to train for the Olympics, so what was he supposed to do pensioned off from active service at thirty-four?

Law enforcement had been his whole life since he left Red Rock at seventeen. It was the only life he knew or wanted to know, so he applied for a private investigator's licence where his police record was favourably looked upon.

As a qualification it was even more enthusiastically received by the volunteer police reserve, part-timers appointed by government decree to help enforce the law. A shrewd and economic move, when they would

25

be wasting the salary of a bright young cop eager for big-time crime sitting around in Blackhawk Creek waiting for the next traffic accident to happen.

The police reserve were tradesmen or professional men, enthusiastic amateurs, armchair detectives inspired by too many crime movies. Basking in the importance of a uniform and a police car, the cream of the crop were the retired city cops with experience and many a gory tale to inspire the fearful. Or those like Chay Bowman, a Navajo with a bravery medal from the President of the United States.

With no excuse to linger Bowman was heading towards the exit when he noticed Golden Hair negotiating a car hire. Heads were being shaken, at last a bargain was struck and dollar bills exchanged hands. Bowman felt angry but helpless. He knew the man, Lopez, a Mexican ex-con, a cheat and swindler who preyed on gullible tourists. He wished he could warn her that she was probably buying trouble, but even as he thought of intervening, she and the boy drove off and Lopez swiftly disappeared from sight.

Crawling slowly through congested traffic towards his office, on an out-of-season weekday with dull overcast skies, the Anglo's confectionary god, the ice cream cone was much in evidence on Main Street, the tourist traps already doing a brisk trade in Indian artefacts, including the sand paintings still

26

regarded as sacred when he was young. Once part of the sacred Healing Way Ceremony, they were now big business.

'Would these Anglos wear their Jesus Christ and the Virgin Mary on T-shirts, do you think?' he had asked Redfeather.

'Only if there were enough dollars to make it worth while,' was the sardonic reply. Grandfather had no illusions about the white man's thirst for gold.

*   *   *

The hallway to his office was dark with a steep flight of stairs leading up to one large storeroom, transformed into a bachelor pad for a private eye who liked the easy convenience of living above the shop. There was the kind of clutter that made it homey, books everywhere for when he had time to read, bought in frequent bouts of enthusiasm and never opened, fighting for space alongside the stacked pictures, to be hung as soon as he found time to drive in a few nails.

Local artists were thick on the ground in Blackhawk Creek with its red rocks and spectacular scenery. All had exhibitions where talent shaded from brilliant to non-existent and Chay, invited to take a glass of wine by some little old lady, would feel obliged to buy one of her pictures.

His compact disc collection received more

attention. Switching on was the first thing he did when he came upstairs. He didn't much care what it was he listened to and couldn't honestly distinguish between Beethoven and Mozart unless he bothered to read the label. One disc played and replayed tended to provide a week's listening but the classics were as soothing as aural wallpaper. Just for a change, depending on his mood, he might switch to country 'n western where long-dead Sean Doe still ranked high on his list, mourned as his favourite of all time singers.

The centre of the room was occupied by a king-sized bed, relic of his grandfather's Hollywood days and craftily donated in the hope that he would re-marry and beget more sons. Mostly Chay enjoyed sleeping there alone. It was good, looking out through the high window and seeing the ghostly outline of the red rocks by moonlight and their rose-flushed heights at dawn.

The bed was flanked to the right, by a shower room. To the left a kitchen, almost as immaculate as the day it had been installed, seeing that Chay never did much more than brew some coffee to drink alongside a sandwich from the deli across the road.

As an unpretentious place of his own, it served his purpose, and few other than Rita had ever crossed the threshold. The untidiness bothered her a lot. When it got too much for her, she would scowl and mutter about having a clear out.

'Touch anything and you're dead,' he would say, making a gun of his fingers and pointing them at her.

Behind the glass door of his office with his nameplate, shiny filing cabinets and immaculately tidy surfaces hinted at a suspicious lack of clients.

This was Rita's domain where she sat mesmerised by the computer's bright screen and flashing messages. Rita Darkcloud was White Mountain Apache, thirty-five years old and already losing the youthful beauty and slim figure she had when Chay had married her elder sister Lora. Lora had died of cancer three years ago and it was the Navajo custom for widowers to marry an eligible sister-in-law. However, Chay couldn't face it. He didn't need anyone to bring up his son Jake who lived with Redfeather and at seventeen thought himself cool enough to be looking around for a wife of his own.

Rita had moved into Redfeather's adobe ranch house to take care of her sister and she was more than willing to follow the old tradition. Clever, college trained, she could also help Chay in his business. A useful and convenient arrangement, but he knew it wasn't all Rita wanted of him and he could never look at her without a feeling of guilt.

Keeping a steady gaze on the computer screen, she said, 'There's a message for you, boss. Folks over by Castle Rock think they've spotted a cougar walking by their jacuzzi. This guy's one of your police reserve so he takes a pot-shot—thinks he wounded it. Asked if you'd care to track it down seeing as how you're the best man hereabouts with a rifle.'

Unimpressed by such flattery, Chay merely nodded. He'd heard it all before. Want a man to do a real unpleasant job, be sure to tell him how good he is, and that no one, but no one else could do it as well.

He consulted the wall map for the quickest route. He could drive till the road met the canyon and ran out, the rest on foot.

Rita smiled. 'How do I book this one, boss. Business or police reserve?'

He knew what she was getting at. Were they to be paid?

He shook his head. 'It's police business, seeing as how this is maybe a killer.'

As he spoke, they both stared bleakly at the cutting from Arizona News on the noticeboard. 'Red Rock Slayings. Brutal deaths of Indian children by wild animals under investigations. Tourists warned.'

Out of date, two months old, its presence was a constant reproach. Chay was always meaning to remove it but knew he could never do so until the killings had been satisfactorily explained and the killer, animal or human, brought to justice.

Rita turned to him frowning. 'You catch him,

boss. We sure don't want any more kids carried off.'

In this day and age it seemed ridiculous that a town could be terrorised by a solitary wild animal. Coyotes there were in plenty, but singly they steered clear of humans and no one had ever heard of them attacking anyone. Perhaps like the grey wolf, they would only do so if they were in a pack and hungry enough.

Chay checked his rifle and drove towards the canyon. He decided he wasn't too sure about the mountain lion theory, either. With mushrooming estates of houses shooting up right to the base of the red rocks, he had a feeling that all the wild creatures had sensibly retreated. A few bold ones, if they were hungry enough, might scavenge at night, but they would make themselve scarce as soon as they got the scent of man.

Chay kept on remembering the police photographs he'd been shown. How neatly the younger boy's chest had been ripped open while the elder brother looked as if he'd been attacked running away from the scene. A grisly killing that maybe an animal—and maybe a machete—could have achieved. There was something too calculated about the precision, like the kind of cuts he had encountered on the lawless streets of San Francisco—which suggested human rather than animal attackers.

Again his progress was halted at the road works, the stretch of the highway being repaired, or renovated, or whatever they damn well called it to cause the maximum discomfort to drivers. With a long line of stationary vehicles ahead moving only yards per minute, he leaned back in his seat, thinking about those killings.

Was it only coincidence that both were male children from the Atalos–Anasazi clan?

According to what his grandfather had told him when he was a small boy eager for gory stories, long after Aztecs, Mayas and Anasazi civilisations had returned to dust, right up to the last century, Los Atalos had secretly clung to the bad old days, ensuring their chief's immortality with the ritual sacrifice of a boy on the threshold of manhood.

As he waited for the traffic to move, he took out his binoculars. He had evolved from this landscape, once sacred to the Anasazi, this fantasy world of red rocks in a rainbow kaleidoscope that still held him in awe each day of his life. Eroded by eons of time and weather into grotesque human shapes, these massive buttes had been revered by his people as the images of long-dead ancestors who watched over them. This was his home, part of every fibre of his being and for him it never lost its magic, nor was he tempted to the blasphemy of taking its splendour for granted, for these once holy places were fast disappearing under wealthy Anglo homes, film star mansions, and the attendant luxuries of golf courses.

Only one home blended so skilfully with its background that the join where house ended and red rocks took over was invisible: the House of Anasazi Fire, so called because it had been built into an ancient cliff dwelling on the site of the legendary Temple of the Sun God, where the last rays of the dying sunset each day bathed its windows, changing colour from fiery red to liquid gold.

This house of mystery was relatively new, said to be the home of a multi-millionaire of the seventies who had opted out of the world of high finance to become a recluse in this eyrie high above the town of Red Rock.

For a while, the district had buzzed with rumours of his identity. Some said he was Navajo. Some said the house was a palace with every goddamned gadget known to modern man. Heads were shaken. What a waste! All for one old man with not even a wife or mistress, only a pack of Indian servants to do his bidding—a secret male community. But unlike the house, the speculation was built on insubstantial theories, since no one other than repairmen had ever set foot inside its walls.

The rumour that most concerned Chay was that the recluse who allegedly preferred animals to people was said to have a pet cougar that followed him round like a dog. And one possible explanation for the boys' brutal deaths was that this animal might have escaped and attacked them in the canyon that bordered his home. This had decided Chay to make a call on Viejo, as the locals called him, the Mexican word for old man.

A twisting, dusty, single-track mountain road led steeply upwards to heavy iron gates where he did not need to ring the bell.

Concealed cameras signalled unwelcome visitors, and the two men who came forward, their expressions grim, were Indian like himself, young and tough. The guns they carried suggested they knew their business and had no problems coping with intruders.

They eyed his uniform and the police car. What did he want they asked in Navajo, testing him out. He replied that this was a routine community service call to enquire whether their wild animals were in safe keeping.

They shrugged. What wild animals?

Chay understood that there was a private zoo.

So? What of it? one demanded.

Chay said he'd like to see their master, talk about them.

They stared at him. What was there to talk about?

Chay believed there was a pet cougar. Perhaps it had gone missing? They must have heard that two boys had been attacked and killed recently.

One of the men sprang forward. There was a suggestion of violence in the sudden move.

'The cougar is dead.'

'Someone poisoned him,' his companion muttered.

Chay looked from one to the other. 'I'd still like to talk to your master.'

'What about?'

Chay couldn't think of an answer offhand and the taller of the two said, 'Our master doesn't receive strangers.'

'What about policemen?' asked Chay casually.

'Only policemen with a warrant,' was the sneering reply. 'You have one? No.'

And before he could ask any more questions, the gates were firmly slammed in his face, the lock clicked home.

So much for evidence thought Chay as they had continued to stare after him until the car was out of sight.

The traffic was moving at last. He put aside the binoculars and headed in the direction of the butte behind the house whose owner had maybe wounded the prowling mountain lion.

Parking the car he began the steady climb over rough ground that would give him access to the canyon's deeper, darker regions unknown to tourists. The sacred caves of his ancestors, the rocks and secret ways, had been familiar to him since childhood. Only the coyotes, and the shyer creatures who never ventured into its lower reaches lived there. As such, he reckoned, this was the most likely place for a hurt animal to go to ground.

In the caves which looked no more than rock fissures in the massive red buttes, he had found fossil bones of dinosaurs that had once stalked the primeval forest, when the rocks had reverberated to their footfalls and cries. He had also found petroglyphs, on the cave walls, of hunters who were his ancestors—the mysterious Anasazi whose identity and strange powers had aroused speculation ranging from fallen angels to inhabitants of the lost world of Atlantis. The surviving artefacts told of a cultured civilisation enjoyed long before the Anglos, who conquered and despised his people, had emerged from their caves, little more than ignorant savages.

At last he found a vantage point near Bear's Point. It commanded a view down the canyon and beyond the rocks across the flat plain to the sacred mountains, the San Francisco Peaks.

He was in no hurry. He let the cool shade absorb the last of a wearing day, and the land, his own earth, hold him for a while. Sitting cross-legged, his back against a rock, with his rifle across his knees he prepared to wait for sunset. In like manner his people had once waited, prepared to ambush their enemies in the canyon below, superior in the knowledge that they had the advantage of surprise.

Surprise was for him this time. A gleam of light in the lengthening shadows alerted him. The setting sun had touched a glass or a mirror. He focussed the binoculars on a distant stationary vehicle far below. A woman was staring down into the engine and looking around helplessly.

It was Golden Hair from the plane.

He grimaced. Her plight was obvious. The hired car had broken down. He could have warned her of that likelihood.

Gesturing to some passenger unseen, presumably the boy, she seized a tote bag and began walking quickly through the canyon. Shit! Where the hell did she think she was going? Didn't she realise the dangers of getting lost in these rocks by night.

And if there was such a thing as a cougar at large. And wounded . . .

CHAPTER THREE

From childhood's hour I have not been
As others were—I have not seen
As others saw.

EDGAR ALLAN POE, Alone

They were making good time in the hired car.

Kate pinned up Hank Wilderbrand's address telling herself—and Luke, that something unforeseen had probably delayed him. He was a busy man and so forth and so on. But she was uneasy. The thought nagged that he would

37

most certainly have a mobile phone in his car and he could have called the airline. Here they were, strangers in a strange land, in spite of the familiarity that began as soon as they reached Red Rock, turning the passing landscape into a high-speed movie, with all that the travel brochures had promised springing into life around them.

Millions of years before Hollywood movies had discovered the west-that-never-was and glamourised those early gunfighters, nature had torn this landscape apart, not with Indian arrows and cavalry bullets, but by mountains turning themselves inside out. Great raging torrents of fire, toppling, heaving, before a great calm and silence descended as this fragment of planet earth passed into yet another geological age.

As the sun dipped towards the horizon, the golden light of late afternoon became the blood-red of a dying day. Rosy clouds rode high in the heavens, folding like majestic curtains above this earthly drama as pink, purple and rainbow-hued tower-clouds mounted into the sky. Ephemeral and ever-changing fantasy shapes toyed with the landscape, building enchanted sky castles and dark secret gorges as they settled into the sleep pattern of untold ages. It was breathtaking, and excitement surged through her replacing anxiety. Somewhere among those red rocks lay Blackhawk Creek.

Hypnotised by the sky's panorama, she glanced occasionally at the milometer hoping it would not be completely dark before they found their destination where, according to the lyrical description in Hank Wilderbrand's letter, a mobile home awaited their arrival, warm and welcoming, by a swift-moving stream, shrouded in cottonwoods and sycamores.

What bliss! Even as the thought entered her head, the car's engine gurgled, coughed and died. Frantically, she tried the ignition, but nothing happened.

She turned round, the noise hadn't awakened Luke sleeping peacefully curled up on the back seat. Not even an earthquake could disturb some kids. How she envied this ability to switch off the world. As for herself, night-time made her uneasy. Darkness had never been her friend, it was the enemy and had been since childhood's demon-ridden nightmares.

Her heart was beating faster now as panic set in. She must keep calm, be practical and think what to do next. She told herself sternly not to be silly and let her imagination run riot. They weren't lost, they had a perfectly reliable map and the worst that could happen was not to arrive in a new house pampered by daylight.

All she had to do was find a payphone and call a petrol station. She gave the car one more chance. Nothing happened, leaving her with the ominous feeling that the petrol gauge had been tampered with, or wasn't working properly, since it had rocketed quite suddenly from half full to zero.

That man. She cursed silently. He'd been a crook.

'Luke, Luke.' She shook him and at last reluctantly he opened his eyes. 'Darling, I think we're out of petrol. I must try and find a petrol station before it gets dark. Do you want to come with me?'

He groaned, shook his head and closed his eyes again.

She didn't really like leaving him alone in the car, but he was completely exhausted by the flight and he'd been airsick too.

The magic sunset was already fading. She mustn't delay. There had been a parked car a mile or so back down the road. Perhaps its owner had returned. At least the presence of a vehicle indicated that they weren't lost on an unfrequented road.

'Luke. Keep the doors and windows locked when I'm gone. Do you hear?'

Again he nodded, unconcerned, and snuggled down into his seat.

She walked as fast as the rough road permitted. A twisted ankle was the last thing she needed. Three times she stopped and signalled cars which merely accelerated. She was angry but forgave them. In her gear she looked like a hitch-hiker. Drivers on lonely roads were naturally suspicious, they had been warned and she could hardly expect consideration from other drivers that she did not herself give to pedestrians wandering about the roads.

A fourth, indifferent driver hurtled past and everything was silent, a world suddenly empty of people.

Damn, damn. If only Hank Wilderbrand had arrived as he promised. He was supposed to be on the same flight. Where the hell was he when he was needed? Why had there been no message?

Luke's prize, this trip won in a kid's quiz competition on the Internet, had seemed so marvellous on a bleak winter day in Edinburgh. They were just back from Gran's funeral, and the letter had been lying on the mat, waiting for them; waiting with all its promises to open up new worlds. It had seemed like a miracle sent to banish their sadness and desolation.

Of course it was genuine. She had tickets, a substantial cheque to cover expenses and a letter from Red Butte Enterprises. All that had gone wrong so far was being rented a dud car.

The sun vanished behind the rocks, the heat of day extinguished like a snuffed candle. Chill shadows replaced the warm sunlight on her shoulders. She felt cold and very vulnerable.

Prize or no prize, what she wouldn't have given at this moment to be waiting for a bus home on Edinburgh's bustling Princes Street.

Then suddenly, the road ahead was no

41

longer empty.

It was occupied by a pick-up truck. She'd try once more. Running into the middle of the road, she waved her arms frantically. As the truck slowed down and came to a stop Kate realised that she was an object of interested attention to the men riding in the back. She was conscious of a watchful alertness about them, almost as if—but that was impossible—as if they had been expecting to find her here.

They were Indians. Not that such an observation should have worried her. This was their country after all and logically there should be more of them than whites in Arizona. The ones she had seen in the airport at Phoenix walked the white man's way in jeans, cowboy boots and stetsons.

Maybe Mr Wilderbrand was Indian. She hadn't thought of that.

She flourished his letter. 'Did Mr Wilderbrand send you?'

Presumably they spoke English but their expressions remained blank and they continued to stare at her as if she and not they were the anachronism on this twentieth-century road. For these Indians should have been on horses. Paint ponies were the right accessories for the full tribal dress they wore. That was surprising enough but they were also in warpaint, their faces striped red, or yellow and white.

Weird and a bit scary, she thought. They

must be extras in a movie. That was it. She felt quite triumphant in her deduction. They had finished a long day's filming somewhere nearby and were returning to their homes on the reservation.

Suddenly one of the men sprang into life, leapt from the truck and walked towards her on moccasin-clad feet, his curious loping stride full of animal grace; a young man's walk in an old man's body. His white hair hung in two thick plaits. Under the paint, his face was heavily lined, the ancient map of a long life. Kate was tall but he towered over her. Tall, proud, his back still ramrod straight, untouched by the years.

'Why have you come?' he asked.

The question was an odd one, but she decided to try again with Mr Wilderbrand.

The man shook his head impatiently and repeated, 'Why are you here?' His voice had a strange metallic ring, halting, as if English was a language he seldom used.

'My car's run out of petrol—' she said and pointed, '—back down the road there. Can you help me? We're going to Blackhawk Creek.'

'Blackhawk Creek,' the Indian repeated and there was a palpable stir of excitement, like the rustling of many leaves, in the group behind him.

He nodded eagerly as if this was the reply he had hoped for. 'Come, we will take you.'

And so saying he took her firmly by the arm

43

and led her towards the truck with its waiting occupants. Someone started up the engine.

'Stop!' It was heading in the wrong direction. 'Wait! My little boy is back there.'

Suddenly Kate's gratitude turned into panic. Was she being abducted, marked down for gang-rape by the silent, watchful group? Ridiculously a scene flashed into her mind like a warning bell. It was from D. H. Lawrence's *The Woman Who Rode Away*; the golden-haired woman who had been taken by Indians to be a sacrifice. The character's 'unhuman eyes' had impressed Kate and she decided that the description might also have been written for these silent watchers.

The old man had her arm in an iron grip.

There was no way she was going to get on that truck without a fight. No way. She tried to struggle free, but the old man did not seem to notice.

One of the young men had turned up a radio. The heavy metal music was jarring, loud enough to obliterate her screams, even if there had been anyone near enough or interested enough to try come to her assistance.

Near to tears now, she couldn't believe this was happening, such things only happened to other people, you read about them in the papers.

That grip on her arm, gentle but strong and somehow relentless, transformed fear into fury. She thought of Luke sleeping peacefully in the

44

abandoned car as she was propelled towards the truck, where eager hands stretched out to heave her aboard.

Now she knew she was being kidnapped. She would never see Luke again.

'Let me go!' she yelled.

And at that moment, as in all the best movies, the US cavalry arrived in the blessed shape of a police car that screeched to a standstill alongside.

Another Indian, his hair tied back in a ponytail, emerged. But he was wearing an official-looking uniform jacket. 'That your car back there, lady?'

'Yes, we ran out of petrol.'

And the men whose hands had been so strong on her moments ago, now hung limply at their sides.

The policeman got out and opened the passenger door. 'Step inside, lady.'

She did so gladly. And as they watched her go, their faces impassive, her rescuer sauntered over, spoke to them in some dialect they understood. He spoke quietly but firmly to the old man who shrugged and smiling briefly, touched her rescuer's shoulder in a friendly, almost reassuring, gesture before leaping back aboard the truck.

The policeman returned to the car, with the same easy, loping stride as the old man.

Now that she was safe, suddenly contrite and ashamed of having made such a fuss, Kate said,

'Thank you again. I don't think your friends understood. They seemed to want to take me with them, wherever they were going.'

The man at her side merely nodded.

Looking back, she saw that the truck and its occupants were still there. Statue-like, unreal figures silhouetted against a stage set of eerie red rocks thrusting against a fast-darkening sky.

'My little boy is back there in the car. I had to leave him. I was going to accept a lift in desperation,' she explained.

In the dim light, squinting at the truck in the driving mirror, Chay Bowman said, 'I wouldn't ever be that desperate, lady.'

'What do you mean? Who are they? Aren't they actors or something?'

Bowman concentrated on a sharp bend. 'On vacation are you?'

'Yes, we're staying in Blackhawk Creek.'

'You're a long way from England.'

'From Scotland actually.'

Her answers were short, she was too anxious for social chat, with all her being intent on getting back to Luke as soon as possible.

There was the car. At last.

She jumped out. Luke was still fast asleep, lying curled up just as she had left him.

'I'm back, dear.'

In answer he opened his eyes and yawned.

'This kind policeman is going to get us some petrol,' she said holding his hand tightly while

Bowman tried to get the car started, after filling it from his emergency can.

In the occasional flickers of his flashlight, she saw that he wasn't as young as she had first thought. He was tall and slim but strong-looking. A nice friendly face, he looked reliable.

The nice friendly face looked in at them. 'It's not just gas it needs. We'll leave it here till daylight and I'll have a garage bring it in. Meanwhile, I'll take you and the boy to the Creek.'

'Oh, I'd be so grateful.'

Luke sat up, rubbing his eyes fully awake. He jumped out of the car, helping their rescuer transfer the luggage.

Kate smiled, realising he was delighted with this new adventure and thrilled to be riding in a police car as he clambered into the back seat.

'Right. Got all your gear? Let's go. Got the address?'

Kate handed him the letter. She only meant for him to see the address not read the contents.

'I hope this isn't taking you too far out of your way,' she said politely and when he replied that it was no trouble, her interest in the adventure with the pick-up truck suddenly revived.

'Who were those men back there?'

Bowman hesitated. 'Magic Men.'

Kate laughed disbelievingly. 'Magic Men!'

she repeated.

Bowman shrugged. 'Yeah. Guardians of the Earth and so forth. They mean well.'

Kate was silent. She wasn't sure about that, and he said, 'Ever hear tell of collective consciousness, telepathy?'

'I suppose so. In animals and birds,' she said vaguely. She wasn't prepared to discuss with this stranger that she and Luke were often weirdly telepathic, more so since his accident.

'Folks hereabouts are pretty superstitious about the Magic Men—that's what they call them. They believe that what one knows, they all know.' He was suddenly serious. 'I'd give them a wide berth if I were you.'

Kate squinted out of the back window. 'I'd be glad to. But I think they're following us.'

This dramatic piece of information didn't seem to bother Bowman. 'It's all right, ma'am. Don't you worry none. We'll shake them off at the next turn-off.'

As the car accelerated, so did the truck and Kate felt faintly sick. There was no longer the slightest possibility that this was coincidence. What if there was a confrontation? Her rescuer looked tough and strong, but what were the odds of two against ten?

The distance between the two vehicles diminished, turning the whole episode into a ridiculous parody of a western movie. Clinging to her seat, Kate decided that all it lacked was the chase music on the soundtrack.

Never in her young days of addiction to westerns had she imagined finding herself in the heart-hammering position of a Victorian heroine escaping from Indians. With swaying stagecoach replaced by 1992 Dodge, and sweating horses by an old pick-up truck. Even the bumpy road was more like a desert track.

'Sorry, lady.'

She opened her eyes with a start. What had happened? She had been once again on that strange frontier of a past world that Gran had called stepping off the time circle.

'Gets a bit rough here,' Bowman had mistaken her confusion for fright. 'But we've lost our followers. You need good brakes and that's what they don't have,' he added proudly.

Looking at his profile, she suspected he was thoroughly enjoying this unexpected drama. She could imagine him telling all his friends, bragging a bit, exaggerating the possible dangers. But she had been right to have confidence in him. He drove superbly, swiftly negotiating the twisting road lined by cottonwoods which occasionally afforded a glimpse of costly-looking executive houses above terraced gardens.

She turned and glanced back the way they had come. And there on the road far above she saw the lights of the truck. The fact that it was stationary gave no immediate comfort. There was still enough light to outline the Indians who stood at the road edge, motionless,

49

watching their progress.

Luke was kneeling on his seat now, looking back at them too, as if he knew the danger she had been in.

'They're up there watching us,' she whispered to Bowman so that Luke wouldn't overhear. 'What do they want?' she added crossly.

Bowman thought for a moment, then smiled at her reassuringly, 'You're a pretty lady, ma'am. That hair of yours is very striking.'

His remark was casual enough for her not to mistake it for flattery, but she gave him a sharp look.

'I didn't think Indians still took scalps,' she said with an attempt at humour which failed to raise a smile. That was tactless of me, she thought and said quickly, 'They're not acting in some movie?'

'No, ma'am.'

'Then why do they dress like that?'

'Ceremonial gear, I guess.'

'What kind of ceremonial?'

The car slid smoothly down the last incline into a tiny square where houses elegant enough to belie the description of mobile homes, encircled a lawn with water sprinklers and a flagpole.

'This is it, ma'am. You'll be safe enough now.'

Safe enough. For some reason the words chilled her. Had he seriously thought she was in danger?

Their arrival had set up a chorus of guard dogs baying. He hadn't answered her question about the Indians and she didn't want to bring it up again as he carried their holdalls and backpacks to the door. Luke sprang out of the car with the remaining bags, waiting while Kate opened the door and switched on the lights.

Chay Bowman followed her through the hall and into the kitchen. The first thing she did was open the refrigerator door. It was well-packed. She gave a sigh of relief.

'Thank goodness something went right,' she said, 'Mr Wilderbrand said he'd have the house prepared. And he did.' She opened the freezer and handed Luke an ice cream.

He laughed and unwrapping it, ran into the lounge and switched on the television. That worked too.

Kate saw that the policeman was watching Luke. She was too tired to start explaining Luke's infirmity to a man she'd never meet again. In the light she noticed that he was even better looking than she had thought at first. Fine lean features, high cheekbones, a well-shaped mouth with what Gran used to call 'kissing lips'.

The thought made her suddenly shy as he turned towards her.

'Got everything you need, ma'am?'

'Yes. And I can't begin to thank you.'

He grinned at her. 'No need, that's what

51

we're here for. Glad to be of service.'

She held out her hand. 'Kate—Kate Fenner.' She pointed to the boy absorbed by the television. 'That's Luke,' she added with an apologetic shrug.

'Chay Bowman.' He smiled at her. His hand was strong, she could feel the bones through the warm flesh.

At the door he handed back the letter. 'You'll need this.'

She frowned at it. 'He was supposed to be catching the plane with us from Phoenix. I presume he didn't make it.' And when Bowman didn't respond she said brightly, to cover up her anxiety, 'I expect he'll be getting in touch.'

Bowman nodded. 'Sure he will. But any problems, you just call my office.' There was a phone pad on the hall table and he scribbled down two numbers. 'If I'm not there, try the second, I carry it around. Now you just lock up and get some rest.'

As he walked down the path, he heard sounds from inside the house. Turning, he saw through the uncurtained window that there was a horror movie on television.

Bloodcurdling screams echoed into the night.

He shook his head sadly. Golden Hair—Miz Fenner—was one beautiful Anglo woman. But this Wilderbrand's letter puzzled him. He just might look into that.

As for the boy, from the occasional glances in the car mirror, he'd noticed his eyes and he hadn't said one single word either. A weird kid all right. And he must be deaf as well as dumb.

CHAPTER FOUR

Which of us has looked into his father's heart? Which of us is not forever a stranger and alone.

THOMAS WOLFE,
Look Homeward, Angel

As Bowman walked down the path, Kate wished he had stayed for a while. She needed consolation for her fears and felt suddenly threatened by the empty house.

At least there were lights in neighbouring windows, the flicker of a television screen across the road. Although it was reassuring to be surrounded by so many houses and dogs, she wanted to be safe inside with Luke, the door locked firmly against the growing darkness of night. Twilight had never appealed to her, there was something sinister about it. There was an old Scots saying, the hour between dog and wolf.

She realised that the policeman was leaning out of the car window watching her. Such concern should have helped but instead it made her feel even more vulnerable.

When she waved he raised his hand in salute and drove off. Turning, she went back indoors where the horror movie was spilling out its entrails, wasting its gore on an empty room.

Luke had disappeared and, having decided on his bedroom, was energetically unpacking.

The Internet equipment, software and modem, which was part of his holiday prize would probably arrive tomorrow, she said, and left him with a glass of milk stacking his books on shelves and rehanging the poster of Red Rock Crossing brought from his bedroom at home.

'It's come a long way, darling.' She kissed him goodnight. 'You'll be able to see it in real life soon. Won't that be super?'

She was pleased with the house Wilderbrand had chosen for them. To the ignorant British traveller, mobile homes meant overcrowded caravan sites with noisy neighbours, poor sanitation and howling babies breaking the stillness of the night.

She had resolved to discreetly invest some of Luke's prize money on hotel accommodation but there was no need. The house's box-like exterior hid rooms cleverly designed with mirrored walls to create an illusion of space, terracotta and cerulean blue décor harmonised with the landscape where the red rocks were now ghostly sentinels touched by the glow of moonrise.

Beyond the sliding doors to the terrace, the sound of a fast-moving creek shaded by sycamores. She would enjoy listening to its faint music under that vast canopy of stars, a privilege unknown to city dwellers whose smoking chimneys of the past had been replaced by the deadly pollution of an overburdened traffic system.

She breathed deeply. This part of Arizona was four and a half thousand feet above sea level and its wine-chilled air reminded her of holidays in the Scottish highlands.

It also brought a feeling of infinity and looking up at the rocks she was suitably humbled, aware that this land tolerated human life and was quite capable of brushing her aside with the same indifference she now shook off a busy ant crawling on her sleeve. As it fell to the ground and bustled away, she remembered that its miniscule body had a preordained pattern of existence, a purpose in life, a beating heart kept that tiny machine alive and gave it powers of reproduction, of creating future generations.

The thought pleased her. She found it gratifying that man had not yet mastered the breath of life, refusing to accept that only the present was real and blaming it on the genes inherited from her minister grandfather and the enforced churchgoing of her childhood. Her faith had fluctuated through the years, but she never doubted that there was Someone out there, available to be called upon, like a failsafe ambulance service, in moments of dire peril.

She slept well that first night and opened her eyes on a new day with a glorious sense of well-being, the dreaded jetlag she had been warned about was mercifully absent.

Surprises were in store. Normally a reluctant riser, Luke was out on the terrace in his dressing gown playing host to a score of wild creatures who had gathered to greet him. A pair of squirrels, larger than those in Britain, and a jackrabbit, were close to his feet while a rock-squirrel no bigger than a gerbil was eagerly taking crumbs from Luke's hands. He laughed delightedly as an abundance of birds chirped from every branch and hopped towards him, beaks dipping towards the ground cautiously eyeing him and the bread he was breaking.

Kate stood back, touched and amazed at how good he had always been with animals. Even as a tiny child they seemed to trust him and domestic pets sought him out. You should have called him after Saint Francis, not after Saint Luke, one of her friends had said when they strolled in the Botanic Gardens where her own small brat chased every pigeon in sight.

This was a scene to be recorded. But by the time she had loaded the camera the terrace was deserted, the scene had dissolved with every animal and bird vanished. The garden, now silent of birdsong, the trees unmoving gave her a sense of guilt that somehow she had touched on a lost Eden only to lose it again.

She looked at the camera, one of man's modern miracles. If only all his miracles were as innocent and brought such pleasure, instead of holes in ozone layers and the dramatic devastation of the planet, as he heedlessly poisoned the atmosphere that gave him life, like a modern lemming fleeing down the path of self-destruction.

At the kitchen table, Luke was solemnly reading the back of the cereal packet as he ate.

She put an arm around his thin shoulders. 'We're going to be so happy here, darling, aren't we? I can feel it, can't you?'

In answer, Luke grinned and continued to spoon cornflakes into his mouth. She was relieved to see him so settled and contented, as if he had known this place all his life, a child who had come home at last. She had no such complacency, remembering that moment in Chay Bowman's car when time turned topsy-turvy and she was another girl in a world long lost, travelling in a stagecoach surrounded by Indians.

And somewhere deep inside her, the warning bell of disaster tolled anew. The demon she thought she had long outgrown stirred once more.

*   *   *

Chay Bowman was a worried man.

He knew at first glance there was no such address in Red Rock as the one Golden Hair—no, he must start calling her Miz Fenner—had shown him. Nor was there any trace of a firm called Red Butte Enterprises whose director the headed notepaper said was Hank Wilderbrand.

Blessed with a photographic memory, he recalled the contents of the letter enclosing the plane tickets, stating that business commitments might prevent Wilderbrand catching the plane but promising a hired car at the airport. The name Lopez had stood out and gave Chay his first indication that Miz Fenner was the victim of a scam. No honest guy such as Wilderbrand purported to be, would have trusted the Mexican ex-con with a wheelbarrow much less a car.

Chay's suspicions made sense of the faulty car. Had the Magic Men been warned that it would run out of gas? And what about that strange kid? He remembered vividly how Luke had knelt on the back seat staring back at them, so still and watchful he could almost feel the vibrations.

He shook his head. He wasn't prone to imagining things and he mustn't get carried away just because he'd met a beautiful Anglo woman whose son was—well, what? Simple? No. Spastic? No. Super intelligent, perhaps.

He had no logical answer to why these

visitors from Britain should be of the slightest interest to Los Atalos or why his grandfather Redfeather's cousin Tomas should be involved. Not that he knew much about the old medicine man, a mysterious and enigmatic figure lurking in the shadows of his life since childhood.

There was another possibility. That Wilderbrand had set them up as hostages for some greater ploy. And if a large ransom was involved that would definitely fit in with Lopez getting into the act. He had better acquaint himself with Miz Fenner's background, see if she had some wealthy connections which would give a plausible reason.

First, he'd set Rita to work, contacting the airport and checking the passenger list from the Fenners' plane.

*　　　*　　　*

As he suspected there was no Mr Wilderbrand listed, no late cancellation either.

'See what that magic box of yours can track down farther afield,' he told Rita, watching her fingers busily conjuring up data on the small screen.

She grinned at him and shook her head. 'Nothing magic involved, boss, just plain electronics, microchips and science.'

'So they tell me,' he said solemnly.

'You should try it sometime. It's a lot of fun.'

Chay shrugged. 'Give me a break, will you?

59

It takes me all my time to get results from an old-fashioned typewriter.'

'So I've noticed,' she said drily. 'Sometimes I think you've inherited Redfeather's deep distrust of machines.'

'Could be.'

'You could skip a few generations of electronics—' she said encouragingly.

He interrupted by laying a heavy hand on her shoulder. 'No—that's why I hired you—to do it for me. I'll keep to my side of the business, do the easy stuff like tracking down missing persons and dicing with death every day by solving crimes that have baffled the law,' he added sarcastically as they bleakly regarded his empty desk.

There hadn't been many enquiries lately.

'Absconding husbands and wives are sure getting smart these days,' sighed Rita.

He nodded. 'Even domestic pets are turning right crafty and hiding their tracks when they take off from home. Learning a thing or two from their owners, I guess.'

Rita looked back at the screen. 'Is this thing I'm looking into police reserve or us?'

'Us, so far. If any urgent messages come in, I'm off to the Creek to tell Miz Fenner the bad news that the car's a write-off and the good news that there's a replacement on its way.' He grinned. 'Thanks for arranging that, Rita. Real smart of you.'

'I thought you'd be pleased. All it needed

was the mention of Phoenix City Police and the fact that the young woman was a friend of yours and Señor Lopez nearly fell off his perch in his eagerness to be right accommodating.'

Chay slung his jacket over his shoulder and went out to the car. As he drove down the road, he wondered why he didn't marry Rita and be done with it, especially as she was more like a partner in the business than a secretary, or personal assistant as they liked to call themselves these days.

She had been with him ever since he got his licence. She was one hell of a clever Apache lady who had been to college, majored in environmental studies and came home after ten years in Phoenix, quitting a good job and a great future to look after an ailing mother who refused to move from the reservation. That was a trap Rita would never escape from until her mother passed away. Chay wondered how much was real sickness and how much was emotional blackmail. Her mother had reverted to the old Indian way which said parents were to be revered and her daughter was too soft hearted to disobey and remind her that there was another kind of life, too, for an unmarried girl these days.

He felt badly about Rita, knowing how accommodating she was and could be with men, and with him in particular. When Lora was sick she had taken husband and son under that umbrella of unbounded kindness.

When Lora died, she had taken Chay to her bed under the same amicable conditions.

'No ties,' she had said firmly, fully aware of their customs regarding sisters-in-law as suitable wives, 'We're good for each other just the way we are, like this.'

But Chay felt too good and comfortable in the situation to let it continue. He had a conscience about Rita, who he was sure was in love with him. The problem was he didn't reciprocate emotionally and although she was good in bed and even better in the kitchen it wasn't enough for him.

The problem was he had never been in love with Lora either. He'd got her pregnant with Jake and felt obliged to marry her. And he sure as hell didn't feel like a second marriage without love.

Sometimes he felt cheated. As if he was waiting for the great emotional experience, the love that drove men crazy with desire, but that touching forty, it wasn't likely to come along now anyway.

Redfeather thought he was crazy and that he should marry Rita. Her mother was no problem. As far as grandfather was concerned, there were no problems for his people with ageing or sick parents or grandparents. They were just herded all together in one great happy, raucous family who had never heard or wished to hear of retirement homes or geriatric wards.

It had to be added that Redfeather's ranch, acquired from the days of his movie star affluence, was beginning to resemble a small reservation with innumerable hogans sprouting for custom-conscious older folk to end their days in, and mobile homes for the many jobless and often bone idle cousins and hangers-on.

Geez! Chay shuddered at the idea of this *en famille* life-style. How could the old man cope with that and all his other activities, including medicine man, conservationist and some vaguely illegal connections, like the Magic Men, which Chay preferred not to think about. Redfeather had also acquired over the years a reputation for witchcraft, doubtless inspired by his boundless energy which could be thought of as supernatural. At ninety he still retained a young man's zest for life that had characterised his early days in films.

*　　　*　　　*

Following the twisting road down to the Creek Chay wondered how he was going to tell Miz Fenner about the mysterious Hank Wilderbrand and the non-existing Red Butte Enterprises.

She opened the door and smiled at him. She was looking good, one of the few women who look great first thing in the morning, with hair unbound and a well-scrubbed face. She smelt soft and inviting, like one of those fancy soaps that Rita liked to leave in his shower room.

Following her through the sitting room, he decided to begin with the good news about the car, but decided not to tell her that Lopez was a crook.

'You should have the replacement car this morning sometime.'

'That's very good of you to go to all that trouble, Mr Bowman, but it's only until Mr Wilderbrand appears and sorts it out.'

Chay said nothing but, as they went into the kitchen, he saw Luke and most of the table occupied by a huge computer, plus screen, modem and telephone. Costly-looking equipment which would have brought cries of rapture from Rita.

Kate smiled. 'That has just arrived.' At his blank expression, she said, 'It's for Luke to use while he's on holiday.'

Chay grinned. 'Don't kids ever play with baseball bats and roller skates in the yard anymore like they did in my young day?'

'It was part of his prize.'

Now that was interesting. 'What prize was that, Ma'am?'

Kate gestured round the room. 'He won first prize in a quiz. All of this. Luke's a whizz kid with the Internet, the World Wide Web. You know, e-mail and that sort of thing.'

He didn't, but let her continue.

'We've been told he's an electronic genius. He speaks to people all over the world. There are forty million people who use the Internet. Can you imagine that? There are often competitions with big prizes.'

She paused and looking towards Luke said hastily, 'I hope nothing goes wrong with this—like the car. I haven't a clue about that kind of machine. It's beyond me, the simple typewriter is all I can manage.'

'Me too,' said Chay, warming to that confession. 'Do you work in an office?'

'No, I have a guest house in Edinburgh. It used to be a family home once, but it was too big for my grandmother alone. She died recently,' she added. But before he could murmur something sympathetic, she went on quickly, 'Summer and the Edinburgh Festival, those are the busy times. There isn't a lot of business in the early part of the year though, which made winning Luke's competition so convenient.'

She looked at him and sighed happily. 'A holiday in Arizona—four weeks in a mobile home in Blackhawk Creek, plus a car and an Internet's use for the holiday. As you can imagine, Luke was absolutely thrilled. Weren't you, dear?'

Luke was frowning over his labours, calling up images on the screen. He looked across and gave them a polite but vague smile.

'You see, he's always been crazy about westerns, and this part of Arizona in particular. He even had a poster of Red Rock Crossing on his bedroom wall at home. When he realised that we would be able to come—well, it was like a dream come true. All the travel arrangements were made for us, plus two thousand dollars for spending money.'

Two thousand bucks. Chay whistled. 'The car too?'

'Oh, that was included.' She frowned. 'But when we got to the airport, apparently there had been some mistake, and Mr Lopez said he hadn't been paid for it and that I'd better reclaim the cost from Mr Wilderbrand.'

Listening to her so cheerful and confident, Chay's gloomy feelings increased. He didn't like any of this, it sounded like the kind of super-con Lopez would be associated with. In fact it stank. As for the mysterious Mr Wilderbrand, he would be very surprised indeed if he ever showed his face, or if he ever existed at all—mythical as the Red Butte Enterprises.

He looked at the boy so absorbed by the machine. He had heard all sorts of rumours about Internet connections with pornography, and with paedophiles. He couldn't offer much help there. Miracles of modern technology had always been beyond him, presumably it hadn't yet evolved into the Atalos–Anasazi genes.

'The letter you got. Can I have a look at it?'

'Of course.' Fortunately she didn't think that an odd question. 'Luke took extra copies in case we needed them—coming through

66

customs can be tricky. Keep it.'

* * *

Chay decided to suss out Wilderbrand & Co before breaking the bad news. He knew his reason, an excuse to keep Miz Fenner in his sights for a while. He headed towards the sleazy district bordering the airport for some frankly threatening conversation with Lopez regarding his association with Red Butte Enterprises aka Hank Wilderbrand.

On the way he called into the office and gave Rita the details.

'How much are we getting?' was Rita's first question.

'I haven't even thought about it.'

'You're impossible.'

'I know, but this is a stranger in a strange land. Even if she is an Anglo, we owe her that. It's bad for our image, this sort of thing.'

'Pul-ease, don't go all virtuous on me,' said Rita crossly and went back to her screen. 'Just say she's a pretty woman and you're feeling mighty chivalrous all of a sudden.'

* * *

Lopez wasn't around his usual haunts. Presumably Rita's enquiry and the possible entrance of the law on the scene had scared him off. Chay sighed. A wasted journey.

Rejoining the long tailback at the roadworks once more, he hoped that there was never a chase for a hardened criminal or someone with a heart attack needing an ambulance on this now single track road, where repairs and reconstruction were interminable.

Drumming his fingers on the wheel he reread the letter. It was addressed to 'Miss Fenner' which indicated that she was either a single parent or divorced.

His thoughts turned again to the boy, Luke, who had seemed to be following their conversation with considerable interest, despite his addiction to the small screen. When his mother had said, 'Mr Bowman is leaving,' he'd looked over and smiled politely.

He wasn't a deaf mute. But could it be that he was dumb?

A strange child. A closer encounter did little to reassure him. As for those eyes. He had seen them before but not for a very long time. They were amber, large and crystal clear. What the Anasazi and grandfather Redfeather called: Light Behind the Eyes.

When he reached the office again, all thoughts of Miz Fenner's strangely silent son were banished.

'Well, that was a wasted journey—' he began and Rita cut him short.

'You're telling me. That car, presumably the one Lopez was bringing over for your new client, ran off the Flagstaff road. Some witnesses said a truck was heading towards him at high speed and there wasn't room to pass.' She sighed, 'It's the late Señor Lopez now.'

CHAPTER FIVE

. . . Present fears
Are less than horrible imaginings;

WILLIAM SHAKESPEARE, Macbeth

Luke was eager to explore. He wanted to see the town, home of his beloved western movies. He wanted a cowboy hat.

Kate smiled. 'All right, all right, let's go. It's a long uphill climb, the exercise will do us good.'

The early spring morning was warm enough for Edinburgh at midsummer. T-shirts, shorts and sandals weather, Kate decided, guessing that the gentle breeze with its sharp scent of sage brush would have died by midday to be replaced by cloudless skies, relentless sunshine and a soaring temperature.

Luke hoisted a small backpack over his shoulder and, as they set off across the square, it seemed that every one of the mobile homes housed a dog. Eagerly they rushed out to inspect these newcomers. Large and fierce-looking guard dogs, small and cuddly lapdogs, all standing on their hindlegs against gate and wire enclosure, air-sniffing, tail-wagging, as excited as if they were recognising old friends rather than these strangers in their midst.

Luke was delighted. He wanted to stop by each one, frustrated that he couldn't pat heads through the wire mesh. Kate had never succeeded in restraining his fearless approach to all animals, particularly strange dogs.

In an effort to share his enthusiasm, she murmured, 'Good dogs.' They weren't interested in her and she managed to drag Luke away at last, heartened that their friendly reactions indicated a lack of crime in the neighbourhood and made nonsense of those imposing warning notices: 'Beware of the Dog'.

As they climbed the steep incline, low thickets of shrubs, manzaritas and chaparral offered shade that would be welcome on their return journey later in the day. Before the road was made to accommodate the extravagant houses on their expensive perches built a quarter of century earlier, this vegetation must have stretched solidly down to the creek, a tangled impenetrable mass.

Only shadowy half-strangled remnants of long-lost groves of sycamores and oak had escaped the bulldozers, evidence that the new residents had not altogether tamed this land. Streams had gone discreetly underground but refused to be quelled. Occasional springs gushed out, bubbling from the dark earth, eagerly disguised by keen gardeners as improbable waterfalls. An even more improbable rash of garden gnomes sprouted from well-disciplined, trouble-free, gravelled drive-ins, along with sculptures of coyotes and roadrunners.

No other walkers occupied the narrow, twisting road and there was little refuge from passing cars whose occupants regarded their presence with undisguised curiosity.

Luke grinned and waved to them.

Kate shook her head. 'Be careful. They're not used to pedestrians. They probably see so few they might think we're a new kind of wildlife worth investigating,' she added, emerging from their latest hasty retreat to a non-existent sidewalk.

Open sandals were a great mistake, she decided, leaning on Luke as she shook out yet another pebble.

Looking back towards the creek, the way they had come, they saw the trees were flushed with spring blossom in a dazzling array of paintbox colours. Wild flowers blazed across the one-time wilderness in a profusion of scarlets, purples, yellows and an almost luminous white.

Ahead, the road climbed once more. The red rocks of evening sunset were even more dramatic in daylight, rising like sandstone monoliths. A fantastic landscape fashioned by the prehistoric glacial ages that had reshaped the planet, leaving crudely sculpted faces, the

71

images of a long-forgotten race of giants.

At her side Luke held her hand tightly, awed by the magnificence of the scene spread out before them, captured so often through the camera lens but totally eclipsed by the reality.

Still holding hands they reached the peak of the steep road where the distant buzz of Highway 89 became the main street, cluttered with neon signs and craft shops.

Kate was glad to see so many Indians in evidence and wondered if the older generations felt that there was something blasphemous in the sale of those delicately executed sand paintings once used in healing ceremonies and afterwards destroyed. How would dedicated Christians react to the Crucifixion on T-shirts?

Turning her attention to Luke among the cowboy hats, she decided that being a privileged visitor in this country didn't include rights to make judgements and raise her standard on behalf of the Indians. She could do without yet another worthy cause for her list of contributions, or one more T-shirt for Luke bearing pleas for planet earth and its many threatened species.

She thought fleetingly of the lost causes back home in Britain, like the rape of ancient woods and meadows to put through even more spaghetti junctions and petrol stations to add more pollution to the world's atmosphere and ultimately wipe out its inhabitants.

She thought she caught a glimpse of Chay Bowman in his patrol car driving slowly along the street, obviously searching for a parking place. His passenger was a young Indian woman with long black hair wearing sunglasses. Disappointed that he didn't see them, and hoping that he might have some information on Mr Wilderbrand, Kate walked quickly in the direction the car had taken.

At the end of the street, she gave up. Luke, proudly wearing his cowboy hat, indicated that he had had enough window shopping and wanted a Coke. All her purchases amounted to were a few picture postcards and knowing that Luke, like all kids, soon got bored with shopping, she resolved to come back alone later.

The cafes were crowded but Kate had noticed one near the Texaco station away from the busy main street.

Luke's Coke became a hamburger with fries and an ice cream. Kate added a club sandwich and coffee for herself. So much food! Far too much, she thought and, ashamed to be leaving half-empty plates, was both surprised and relieved when the waitress tactfully suggested, 'You folks like to take that with you?' Brought up to regard wasted food as a crime, Kate was delighted with such a sensible solution. At this rate they would be able to cut their grocery bills by half.

About to leave, Kate was suddenly conscious

of being under close observation. Two men, their faces pressed against the window, shading their eyes, were gazing straight at her.

Her heart beat faster. They were Indians and she could have sworn that, despite leather jackets and jeans, long hair and sweatbands, they belonged to the sinister group who had tried to drag her onto the pick-up truck.

Realising that she had seen them, they turned away, whispering together, trying to look casual but with an undisguised alertness, like plain clothes detectives at home. She remembered how Gran, with her sharp eyes, had maintained that you could always spot a policeman out of uniform.

Seeing their faces clearly as they turned and looked through the window again she thought they might be brothers. Or was she falling into that age-old Caucasian trap, that all other races except the superior whites looked alike. High cheekbones, cleft chins, broad well-shaped mouths, they touched a faint chord of a face seen before, long ago.

Suddenly she panicked, remembering the almost deserted road back down to the creek. What if they decided to follow her? Would they be deterred by Luke's presence? But he was just a boy, how could he protect her?

Luke seemed aware of her thoughts. He touched her hand and mouthed, 'Don't be afraid, we'll be all right.'

Paying the bill, she took his hand and walked

swiftly towards the gas station two hundred yards away. There were payphones on the wall outside.

'We'll get a cab,' she said to Luke.

But the phone system was new to her and she couldn't find a directory and didn't have any dimes. She was wasting precious minutes for each time a car appeared and slowed down, she looked fearfully over her shoulder expecting it to be the two Indians, expecting them to leap out and seize her, ignoring her resistance as effectively as the Magic Men with their pick-up truck. The deafening sound of heavy metal music played at full pitch from inside the gas station would stifle her cries for help.

This time there would be no cavalry to the rescue in the shape of Chay Bowman.

A car slowed down and stopped. She saw movement in it, a door opened.

Waiting no longer, she took Luke's arm and rushed into the supermarket section of the gas station. Seizing the first thing that came to hand, a packet of cookies, she asked for dimes in her change and could they please give her the number to call for a taxi.

Obviously they had few such requests but the assistant was polite, asked her to wait and said he'd enquire.

Kate turned and murmured apologetically to another customer waiting to pay for a basket of groceries.

She smiled at Kate. 'Hi, there. Thought I recognised you. I'm Tessa Rhodes, we're neighbours.' At Kate's puzzled look, she said, 'Saw you move in yesterday.'

'Here's the number, ma'am,' the assistant said to Kate.

Quickly paying her bill, Mrs Rhodes followed her out.

'Did you have a breakdown—where are you parked?'

'I'm not. We walked.'

Mrs Rhodes stared from Kate to Luke. 'You never did. All that way. Why, you should have called me. It's no distance with a car, but that long hill. I'd die!' And opening the car door said firmly, 'Hop in. At least you won't have to walk back.'

Kate sighed gratefully. The US cavalry, as Luke would put it, had arrived again. In a different guise but in the nick of time.

One of the Indians had emerged from the gas station. So she had been right. They had followed her. His companion was making a phone call, staring straight across at her.

As Luke scrambled into the back seat, Mrs Rhodes asked, 'What's your boy called?'

'Luke,' said Kate.

Mrs Rhodes looked at her. 'He's like you.' And seeing Kate's anxious expression as she stared out of the window. 'Something wrong, honey?'

'Yes. Did you see those two men back

76

there?'

'Sure. They're Indians.'

'I know that, but I think they were following me.'

Mrs Rhodes smiled. 'You've seen too many movies. All our Indians are harmless, their teeth and their sharp claws drawn more than a century ago, so Warren—my husband—tells me.' With a sideways glance, she added, 'There could be another reason. They're young 'uns and you're a pretty woman. You have wonderful hair.' She paused. 'Can I be personal?'

'If you mean, is it natural, then it is. And I've always hated the colour. Ever since I could remember I've longed for raven black tresses.'

'What a sacrilege. But that's always the way, I guess.' Mrs Rhodes touched her short, tightly permed curls. 'I've long forgotten what my real colour was—haven't seen it for twenty years. Rich mouse, I think—what they call "fair". I longed to be a blonde without all the bore of peroxide . . .'

But Kate was hardly listening, all her attention was nervously directed to watching through the back window, to see if they were being followed. Once they turned off towards the creek, they had the road to themselves. There was no sign of the Indians.

She sat back. Perhaps Mrs Rhodes had been right and they were just two unknown admirers. Relaxing she was surprised to discover that the road back seemed considerably shorter downhill.

Outside her temporary home, Kate was introduced to Raj, the Rhodes German shepherd who bounded out to greet them and after a polite but cursory sniff at Kate, rushed eagerly to Luke.

'He likes you both,' said Tessa, as the big dog, who on his hind legs was as tall as Luke, leaped round him, tail wagging delightedly.

Mrs Rhodes looked quickly at Kate, said reassuringly. 'He won't hurt your boy. He's mild as a lamb, like most of the dogs here.'

'So I've noticed.'

Mrs Rhodes laughed. 'Noisy, but harmless. They get used to their owners' cars, but if anyone comes on foot, they raise one hell of a row and the whole place is on the alert. Our own neighbourhood watch and better than any burglar alarms. Neat, isn't it?'

She shook her head. 'Makes us kind of careless about bothering to lock doors and so forth. We can't keep pussycats, of course. The coyotes would have them for breakfast. Or any small domestic pet that wandered away. Some folks ignored the warning and tried, but the moggies were never seen again.'

She waved towards the wire mesh enclosures. 'Small dogs too. They have to be kept behind those for safety and walked out on chains. Come, Raj,' she called, 'let that boy be. You can eat him up later.' And smiling at Kate.

'Come and have a drink with us, meet Warren. He's a retired history professor, UCLA—he'll tell you all about the Indians, the undiluted history of Blackhawk Creek's past.' She laughed. 'More than a person would ever want to know, I guess. He has mountains of files, his granny's old letters and so forth. And he just adores a captive audience. 'Bye, for now.'

Kate left her thoughtfully. Mrs Rhodes's attitude to the creek's dog population suggested over-optimism. She didn't want to dampen her faith in them as guard dogs by telling her that she and Luke, perfect strangers, had walked up the hill past all the houses accompanied by friendly tail-wagging and not so much as one solitary warning growl. It made her uneasy after her experience with the Magic Men and the two Indians who, she was still certain, had been watching her. She would have felt happier and more secure pinning her faith on a good anti-burglar device, some highly neurotic dogs and a less flimsy Yale lock.

*   *   *

Tessa Rhodes watched her go indoors.

When Warren came back from golf, she was waiting to tell him of her meeting with Mrs Fenner and her boy.

'Fine looking woman. Saw her out on the deck this morning. Great shape,' said Warren who had an eye for that sort of thing.

79

'Boy's good-looking too. And he has good manners.'

That he hadn't spoken a single word, she had never noticed, impressed at how he had smiled and inclined his head ever so politely. She didn't care to remind Warren that such cute behaviour had been unknown to their boys. It was her constant grumble that young 'uns pretended that grown-ups, particularly their own parents, were invisible these days.

'Boy's like his mother. Inherited that blonde hair,' said Warren.

Mrs Rhodes shook her head. 'I know. But it's the oddest damn thing. He's got the strangest eyes, sort of luminous.' She shivered. 'Not a bit like hers. More like some of the Indians . . .'

But Warren wasn't listening.

CHAPTER SIX

Go, and catch a falling star,
Get with child a mandrake root,
Tell me where all past years are,
And who cleft the Devil's foot.

JOHN DONNE, Songs and Sonnets,
'Song: Go and catch a falling star'

Chay Bowman had seen dead men in plenty

during his time as a cop on the San Francisco streets and in many a street fight before the supermarket massacre put an end to his promising career. The spray of bullets had narrowly missed his lungs, but they sure as hell hurt sometimes, especially the one in his thigh. Vague aches and pains reminded him that his body hadn't forgotten or forgiven the damage that was done, but made him thankful to be alive each new day.

He averted his eyes from Lopez's mangled body. The car was a write-off too. The gas tank had burst into flames as it hit the bottom of the canyon.

The cops from Flagstaff were already on the scene. Eyeing Chay's police reserve uniform one said sternly, 'You're a long way off limits, fellow, this guy hails from outside Phoenix.'

Another officer came forward. 'What's your interest?' he asked curiously.

Bowman shrugged. 'Just a dud car he sold to a client of mine. I wondered if he was working a scam for someone we think might be a murder suspect.'

'What was this case?' demanded the second cop.

'Two Navajo boys who were killed back at Blackhawk Creek two months ago.'

The officer shook his head. 'That's old news. Seem to remember the killer was an escaped cougar,' he added with an amused expression that plainly said: this is some naive guy.

'Maybe,' said Chay turning his attention to the burnt-out wreckage. There wasn't much left that could be used as evidence or in Lopez's partially charred body.

Turning to leave the scene, he decided to have one more try. 'Had any dealings with a guy called Wilderbrand from Red Butte Enterprises?'

'Nope,' The officer looked at him blankly. 'But we'll keep a lookout. Drugs is it?'

'Maybe,' repeated Bowman and drove off.

Back on the main highway, he gave way to a patrol car heading towards the accident and was hailed by a familiar face.

Rudd Shashtso, a friend from his schooldays, explained that he had been recently transferred to the detective squad at Flagstaff. In the customary Navajo fashion they politely discussed family matters. Rudd had spent holidays with Chay on Redfeather's ranch and sent his regards to the old man before nodding towards Chay's car.

'So the reserve recruited you. Heard you were in the private eye business.' He paused. 'Is this a case or is it just curiosity that brought you here?'

When Chay told him about Lopez and mentioned the two Navajo boys, Rudd gave him an odd look.

'I was on a similar case—open and shut, just like that—a couple of years ago. Might interest you.'

'Sure would.'

The bleep of Chay's mobile phone interrupted what showed prospects of becoming an interesting conversation.

'I'll fax it to you,' said Rudd, and leaning out of the car window. 'For your eyes only, remember. Seeing as how you're an old buddy.'

*   *   *

In the office, Chay told Rita. 'You can take the rest of the afternoon off.'

'Brilliant!'

'There's just one little thing.'

Her smile faded. 'And what's that?' she demanded suspiciously.

'There's a car outside, I want you to deliver it to Miz Fenner.'

'Mr Lopez's customer?' She looked at him curiously.

'The same. Seeing he can't deliver, I've got her one from the hiring firm down the road.'

'She's paying for it, of course?' demanded Rita sharply.

'Naturally. We're not a benevolent society.'

'No, just a new order of chivalry,' was the reply. Rita shook her head sadly but she wasn't too displeased. This gave her a chance to see what this Anglo woman was like, a potential female client who was capable of turning Chay into a mother hen. She hadn't encountered him in this role before and it suggested possibilities that she would be wise to investigate carefully.

'I'll go ahead in my car. Show you the way.'

'Gee thanks. I was wondering if I'd have to walk back.'

Her look spoke volumes and he added hastily. 'This Wilderbrand business—I'm sure he was behind Lopez's death.'

'You think the road accident was murder?'

'That's how it adds up to me.' He frowned towards the news cutting on the board. 'And I can't get rid of this gut feeling that there's a definite link somewhere with those two boys.'

Rita sighed and pulled on a cardigan. 'OK, you're the boss.' Her attitude as she turned the notice on the office door to 'Closed' told Chay what she thought of that theory.

*   *   *

At the creek Miz Fenner answered the door.

Introduced, Rita's worst fears were realised. She took one look at that long blonde mane no Indian could ever resist. A beautiful Anglo scalp, not to be hung on a pole but to be taken to bed. Just what she suspected Chay had been dreaming about ever since he started collecting old British videos of long-ago movie stars like Madelaine Carroll and Deborah Kerr.

Fear gave way to certainty and mild despair as she watched him, suddenly gauche and awkward, twisting the brim of his hat like a teenager looking shyly into long-lashed blue

84

eyes, the colour that had earned all Anglos the name 'White Eyes' from her people. She suppressed a sigh of disgust at Chay Bowman, tough, strong ex-cop, shrewd private investigator, behaving like a schoolboy with the hots for the girl next door.

Eager to get away, she hardly listened to the conversation between them as Chay handed over the documents. She had been forgotten and was wondering how she could get into Chay's car without appearing huffy and drawing attention to her humiliation, when a young boy came out. He was wearing a cowboy hat rather self-consciously and ignoring the grown-ups he went out to look at the Dodge.

Aware of Rita's presence again, Chay turned to look for her. 'Come and meet Luke.'

Introduced as Chay's partner which wasn't a bad description all told, and hoping Miz Fenner had noted that too, Rita said, 'Hi, Luke.'

The boy bowed over her outstretched hand. Kinda cute, she thought, always impressed by good manners. 'How do you like it here?'

In answer he looked around, held out his hands in a gesture that took in their surroundings and nodded. Then he smiled and went back to examining the car.

Rita waited politely on the sidelines watching Chay and the boy's mother narrowly. A few minutes can seem an eternity when you love a man, when he is your whole world and he

85

doesn't care a damn about you. It's then you notice every little thing like a knife in the heart when he talks to another woman.

They were going inside the house and almost as an afterthought, Chay turned and waved to her to follow. As she trailed after them, taking stock of the surroundings, she heard Chay explaining something about adjusting the temperature controls on the central heating.

The kitchen table was occupied by Luke's Internet, a mighty handsome outfit, Rita decided. The empty container it was delivered in had been pushed into one corner and she made a quick note of the supplier's name.

There weren't many personal possessions in the lounge, a concertina photo frame with some ancient family photographs. Looked like this lady had brought all her ancestors along with her.

At last they were ready to leave and polite farewells were exchanged. Chay leaned out of the window and saluted Miz Fenner. As they started back up the hill, Rita sighed and leaned back in her seat.

'Is that us finished with Miz Fenner then?'

Chay thought some before replying. 'That depends on the whereabouts of Mr Wilderbrand.'

Rita sighed, less patiently this time. 'Don't you think you've done more than your share, finding her a car and so forth. Let her take it to the cops if she's worried about this guy who let her down. Although, if she's got her money and the vacation, everything included, and her return ticket home, I don't see what she's got to moan on about.'

As she paused to see the effect of her words, Chay's face was impassive. 'Ever considered that he might just be a good guy with a taste for helping waifs and strays. Just like you,' she added a trifle acidly.

Chay ignored that. 'Let's just say I don't like cases left unsolved and anything I've had a hand in no matter how slight, I want to see it all neatly tied up—and explained.' he added doggedly.

'I thought it was only the Scots who were known for their cautious natures.'

'Why do you say that?'

'Chay, didn't you notice her accent.'

Chay grinned. 'That was pretty sharp. Sounded like English to me.'

'You were wrong,' she said triumphantly. 'We had a teacher from Scotland at the mission school and I was friendly with two girls whose parents were from Edinburgh.'

'That's where she's from.'

A moment later Rita asked what she was dying to know. 'Is she a widow?'

'I don't know. She hasn't mentioned any husband, but it's not the kind of question that I'd consider polite.'

'For heaven's sake,' said Rita impatiently, 'you could have asked to see her passport. All very right and proper when you're dealing with hired cars.'

They were waiting at the intersection on the highway for the lights to change. A glance at Rita's face told him she was sulking.

'Single parent, alone in the world. That's what I'd reckon,' she said.

'Turned psychic, have you?' He grinned at, her.

'No, just observant. If there had been a husband, he'd have been included in the deal. If she was a widow then she would almost certainly have had his picture there with the others.'

'What others?'

'All those on the window sill, grannies and so forth going back to the year dot by the look of them.'

'Maybe she's sentimental about the past.'

'Which rather suggests that I'm right. I can imagine the devotion of a single mother to a handicapped child. Any woman can.'

'What gives you the idea he's handicapped?'

'Well, he's not deaf, unless he lip reads, but he sure doesn't say a lot. I'd say he was a mute. You know, at first glance when he was wearing that cowboy hat and I didn't see his fair hair, I'd have sworn he was one of our people.'

Chay was impressed by Rita's deductions and realised he'd been too concerned with his reactions to the lovely mother today to take any more notice of the strange son. Never mind.

He'd soon remedy that. Find some excuse to call on her again, but next time he'd make sure that he went by himself, without Rita's sharp eyes boring into the back of his neck. However the idea of Kate Fenner being so alone in the world with her mute boy that she had to bring images of her ancestors with her, he found both moving and appealing.

*   *   *

Kate had never loved anyone but Luke's father.

In the years since his birth she had met many men, always with the hope that this might be the one, but fleeting 'mini-flings', as she described them to Gran, always left her disillusioned.

If men came in DIY kits, then with the brains of one, the body of another, the humour of a third and so forth, she might have been able to make up her ideal lover. But the passing years left her increasingly certain that the prospect of her secret requirements ever coming together in one man was bleak indeed.

Like thousands of other girls she had been madly, insanely in love with Sean Doe, the Western singer, for a long time and had a life-size poster of him above her bed. His smiling face was the last thing she saw when she put out the light and the first thing she saw when she opened her eyes in the morning. His songs serenaded every mealtime. She lived, breathed and dreamed Sean Doe long before she went to London and queued all night for a concert ticket, to see him play at the Albert Hall.

She thought how lucky she had been. Lucky, after the concert, to have run across the street to try to get a taxi in the rain when, stumbling she had fallen almost beneath the wheels of an approaching car. The beautiful limousine had stopped and Sean Doe himself jumped out and picked her up. He had taken her back to his hotel, saying that she was in shock and he couldn't think of letting her go back to a bed and breakfast hostel when he had a whole suite. After all, it was his fault, he had nearly run her down.

Her thin summer dress was mud-splashed and grimy. While she stood in the hotel's penthouse, blinking at the magnificence of her surroundings, he emerged with a bathrobe for her to wear.

'Take off your dress.'

When she looked startled he said, 'The hotel laundry has a one-hour service.'

To this day, every single time she showered, she remembered that night. She couldn't turn the shower off properly, and he had come to help. In the cool-scented water, his hands were so warm.

What happened afterwards was inevitable and she would have believed the whole episode was a fantasy if it hadn't been for Luke. Sometimes she thought she had been fortunate. Unlike so many women who know only a brief passion that soon fades into a lifetime of mediocrity, cold and sour, stretched out into years of compromise and indifference, her brief relationship remained immutable.

But what would life have been had she stayed with Sean—if he had asked her to? For, despite his notoriously fickle reputation, she always pretended that, knowing about Luke, he would have insisted on marrying her. But would he really? And most important, would she have been able to live up to his bright flame which quenched her own?

The emptiness of the years since his death made her certain that her first experience of sex had been the one and only emotional impact in her life. As it retreated, became remote, imagination added wistful enchantment and a kind of deification.

She was touched to hear that thirteen years after his death there was still a Sean Doe fan club in existence. Occasionally his songs on radio brought back vividly to life the bitter sweetness of that one night of love.

He had been oddly touched to realise that she was a virgin—made a joke of it. Next morning he had kissed her lightly in reception in front of everyone and whispered that he'd keep in touch when he got back to America. She hung on to the belief that he would have done so if his private plane hadn't crashed in a storm over New Mexico. Only the burnt-out wreckage and bodies of the four men had been found.

The obituaries told grieving fans very little about Sean Doe's background. Some said that he was Argentinian, others that he was part Mexican. Even his name was an enigma, but whatever the truth of his extraordinary life, it went to the grave with him.

His rise to fame had been sudden and meteoric and the newspapers concentrated on the last four years of his life. A womaniser, shallow, vain, he might well have been to others, but to Kate the strangest and most beautiful man she had ever met. That brief contact with perfection had spoilt her and Sean Doe became the mirror she held up before every man she met afterwards.

And he had left her something, part of himself for ever in his son, a child who defied all the natural laws of conception. Conceived in the allegedly safe period of the menstrual cycle, obeying some other cosmic law unheeded by man, despite all manner of contraception.

Gran's old wives tales were in total agreement, 'A child determined to be born will force its way into the world no matter what you do to prevent it.' She could quote chapter and verse on a dozen such cases.

And looking back on those hazy events of thirteen years ago, Kate wondered rather forlornly if the sole purpose of her own creation had been to bring Sean Doe's son into the world. Why had her path crossed his that night? Why had he loved her, bewitched by a beauty he imagined he saw in her long golden hair, her 'Englishness' as he called it.

Luke accepted that his father had died in a flying accident and that he was American, leaving her to consider whether his addiction to westerns had somehow been inherited in his genes.

She looked out of the window and once again the unreality of this movie-set red rock exterior had her feeling that she would wake up back home in Edinburgh to find there was no winning competition for Luke and that Gran was still alive.

Gran had died the week before Luke knew he had won the competition. And for the first time Kate knew she was free. Not that Gran had been demanding, but at ninety she needed someone to look after her. She had long since turned the running of the guest house over to a reliable couple with Kate there to supervise and keep an eye on the accounts.

Kate looked at the family photographs. Gran had brought her up, the nearest thing she had ever had to a mother. Losing her had left a deep, empty well of sorrow that only time could heal.

Family History

NOTE: *Readers who are not interested in such*

information and find it an unnecessary interruption should proceed to page 101.

It was a measure of Kate's insecurity that she never travelled anywhere without her three generations of ancestors. Few in number, her entire family could be accommodated in one small plastic frame, and such photographs were to her what teddies and St Christopher medals were to those of nervous disposition.

First, great-grandmama Donna Anna, the one they called 'the Spaniard', rigid but slightly out of focus in unbridal sepia. Brought back to Montrose by her sea captain great-grandfather Peter Alexander, his allegedly 'high-born Castilian lady' had died giving birth to Kate's grandmother Jetta.

The bereaved husband had to return to the sea. His infant daughter needed a nanny. There were offers in plenty from the Alexander females, but he had no intention of leaving his motherless bairn to their tender mercies. Especially as he had never allowed them across the threshold, even for the funeral, after their shabby treatment of his young wife while she lived.

The captain's first officer had a cousin looking after his wife who had been poorly. The captain took a long look at Lizzie Fleming. He liked what he saw, the right stuff for a nanny, sharp and practical as himself. Lizzie was comely too, and so by all accounts was

94

Captain Alexander. After burying two wives he wasn't finished with matrimony and on his next voyage home he married Lizzie and in due course Amy, Kate's step-grandmother (who she called Gran) was born, thereby deepening the rift in the Alexander family.

No doubt there would have been more bairns but the captain, who believed in his own immortality and his ship's impeccable seaworthiness, went down with all hands in a hurricane off the Florida coast. Disinherited by the Alexanders, Lizzie took both bairns back to Edinburgh where Jetta howled in misery wanting to go back to the seaside at Montrose, where she used to play for hours with the rosy pink sandstone pebbles on the beach and now had to make do with the perfectly ordinary, less agreeable, variety offered by Portobello beach.

Jetta was five years older than Gran, a fey sort of creature who never played with dolls and talked to herself in a funny sort of language. As Jetta got older, Gran thought secretly that she wasn't 'all there'.

'Folk were scared of her. They would have had her for a witch, burned her in the Grassmarket, in the old days,' she told Kate. 'Especially when she "saw" things. Things that never boded good to anyone. There weren't stacks of books on psychology in the libraries then. No social services to try to sort out a bewildered little lass who walked for miles, running away from home with a basket over her arm picking up pink stones till they got too heavy to carry any further. Then she'd sit down by the roadside, until someone, usually me, found her and brought her home. With that passion for collecting rocks and pebbles she'd have been a geologist these days, but there was nothing for lasses before the First World War. Just get yourself a husband and have some bairns.'

Kate had the only surviving childhood photo of Jetta as an improbable fairy posed against a hideous potted palm, long before she went off to be a servant to a well-off family in the Grange where, touching forty, she met Reverend Thadeus Fenner.

'He was impressed by her lack of worldliness, which poor man, he mistook for godliness,' Gran told her. 'Whether he ever found out his mistake, we'll never know. Your mother, Florence was born the next year but she never knew her parents either. Thadeus went to preach at Skye and both he and Jetta drowned in a sailing accident.'

In common with many other women, the First World War had deprived Gran of her one love, leaving only a faded photograph of a smiling, handsome young soldier. Destined to be neither wife nor mother, looking after her mother Lizzie, painfully wasting away with cancer, Gran took on the task of bringing up Florence. A difficult child, she had screaming tantrums as well as her mother's weird tendency for seeing things and her passion for wandering off to collect pretty red rocks and pebbles, which Gran conscientiously added to the rockery begun by Jetta in her pre-marriage days.

The money left by Reverend Fenner soon vanished. Always practical, Gran did her sums and decided to take in boarders to fill the twelve rooms of a Victorian manse, destined for a minister's vast family of children and servants. And so, the guest house on the south side of Edinburgh was born.

At sixteen, Florence showed little inclination for scholarship and went to work in a cake shop, bought a bicycle and spent all her leisure hours on the beach at Portobello hunting for coloured rocks to paint into her wildly imaginative landscapes.

'The kind that go down well in the Museum of Modern Art these days,' said Gran, 'but I couldn't make head nor tail of them. Great towering red rocks, like something from Dante's "Inferno". When I used to ask her where she got all her ideas from she said it was easy, the pictures were all in her head, as if part of her lived in a different place. She said once, "I feel like a pilgrim out on a journey, but no one has told me where I'm going."

'Weird it was. Like a bairn left in a strange house after a party, always waiting for someone to collect her, but they never came—that is, until a good-looking young boarder came to

97

stay. An art student from Australia. His father, he said, was a wealthy sheep farmer.'

Gran regarded this miracle as the answer to her prayers. Florence had a sweetheart at last. She'd get married and be someone else's responsibility for a change. Tom stayed all that summer, quite forgetting, on the day he left, to settle his last month's bill in the excitement of taking Florence with him.

Kate knew the rest of the story. How a year later her mother had trudged up the street, heavily pregnant but alone. Tom had taken all her savings and gone to Australia to tell his parents the glad tidings and get their blessing. His mother would be so thrilled having a grandchild to knit for. That was six months ago and she hadn't had a word from him since.

Gran said nothing, surprised that Florence was naive enough not to smell a very outsize rat. But blissfully optimistic, she could hardly wait until Kate was on solids to hightail off to Australia in search of her missing husband.

Several months later, in a foul temper, she returned with hardly a glance for the baby, Kate, who now regarded Gran as her mother.

'And where is Tom? Did you find him?'

Oh, she had found him all right. Comfortably ensconced in Sydney with his legal wife and two children.

Gran hated to admit it to anyone, but Florence took out her spite on Kate. If ever a mother hated her child, then she hated the

98

little girl whose father had betrayed her. Gran never told Kate how she had snatched her many a time, sobbing, from her mother's blows. How she had told Florence in no uncertain manner that she was a rotten bitch to take her spite out on a helpless bairn.

'Get away from Edinburgh if that's what you want. No one needs you here. I'll bring Kate up. As I did you,' she reminded her, 'and a fat lot of good you were to me.'

Florence never returned. Until Kate was old enough to hear the truth, Gran told her that her mother had died when she was a baby. Perhaps it was true. She had often hoped so.

As for Gran, her sacrifices were rewarded at last. Right from the beginning Kate made up for all the faulty genes, the deficiencies in Jetta and Florence. Such strange bairns, unformed in many ways, drawing beings from other worlds in the days before science fiction and *Dr Who* on TV.

When Kate asked what happened to her mother's paintings, as she had never seen them, Gran shook her head.

'Nobody but me ever saw them. She kept them with her poetry and burnt the lot before she went to Australia.'

There was a lot Gran could have told Kate about her mother, things the poor lass would be happier not knowing. Like how well she remembered Florence destroying the paintings and notebooks, setting fire to them in the garden, watching over them till they turned to ashes. Like someone burning love letters. Perhaps she thought that way her hurt could be burnt out of her too.

Kate had only one picture of Florence in bouffant skirts at someone's wedding, looking happy as Kate never remembered her.

The quintet of photographs was completed by Gran and Luke, but a family history so devoid of males suggested similarities to more primitive amoeba-like creatures whose lineage was of entirely female descent.

It would all change with Luke, Gran had prophesied, when his birth was over. She had been shocked at first, since the fastidious Kate had never shown any tendency to indulge in the free and easy sexual associations of her fellow students at the university.

There had never been any question in the minds of either of them that she should not have the baby. Gran's qualms were superstitious, based on the curious fact that in their family few mothers survived long enough to see their bairns to school.

But with Luke safely delivered, he became the embodiment of her devotion to three generations, the son and grandson she had never known, the perfect child. Clever too. Proud of him, she insisted that he must meet the 'right' people and get on in the world. When he won a scholarship to boarding school, she insisted he should go there; she'd pay his fees and he would live in with other lads as was right and proper, instead of living at home with females all the time. Always ready to indulge him, the Internet had been her present for being so clever.

'He'll go far, that bairn. Mark my words,' she had predicted and Kate wondered if in paradise she smiled proudly at Luke winning a holiday in this magic land beyond her own comprehension.

But God had been kind, Kate thought. Gran never knew of the death of Togger, who had been Luke's best friend, or of the mysterious fire which had forced the governors to request that his mother remove him from the school until the outcome of their enquiries was complete.

CHAPTER SEVEN

If we want to feel humility . . . it suffices to gaze upon the world cultures that existed before us, achieved greatness before us, and perished before us.

C. W. CERAM, Gods, Graves & Scholars

Rita was misjudging him again, Chay decided. It wasn't true that he was interested in Miz Fenner's mysterious benefactor just because she was a pretty woman.

'You should know me better than that by now,' he told her trying to sound wounded. 'You know unsolved mysteries bug me.'

'Oh, yeah,' was the laconic response as Rita swung round from her contemplation of the fax which for some time past had only ever spewed up bills. 'Private investigator' was beginning to sound like an expensive hobby and, if it wasn't for Chay's police pension, they'd be closing shop.

'All the estate agents would say was that the house was rented by a firm called Red Butte Enterprises in Miz Fenner's name and as far as the clerk could remember, someone paid the rent in cash—in hundred dollar bills.' Rita shrugged. 'Same with the Internet equipment. I phoned the dealer when we got back and what does he tell me? That it was ordered by Red Butte Enterprises—and paid for in cash.'

'Doesn't that strike you as suspicious?'

'Not really.'

'Come on. Everyone uses plastic these days.'

'You could try asking Miz Fenner how she received the prize money. We might have had more luck with the boy, about this competition and so forth—if he could speak, and if we could understand the intricacies of the World Wide Web.'

Chay thought. 'Seems we just have to find out what happened to Wilderbrand. The firm doesn't exist, the street doesn't exist. What does that suggest to you?'

'One way to find out is to make it an official police enquiry, but unless we can prove that there are criminal activities involved they won't touch it. After all there's nothing illegal about having stationery printed in some fancy name unless you are using it for fraudulent purposes. And no crime has been committed. Everything has been above board. Our Mr Wilderbrand has been very careful not to step outside of the law, everything ordered and paid for. So what have we to go on?' She looked at Chay. 'You might have got some valuable information out of Lopez if he'd survived.'

'Maybe he knew too much and had some blackmail in mind, and that was the reason for his accident.'

'Delivered and paid for in dollar bills again, no doubt,' was Rita's cynical response.

Chay couldn't take on board Kate's kidnapping hysteria but he could smell something phoney about the whole deal. If Wilderbrand wasn't just some harmless loony benefactor, then someone was mighty anxious to get Kate Fenner and her son over here. What he didn't know yet was who—and more important, why? He just couldn't shake off the gut feeling that Lopez's death was linked with the killing of the Begay brothers. Worse, that his own grandfather might be implicated by association with the Magic Men.

Rita swung her chair round. 'I'll keep on

digging if that's what you want.'

'Good.' Seeing her expression, he said, 'Aren't you intrigued?'

She stared at the screen, tapping at a few keys. 'I could be. If it was Mel Gibson you were investigating.'

She watched him go out and dutifully considered her enquiries. She had covered all the usual procedures but no one knew what went on in the minds of Internet addicts, although there were rumours in plenty, pornography for one. Could be Wilderbrand fancied pretty young boys. But unless he had committed some crime and wasn't just a harmless dotty benefactor that Luke had tuned into on the World Wide Web, who felt sorry for the mute boy from Edinburgh and wanted to give him a treat, then Chay Bowman, Private Investigator, had reached an impasse.

She couldn't go much further without a lot of information from Luke's mother since, according to Chay's report, the prize had been a total surprise to her, and without knowledge of the workings of the Internet, she could hardly question a mute eleven-year-old. She probably didn't even think it necessary. She'd have been completely convinced when the letter arrived announcing the prize.

A fax arrived; a married woman in Phoenix who suspected that her husband's business activities in Red Rock were a screen for an affair with his secretary. Her address in

Scottsdale was a pretty fancy place.

Rita sat back. At last. Here was something boring but lucrative they could work on, at one hundred dollars an hour that would pay some bills and divert Chay's attention from Miz Fenner.

*   *   *

Chay hadn't expected to see Kate again so soon.

He went into a jeweller's shop for a new battery for his wristwatch and there she was at the counter trying on Navajo bracelets.

Looking up, she greeted him cordially and said, 'Am I glad to see you! You're just the one who can help me—I don't know a thing about turquoise.'

The bracelet she was twisting round her wrist was heavy and it looked valuable.

'He says it's only forty dollars. Doesn't that seem like a bargain?' She held out her hand for his inspection. 'What do you think?'

Chay knew the piece was worth five times that.

'Hold on.'

He spoke rapidly to the Navajo behind the counter and turned again to Kate who was watching them without understanding a word.

'As I thought. It's an unredeemed pledge.'

'Is that good?'

He shook his head. At her puzzled

105

expression, he explained, 'Jewellery that has been pawned. Brought in over six months ago, the owner never came back for it, so they are free to sell.'

'So that's why it's such a bargain,' said Kate, examining it closely. 'I do like it. It's lovely. What do you think?' she repeated.

Chay frowned. It was large and too heavy for a woman. It was a man's ornament. And dead pawn.

'Came in with several other pieces,' the Navajo dealer had told him. 'I wouldn't have touched it, if I had been in that day. I'll be glad to be rid of it. Guy who brought it in was probably a skinwalker who had stolen it from a corpse.'

Kate, waiting for his opinion, said eagerly, 'Well, shall I buy it?'

He shook his head and, removing the bracelet from her wrist, he replaced it on the tray. 'Let's talk about it, outside.'

'What did he tell you?' she asked him as he followed her out. 'You were both looking very serious.'

'I just didn't think you should buy it.'

'Why ever not?' When he didn't reply, she said, 'Was it stolen property or something?'

'You might call it that. Look, if you have a spare moment, may I buy you a coffee?'

As she thanked him, he steered her into an almost empty cafe.

'You're being very mysterious, Mr Bowman.

106

What was all that about?'

'Dead pawn.'

'Dead pawn?' she repeated. 'I don't understand.'

'Let's just say it's not a very good investment.'

'Why not?'

'When a rich Navajo dies, they put him in a coffin and people, his family and friends, bring gifts of jewellery which they bury with him. It's an old tradition, the dead being accompanied by good things to help them along in the spirit world.' He shrugged. 'Sometimes dishonest people come along and rob the grave, steal the jewellery and sell it.'

She was listening intently and he didn't know how to go on. 'These people are called skinwalkers.'

'Skinwalkers?'

'Yeah. Bad people.' Again he shrugged, trying to explain. 'Like vampires. And if you wear jewellery that they've stolen from graves and you don't have the skinwalker power, then, well—it could bring bad luck. It could even kill you.'

Her eyes widened. 'Do you believe all that?' Her expression said that she didn't.

'It's the way I was brought up to believe, Miz Fenner. My grandfather knows all about such things. It may be wrong, but I'd rather not see you—an Anglo lady—take any chances.'

She considered him for a moment. Then she

107

smiled. 'That's very good of you. And I'm grateful.' She added softly, 'Your grandfather—is he a medicine man?'

'Sort of. He used to be a movie star.'

'Really? Wait until I tell Luke.'

Chay sipped his coffee. 'Where is he?'

'Oh, I couldn't drag him away from his new toy, especially when he knew it was to go shopping.' She drained her coffee. 'But I'd better be getting back.' And indicating her shopping bag. 'I had to pick up a few things for our supper.'

Seizing the bag he led the way out into the warm sunshine.

'Where are you parked?'

'I'm not. I walked.'

Chay stopped, 'Something wrong with the car?'

'No, it's fine. We had a little run last night.' She laughed at his puzzled expression. 'I enjoy the exercise. I do a lot of walking back in Edinburgh.'

'Come along,' he said firmly and taking her arm, ushered her towards his car parked outside the office. 'I'll take you back down the hill.'

When she protested about being too much trouble, he opened the door and pushed her gently into the passenger seat. 'No trouble. I'll enjoy the drive.'

He liked being with her and that was the truth he wasn't prepared to admit to himself as yet, much less to Rita.

'It's so beautiful here,' she said leaning back happily as the road dipped towards the creek and the red rocks towered above them. 'Such peace. I envy the people who lived here long ago.'

He laughed. 'Only the dead lived right here. These rocks were revered—home of the Great Spirit, the sacred hunting grounds.'

He switched off the engine and surveyed the landscape, his eyes narrowed against the sun. 'They brought their dead chiefs here, buried them far beneath the ground. Their horses trampled the earth so that there was no sign of a grave. Not that the bodies would last long. There are so many hungry animals and snakes and other eager scavengers, none of them picky about their food. Vegetable or animal, and that includes humans. Bodies disappear without trace.'

Kate shivered. For some reason it made her think of Sean Doe and his friends in the plane, crashing into the desert. Suddenly she wondered if she was really wise to give her heart to this wild country, to allow its magic to captivate her. Magic, Gran had often told her, everyone with any sense knew, had two faces, good and evil.

'There are an amazing number of wild creatures around our house. Luke seems to attract them,' she added lamely, for that was extraordinary and when she thought about it, a bit sinister too. Especially as their stillness and the bright, eager intensity of their eyes watching him, brought vividly to mind the Indians who had tried to kidnap her.

'Those men, the other night,' she said.

'The Magic Men?' So he knew who she meant. He looked at her and asked sharply, 'What about them?'

'Well, I think I saw two of them again yesterday. I was sure they were following me.'

'What made you think that?'

'Well, they were staring at us through a cafe window back along the street there.'

He regarded her gently and smiled. 'Is that the truth?'

'Yes,' she said solemnly. 'I—I knew I was under surveillance and it was scaring, after what happened the first time.'

Chay thought for a moment. 'Were they all dressed up? Feathers and warpaint.'

'Of course not.' She realised how improbable her story sounded and that he was amused. 'They were dressed like you.'

'So what made you think they were from the Magic Men?'

'When we left the cafe they followed us to the petrol station.'

'And then?'

Now angrily aware that he didn't believe a word of her story, she said, 'My neighbour was in the store, she drove me back down the hill.'

'Another daring rescue?'

She heard the suppressed mirth in his voice and wished she had never mentioned it when he added, 'Were these two men young, old?'

'Young, I think.'

He shrugged. 'Then I think you have the answer.' When she turned to him frowning, he said very patiently 'No mystery, lady. Don't you ever look in the mirror?'

'Not to admire anything I see,' she said crossly.

'And I thought all women were vain.'

His tone made her anxious to change the subject. 'Tell me about these Magic Men.'

'Sure. They go back a long, long way. To the Anasazi. No one knew where they came from, or even when they arrived and they disappeared just as mysteriously, leaving behind evidence of an advanced state of civilisation. They'd built great roads across the south-west, houses too—some of their ruins are still visible.'

'How fascinating. I'd love to see them.'

He looked at her. 'Would you?' Here was a great chance. 'Maybe I could take you there sometime.'

'I'd love that.' The way she said it made him feel good. 'But I interrupted you.'

'Well, a small tribe who claim to be their sole survivors, direct descendants, Los Atalos, were discovered by the first whites to come here during the last century, living in a secret canyon near the creek here. It had been cut off by the collapse of one of the natural rock bridges through erosion and had never encountered the Conquistadores. They were peaceful folk, and left a record of their lives, rock carvings called petroglyphs.'

He paused. 'I can show you some of those too. Like the Anasazi, Los Atalos had strange powers. They were telepathic. I guess they belonged to an earlier strand of evolution when mankind had extra senses which our civilisation has destroyed.'

'What became of them?'

'The white men found a way into the canyon. Those who survived spread a story about an ancient Anasazi temple with walls of pure gold. They brought their own god's representative, a missionary to teach them the way of Christianity. Maybe he meant well, but to men with gold fever a few more damned Indians standing between them and a fortune meant less in terms of human life than going out and shooting a few jackrabbits. There was a massacre and the Los Atalos who survived were bundled off to the Apache and Navajo reservations.'

Kate looked out at the creek with its gently swaying willows, as he spoke, seeing the tragedies the land had witnessed, the rocks reddened not only by their natural sandstone but with human blood.

'From time to time some of their descendants have found their way back to Red

Rock to die in the sacred earth of what was once their homeland.'

It was a sad story, yet another strand in the Indian tragedy well known to her. 'What happened to the missionary?' she asked.

Chay shrugged. 'Story goes that he was murdered, his daughter abducted by the young chief. Some say she had a child by him but what became of them is a mystery the Magic Men are still trying to work out after more than a hundred years.'

'What do you think?' asked Kate.

'I think it's very unlikely that they survived. Those were lawless times.'

He paused and looked up at the canyon walls towering above them. 'There's supposed to be a kind of magnetism in these rocks, a vortex that draws the Los Atalos back, or anyone with their blood. The Magic Men claim to have it.'

'What about this lost temple? Are they still searching for it?'

Reading her eager expression Chay shook his head. 'No one has ever seen it—and survived to tell the story. But it it exists, I reckon it would be behind the cliff dwellings somewhere out there.'

He smiled as she continued to watch the red rocks. 'The Atalos village was right here where the mobile homes are now'.

He wondered about telling her the rest, then said, 'The Navajos think Blackhawk Creek is bad medicine. That it's haunted by chindi—ghosts of the dead.'

She looked faintly alarmed and he added, 'Nothing for you to worry about, just let's say that living close to the earth we've retained some of the primitive senses city life destroys.'

Seeing her surprise, he said, 'Some of us still believe that Nature Rules OK and we haven't been completely overruled—or even come to terms with, the white man's civilisation.'

'If coming to terms means losing the magic of all this,' Kate said, laughing, 'then I'm all for opting out. A very good idea.'

Chay nodded. 'We still have quite a long way to go, if we're to catch up. Los Atalos believed that their chief was immortal, that he never grew old and was constantly renewed by their gods, that he was hundreds of years old, the lone survivor of the Anasazi.

'He was still around when the white men came but I guess he died in the holocaust. The Magic Men never give up. They've been trailing their lost god for more than a hundred years.'

Kate sighed. 'What a fascinating legend.'

But as she said the words, she had the oddest feeling that it was all painfully familiar and that Chay's story had touched gossamer strands deep in some racial memory. But that couldn't be. She had no connection with this land. There was one explanation—

'Did they ever make a movie about Los

114

Atalos?' she asked.

'My grandfather could tell you that. He was a Hollywood Indian and he knows every one that's ever been made.' He grinned. 'Took scalps in quite a few. Metaphorically speaking. He was a great guy for the ladies and the white man's booze.'

Deciding on a change of subject he asked casually, 'Has Mr Wilderbrand contacted you yet?'

'No.' But she didn't seem too worried about his non-appearance. 'Probably been too busy, called away or something. I expect he'll get in touch soon. After all, we still have almost three weeks left.'

There was no point in sharing his misgivings. Letting her out of the car, he found himself looking for some reason for prolonging this meeting, or even better suggesting another one.

Luke had seen the car. He rushed out of the house, smiling and held out his hand.

'How are you today, young fellow?' said Chay.

Luke mouthed, 'Fine, thank you.'

Chay had a sudden inspiration. 'How would you like to meet my grandfather? He's been a movie star and he's a real Indian chief.'

Luke's eyes widened in delight. It was obviously a great idea. He looked at Kate.

'And your mother can come too.'

Kate laughed and put an arm around Luke.

'Oh, yes, please.'

'How about tomorrow then? Say I come around about four o'clock.'

As he left them and drove back up the hill, he realised that he was one other Navajo who had not shed all his primeval senses. He had heard the danger bells ringing, the gift that accounted for about twenty per cent of his success as a private eye. He doubted whether she knew about Lopez and he didn't intend to raise the subject, add to her fears unnecessarily. But he should have warned her about Wilderbrand. Next time, he'd make a point of telling her exactly what he had found out: the false address, the non-existence of Red Butte Enterprises.

Tomorrow, maybe . . .

CHAPTER EIGHT

The dream is the small hidden door in the deepest and most intimate sanctum of the soul.

CARL GUSTAV JUNG,
Psychological Reflections

Kate discovered that Luke was already familiar with the story of Los Atalos and Blackhawk Creek. The Internet apparently had access to every kind of historical material. According to Luke, you just pressed a few keys and there was a whole encyclopedia of the world and everything you could possibly want to know about.

You must learn, he told her. It's easy. There's nothing scary about it.

How had he guessed that this super-intelligence scared her? She didn't even feel terribly comfortable with that omniscient eye sharing her kitchen table. Even when it was switched off she wondered if its miraculous powers were scanning her private thoughts.

Luke had finished his daily chat with his worldwide chums and, watching her pack away the groceries, he decided he needed some action, like going to look for those old cliff dwellings.

She shook her head. 'Tomorrow, Luke. It's too late today, we might still be up there at sunset and it gets dark very quickly.'

*　　*　　*

That night she had a bewildering and frightening dream, doubtless the effect of Chay's revelations about Los Atalos.

She was with her mother Florence, who was wearing that bouffant dress in the photograph. They were passengers in a stagecoach, bumping its way through a canyon. A band of Indians rode towards them. Their leader stared in at the window. He smiled at her, indicating that she was not to be afraid.

The scene changed. Her mother was dead. She was standing by a grave with a cross, then the cross changed into an altar cross. She was being married to the young Indian. The church was suddenly filled with men carrying rifles. The minister, who in the dream was the father she had never known, was refusing to marry them. There was an argument, he sprang forward, a shot rang out and her father lay dead at her feet, his blood on her grey wedding dress.

She was clinging to her strange bridegroom. Crying.

Her cries awakened her. Her pillow was wet with tears.

She sat up in bed. It was moonlight and through the window leading onto the terrace, a solitary figure looked in at her, smiling, beckoning. It was the Indian from her dream. A tall figure in tribal dress, his hair pulled back into plaits.

She blinked, believing she still slept.

But this was no dream. The shimmering figure remained. His features were obscured by vivid stripes of white and red paint.

He smiled. And she saw that he had Luke's eyes.

Perhaps she fainted. Perhaps it was a dream within a dream, for when she opened her eyes again, it was Luke standing outside, staring

118

through the window at her.

Leaping out of bed, she unlocked the glass door.

'Luke! What on earth you doing out there?' she demanded crossly. 'What a terible fright you gave me.'

He indicated that he had heard something. Someone was out there.

Panic seized her. It had been one of the Magic Men. They had discovered where she was living.

Fearfully she stared into the dark shadows. They might still be out there, watching. Every ghostly boulder became a human shape. Terror destroyed all caution, all rational thought. She had to find someone to protect her and Luke. She must get help.

Her hands were shaking so much she could hardly read the telephone directory. Rhodes, that was it. She dialled the number, still watching the window, still seeing the dark shadows, watching them move ever so slightly towards the house.

At last a sleepy voice answered.

'Mrs Rhodes? Please help me. It's Kate Fenner, next door. I think we have a prowler. We've seen someone—out on the terrace. A man.'

The voice was no longer sleepy. 'Warren, you awake?' Then to Kate, 'All right, honey. Stay where you are. Warren's coming. He's got a gun.'

Still clinging tightly to Luke, Kate waited. After what seemed an interminable time, she heard the sound of a front door closing. A dog barking—Raj. Then footsteps round the house, a few scratchings and stumblings. A shadowy figure moved past the kitchen window.

A knock on the front door. Another voice, a woman's.

'Kate. Open up, honey. It's Warren and me.'

The couple were in dressing gowns and, looking at the clock, Kate saw it was three a.m.

She opened the door. Raj ran in first, sniffing around the room eagerly then, tail wagging, he ran to Luke's side and sat down.

'There's no one on the deck,' said Warren, seizing Raj's collar and cutting short her apologies for dragging them out, he allowed the dog to lead the way through the lounge and the bedrooms. 'He's got your scent and he'll know if anyone else has been inside.'

The dog came back without detecting an intruder and with a self-important air settled himself once again at Luke's side.

'Here, Raj.' Warren Rhodes sounded impatient as he unlocked the glass door. Far below they could hear the creek, coursing its way sleepily through the moonlit sycamores.

Tessa peered over her husband's shoulder. 'He could have escaped that way.'

Warren frowned. 'He could, but he'd have to come up somewhere close by and that would have set every dog on the square howling for his blood.'

Tessa turned to Kate reassuringly, 'If he'd come up on our deck, Raj would have let us know and no mistake. He's a great guard dog, the least whisper of a can dropping outside—'

'We know what he's like with strangers,' Warren cut in, 'all hell let loose.'

Kate didn't like to contradict but looking at Raj lamb-like at Luke's side, she found their faith and optimism in his abilities as a fierce guard dog barely credible.

Tessa put an arm around Luke. 'You all right?'

He nodded and smiled up at her.

She turned to Kate with an anxious expression. 'You're all shook up, honey. Look, why don't you both come back with us? We have spare beds in the guest room. You're most welcome.'

Warren, large in height and girth, loomed over them adding agreement to his wife's suggestion. With the gun under his arm, he was a comforting presence but Kate, although sorely tempted to accept, shook her head.

'You're very kind but I can't put you to all that trouble. I'm afraid I had a bad dream. I must have wakened Luke and he panicked.'

The Rhodes looked at them both trying to make sense of that, but too polite to comment on dreams that set all hell loose and brought neighbours out of bed in the middle of the night.

As they were leaving, Kate thanked them again, with profuse apologies. 'I hope you get back to sleep all right,' she added weakly.

'Think nothing about it. All this quietness down here, it does take city folk some time to get used to it.'

Warren paused to look up at the flagpole perched on a stone cairn. 'Different to what it used to be in my grandmother's day. A thriving community with Indians and settlers living happily together. And now nothing.'

His shrug was expressive. 'Hardly one damned stone on another to show for it. Everything vanished into the ground. Goodnight then.'

'It's like that with the old frame buildings,' said Tessa hastily watching Kate's nervous expression. 'If you set fire to them, I mean.'

'What happened?' said Kate.

Tessa's furious look at her departing husband said he was mighty tactless bringing that up.

'Indians, honey. They turned hostile. After the massacre the cavalry burned everything down.'

'How awful,' said Kate.

'Warren has loads of things about it. It's his pet subject. His grandmother had letters the missionary's daughter wrote to her. They were friends. He'll be only too happy to show them to you. He aims to write a book about it some day.'

There was a chill in the air and she shivered. Squeezing Kate's arm, she said, 'Sure you'll be all right?'

'Yes, of course. Thank you again.' Kate stared after her until their door closed.

Luke had already gone back to bed. He regarded her sleepily as she leaned over, kissed him, and tucked the covers around him.

Back in the kitchen the first streaks of dawn were reddening the tips of the red rocks. Not much point in sleeping now she thought so she made tea and toast and carried them through to the bedroom, switching idly from channel to channel on the all-night television.

Trying to concentrate on a programme about rare wild flowers but knowing that she wasn't taking any of it in, she realised she was trying to convince herself that the Indian in the garden had been a figment of a dream and not one of the Magic Men following her. She told herself over and over that if her visitor had been real then, according to Warren, Raj would have detected a stranger's presence. And that applied to a ghost. Even quite ordinary dogs, she knew, were sensitive to the supernatural. Their hackles rise and they snarl but Raj had been quite unperturbed.

A reasonable explanation was that Chay's stories about the chindi had triggered it off and that somehow being a minister's granddaughter also, and a single parent, her subconscious had taken over and formed a sympathetic link between herself and the tragic history of the girl who had lived long ago at Blackhawk Creek.

But the worst part of the nightmare, the part she couldn't shake off, was when the Indian turned into Luke.

Luke, whose eyes were also those of the father he had never known, the long-dead singer Sean Doe.

*   *   *

There were no more dreams. Three hours later she awoke still sitting up in her bed, with a very stiff neck and shoulders. Outside, the creek was bathed in sunlight.

It was morning.

She was safe again. And Luke, the habitual non-riser, was already awake. He had apparently forgotten all about the prowler and was out on the terrace throwing bread to a small tribe of squirrels and birds.

Watching gave her such pleasure. It was like a scene from Walt Disney's *Snow White.*

Dusting his hands of crumbs, he came in and while he was having his own breakfast, he decided what he wanted to do for the day.

The story Chay had told his mother about Blackhawk Creek, combined with his information from the Internet had fired his imagination. He wanted to climb the red rocks behind the house, and look for the cliff dwellings and signs of the lost temple of the Atalos.

As they were leaving the house, Tessa came out.

'All right this morning? No more bad dreams? Good.' Then indicating their boots and backpacks, she said, 'You two look very energetic.'

When Kate told her where they were going, she groaned. 'Lord, it'll get real hot up there in the canyon. There's a road wanders on for a couple of miles before it peters out. Why don't you drive?'

'Luke would like to walk.'

Tessa considered for a moment. 'If you don't feel like driving, I'll take you,' she said tactfully.

'I wouldn't think of it. We have a good map and we're not intending to go too far. We have a date back here at four.'

Tessa stared after their vanishing figures in disbelief. She found it difficult to understand why anyone offered the choice between riding and going on foot should choose the latter.

The mercury was already climbing and people who lived here all the time failed to see the allure of violent exercise to the visitor, on what promised to be a day to stay indoors with the air conditioners full on.

*   *   *

For the first hour, the path rose steadily. A

pleasant undemanding walk with only an occasional boulder needing negotiation or a patch of hazardous scree to be carefully crossed, which had once carried rocks the size of houses tumbling from the top of the butte, and huddled together at its base like a giant's discarded toys. Far below, the creek was still visible and Kate realised that although the terrain looked like an expanse of sloping red rock, smooth with a few fissures, an easy climb and an inoffensive hill scramble, the reality was different.

They were still only halfway up; each time the summit seemed accessible it was merely to find yet another plateau sloping to the horizon. And another, and another.

Luke was unperturbed, walking, climbing, scrambling hand over fist, always onward and upward, as if he had done it all many times before and, sure-footed with the certainty of familiarity, knew exactly where they were heading. Occasionally, seeing her breathless, he stopped, smiled encouragingly and, after waiting for her to catch him up, set off again, his whole demeanour one of eager expectation and absolute confidence.

Once an immense black hawk, startled by their sudden appearance in its domain, rose from a stunted tree and disappeared lazily, flying effortlessly before them, the sound of its wings breaking the silence like the rustle of a taffeta petticoat.

Kate stopped again for breath. She leaned against a boulder and stared down into the valley they had left two thousand feet below where the creek was a tiny ribbon, sun flecked into gleaming radiance, the houses indistinguishable, shrouded in heat haze.

All around them, the red rock monoliths rose straight and clean-cut into the sky, casting their great shadows across their path with a dignity born of utter indifference to the folly of humankind. Here and there she saw evidence of walls, ill-fashioned remains of the tortuous efforts of man, the lesser god than the one who had wrought this miracle of creation.

Long since scoured by wind and storm into crumbling insignificance, a piece flaked off in her hand and disintegrated into the sandstone earth at her feet.

They must be near the cliff houses.

She looked round. There was no sign of Luke. But before she could panic he appeared again, signalling frantically. He had found them.

She had expected a street of some kind but all that remained, some sixty feet above their heads, was almost unrecognisable as a cliff dwelling, except that windows and doors had been carved out of the solid rock. The interiors, black against the relentless sunlight, stared down at them, like giant empty eye sockets.

There was no way of approach. No ladder, nothing but the sheer cliff face. Luke was searching diligently. She joined him, but after half an hour, they knew they were defeated. Once upon a long time ago, the dwellers must have used ladders made of rope, or some other substance which like themselves had vanished into dust.

'We'd better press on,' she said, not altogether disappointed that they were unable to inspect those black holes of doors and windows far above their heads. She was afraid of what they might be hiding, what secrets of the ages might lie on those cool dark floors that had not known the footsteps of man in a thousand years.

It was a sinister place and, with the sun already dipping in the sky, she urged Luke to move on if they were to reach the summit of the butte before beginning the steep descent to the creek.

Once, looking over her shoulder, she shivered, unable to throw off the feeling of being watched from inside those long-deserted doors and windows. Ahead of them there was no exit from this plateau which had become a warren of tiny canyons, like rooms in the palace of a prehistoric world, one opening into another.

The day was cooling, but where they walked was a shallow sea of sunlight offering only the shade of occasional pinnacles, secret alcoves, or the mouth of a cave far above their heads.

Suddenly there was the gentle sound of

running water. They exchanged delighted looks as Luke tracked down a spring flowing from the base of one of the shadowy rocks before being swallowed up by another crevice.

The water was ice cold and clear, far better than the Coke they had brought, now unpleasantly warm. Leaving her to refill their water bottle, Luke ran on ahead to a narrow fissure in the rocks.

Turning he beckoned to her delightedly.

Far below was the last thing she had expected to see. A huge swimming pool in a large, well-cultivated garden with walls and paths and neatly laid out vegetable plots. The house was hidden by willow trees but, as they watched, two Indians came out and moved dishes on a table by the edge of the pool. Sounds travel in the clear air and even at that distance they could hear the faint clink of glass and cutlery and the men's subdued voices.

Kate looked at the sky. Her watch said three o'clock, too early for sunset, but the sky was darkening ominously and the air had changed, turning still and colder, as it did at dusk's approach. The rapid change in temperature signalled only one thing—a storm—and there was no time now to get back the way they had come.

She gazed longingly at the token of civilisation far below. Could they climb down, cut across the garden and find their way back to the creek by the access road that must exist somewhere out of sight? But even as the thought entered her mind, a door opened and four enormous black dogs, guard dogs, rushed out, systematically sniffing the environs of the garden. They stopped in their tracks and seemed to be staring up at the place where she and Luke crouched unseen.

Luke clutched her hand, shook his head. The dogs' search was disciplined to root out intruders and it quelled any thought of clambering down into that garden. Especially as, by leaning over a little further, Kate saw that barbed wires extended some twenty feet from the ground. No doubt it was electrified, the kind of enclosure one would expect to find around a prison camp.

Taking Luke's arm, they slid carefully back from the edge of the rock. The sky above them rattled, a drum roll of the storm to come, and she thought about Blackhawk Creek and Chay who would be arriving to take them to visit his grandfather.

They would never make it back in time.

A faint wind had arisen agitating the cottonwoods and sagebrush with a sound for all the world like faint applause, as if the spirits of the place were mocking their audacity, slow-clapping their persistence.

Anxiously they looked for possible shelter. There was no longer any denying that the storm, a big one, was almost on top of them. The thunderheads were rapidly covering the

130

sky like a great dark eyelid slowly closing on the still sun-bright horizon.

A zigzag of lightning, a distant warning rumble became a giant's faint roar shaking the canyon.

'We must head back the way we came, Luke. Try and beat the storm.'

They were too late for that. The wind increased, hurling sagebrush and dried leaves before it along the ground. The rain fell, a few droplets followed by stinging, giant hailstones, forcing them to turn, and race back towards the sheltering cliffs.

It was at that moment, blinded by rain, crossing a patch of scree that Luke stumbled and fell.

Kate running ahead, heard him cry out. She ran back, tried to seize him, watching in horror, as he slid slowly downwards towards a massive boulder that must either break his fall or break his bones.

*   *   *

From the place they had just left, hidden cameras kept their constant vigilance across the gardens. As was normal practice with all strangers, their presence had been recorded and a still photograph already blown up as a means of identification. They took it into the man known as Viejo who was waiting impatiently.

Studying it intently, he smiled. The woman he dismissed in a single glance, she was of no interest. But the boy—The boy seemed to be looking directly across at him.

Quickly he gave the order. The men nodded. They knew what to do.

CHAPTER NINE

It was if you had come to me and I had turned my head from you—I, who seem to have waited for you through all the lives of Other Worlds.

SE-TEWA, Indian Love Letters

It was three o'clock when Chay Bowman began to read the two-year-old documents that Rudd Shashto had faxed from Flagstaff.

The body of a twelve-year-old Navajo boy had been discovered on the far side of Anasazi Canyon, a considerable distance from the reservation. The details were gruesome. His chest had been ripped open. The official accounts were long-winded but Chay read them with patience, detecting a certain eagerness to dismiss this unsolved death as the work of a mountain lion.

The boy's photograph, circulated across the reservation, was followed by a call from the

132

House of Anasazi Fire notifying the police department that one of their pet cougars had recently escaped. The animal had been tracked down and shot by Mr Viejo's orders. He had sent a personal letter of sympathy to the boy's foster parents with a substantial (unstated) sum of money on the understanding that there be no further publicity of any kind concerning the incident. This was purely in the public interest, he maintained, since the boy's death had been a deplorable accident but one that was unlikely to happen again.

And there the case closed. A newsworthy local item which had not even merited a paragraph in the *Arizona News*.

Absorbed by the implications of this new information, Chay didn't hear Rita come in and he almost leaped into the air when she put a hand on his shoulder.

'Ah, you've got to the part where it was dismissed as an accident. I imagine that the boy's foster parents were not the only ones to be bought off. That goes for authority too. If this Viejo is a millionaire many times over he can sure afford to pay for silence,' she added shrewdly.

When Chay put down the papers, she continued, 'There was another call from the lady from Scottsdale with the straying husband. She sounds kind of anxious—wants to see you Thursday. I've put a note in the diary.'

Chay nodded vaguely and Rita regarded him

133

sadly. 'You're not really interested, are you?'

He shrugged. 'Guess I can't seem to summon up any wild enthusiasm for the project.'

'Just a tiny bit would do. Just for the money.' And fiddling with a pencil on the desk, she said idly, 'I've just found out why you're so determined to prove the Begay boys were murdered.'

He looked at her slowly. 'You have?'

Her smile was challenging as she sat on the desk, swinging her legs. 'Their mother was an old girl friend of yours, wasn't she? The one you were dating when you met my sister.'

Chay went over to the water cooler, poured himself a drink. 'You sure would make an excellent private eye, Rita. I wonder you haven't thought of that. You could go into business on your own account, call it "The No Stone Left Unturned Detective Agency",' he added heavily.

Rita smiled sweetly, happy in her triumph and refusing to be fazed. She handed him some photographs.

'My fax has been very busy today. The best is yet to be.'

The accident photographs of a wrecked car and dead driver made unpleasant viewing. The newspaper headline screamed: Fatal accident.

'For accident read murder,' said Rita. 'The report says there was little in the evidence from the car except that it had faulty brakes. Though anyone driving those canyon roads with faulty brakes amounts to suicide.'

Chay was glad to have Rita agree with him for once. 'So you think it was murder too.'

'I do now.' She handed him a blown-up photograph of the dead man's arm, one of the few areas of his body uncharred. It revealed the tattoo of a petroglyph, a tiny figure playing the flute.

'A Kokopele.' Chay sat upright suddenly. 'The mark of the Magic Men.'

Ruth smiled. 'It wouldn't convey anything to the cops in Flagstaff or Phoenix, but you know and I know that the Magic Men are Atalos–Anasazi and that they are rumoured to have close connections with our reclusive millionaire in the house up there.'

He looked up at her. 'What are you trying to tell me? That Viejo had the boys murdered by Lopez and then had him killed to stop him talking?'

Rita smiled triumphantly. 'Could be. I'm only saying it's worth bearing in mind. In the old days they sacrificed young boys,' she reminded him.

'We all know that, Rita. But this is the twentieth century,' he added impatiently.

She shook her head. 'I agree, but does this Viejo know that? And more to the point, what do we know about him, where he came from, what his early life was like?'

When Chay shrugged, she continued, 'He's

Mex or white, he settled here six years ago, but he's hardly been seen in public since. We're told that that he's filthy rich and looked after by a tribe of close-mouthed servants, with enough money to buy off newspaper speculation and probably the cops as well.'

Tapping the pencil against her teeth, she thought for a moment then said casually, 'You might ask Redfeather's opinion. There isn't much goes on that he doesn't know or can't find out from his connections with the Magic Men.'

Chay regarded her sternly. His grandfather never would admit to such a thing, although he had his suspicions that Rita was right.

'As a matter of fact, Chay, I've often wondered whether it is only a bad scar from an accident in his movie days that makes him wear long sleeves all the time, or whether it's because of that Kokopele tattoo.'

Once during a very hot season they had caught him emerging from the swimming pool. Chay remembering, felt agitated. He had hoped that Sharp Eyes Rita had forgotten the incident. He sure as hell didn't want his grandfather involved in anything to do with breaking the law. He'd go further than that, being family, he was prepared to protect him at all costs.

He looked at the office clock. 'I have to go.'

'Seeing Redfeather, are you?'

'Yeah, I'm taking Miz Fenner and the boy to

meet him.'

Rita scowled. 'I doubt whether you'll get any social chat out of him, seeing as how he doesn't like Anglos.'

'He should know. Married to one once,' was Chay's laconic reply.

Rita pursed her lips and turned away.

Chay preferred to regard himself as pure Navajo. He rarely drew attention to the fact that his grandmother was Irish. A red-headed starlet Redfeather had been crazy about. A couple of years after they married, she left him for a movie director who had more to offer career-wise and money-wise than a stuntman in westerns.

It looked to Rita as if history was in danger of repeating itself. This yellow-haired Anglo woman down at the creek was bad medicine as far as Chay Bowman was concerned. Her own dream of a Sometime with him was rapidly dwindling into Never.

*   *   *

Chay was late. He hadn't hurried, letting the eye of the storm blow itself out. The heavy rains had been carried away by the storm drains in the street and the deluge was almost spent. The thunder growled its way across the creek, where the sycamores and willows remained very still, as if bracing themselves for any high winds calculated to take them by surprise.

As the car slid into the square, he sounded the horn outside the mobile, and again. Only the guard dogs took any notice.

Obviously Kate and the boy hadn't heard it, but the hired car was in the drive-in. He waited a few moments and then ran up the front steps. The doorbell shrilled through the house but there was no answer. He looked around the patio. It was empty. His watch said four thirty.

Chay stared up at the windows. He was disappointed. They had gone out and forgotten all about the visit to Redfeather they had greeted so enthusiastically. Maybe they'd just gotten the day—or the time—wrong, he thought charitably as, hastily scribbling on the back of a card, he shoved it under the door.

With a final look at the silent house, he was about to drive away when a woman appeared at the door opposite, obviously curious about the patrol car in the square and the dogs' uproar.

She ran down the path. 'Is there anything wrong, officer?'

'No, ma'am, not a thing . . .' He felt bound to explain. 'Just a social call.'

Tessa Rhodes looked relieved. 'I thought it might be something to do with the prowler Miss Fenner heard last night.'

'What prowler?' Chay demanded.

Tessa continued hastily, 'Just a false alarm as it turned out. She thought she saw someone on the deck and, er—' she paused and knowing he was Indian looked embarrassed. 'Well, she

138

thought he was in tribal dress. It was three in the morning when she phoned us. We went across, took the dog, but there was no one there.'

Chay listening, felt suddenly chilled.

'I guess it was just a bad dream,' said Mrs Rhodes. 'Anyway, they both set off at ten this morning, none the worse for the experience, bright eyed as a couple of squirrels, off to climb the Anasazi rocks back there. Said she'd only be gone for a couple of hours, that she had to be back at four.' She smiled. 'I guess she was expecting you.' When there was no affirmation, her curiosity unappeased she went on, 'I expect they got caught in the storm, took shelter somewhere.'

Chay was thinking that six hours was a long time for a short stroll. The wind was striking up a faint orchestra among the windbells on the houses and the rain began again.

As he levered up the hood of the car, he shouted to the fast retreating Mrs Rhodes, 'Ma'am, which way did they go?'

'Straight up the rocks there. Miss Fenner said she had a good map.'

Thanking her, Chay drove parallel with the canyon, until he reached the place where the road ended and became an overgrown track. Fine as long as you kept to the rough paths and were knowledgeable about flash floods. You had to know where to find shelter in a hurry in the vanguard of an approaching storm.

Parking the car, he took out a backpack containing survival gear, water, candles, food and a rope. Discarding shoes for moccasins, he tied back his hair and added a sweatband. Lightly clad now he could climb fast and easy.

He hoped he would get to them before the storm returned and rainsheets obliterated all landmarks, reducing visibility to nil.

As he climbed he was haunted by those flash floods that rushed through small canyons like raging torrents, drowning plants, animals and humans alike in their relentless path.

And at the back of his mind was the account he had read about the first Navajo boy who was attacked by one of Viejo's pet cougars. What was the boy doing there in the first place, alone and far away from the reservation in the canyon near the House of Anasazi Fire?

Kate Fenner's neighbour's disclosure about the prowler left another scaring possibility gnawing away at his mind. Whoever he was, the description fitted almost any of the Magic Men.

*　　　*　　　*

The boulder that had broken Luke's fall, but not his bones, hid the entrance to a cave. He was unhurt apart from a few grazes.

Kate was not so fortunate.

She was clambering towards the cave, carrying Luke's backpack over her arm, when a small avalanche of stones dislodged by his fall hurtled down towards her. A piece of rock no bigger than a golf ball struck her forehead and felled her to the ground.

Tearfully, Luke dragged her into the cave. Blood was pouring down her cheek. He took out a tissue and dabbed at it.

Protesting that she was all right, Kate smiled with a reassurance she did not feel. Scalp wounds bled profusely and she was scared he might be frightened at the sight of so much blood.

Holding the tissue to her face, she lay on the ground. At least they were safe from the storm that now unleashed itself upon the mountains and shook the walls of their natural shelter. Flash upon flash of lightning lit up the interior revealing that the cave stretched back some distance and that the smooth surfaces of the walls were covered with petroglyphs, ancient carvings of animals and hunters with spears.

Fascinated, she stared at this chronicle of a race of long-lost humans who perhaps, terrified like themselves, had once taken shelter in this secret stronghold, but from a more dreadful fate than a raging storm. The hunters had become the hunted.

'Afraid?' She put an arm around Luke,

No, he wasn't afraid. Luke smiled, shook his head. It was too exciting for that. He was eager to explore their surroundings and as she watched him move around inspecting the carvings, touching each one, she leaned back against the wall.

Suddenly she was overcome with exhaustion, perhaps the result of the long climb. She had a sore head, felt sick and recognised the beginnings of a fierce headache. A malady she rarely suffered from and, with no medication, she decided the best treatment was just to close her eyes and hope that it would pass.

She was drifting into sleep, when Luke returned. He held out two tiny turquoise beads which he dropped into her hand, delighted at his find. Then he looked into her face anxiously, touched her cheek. Was she all right?

'Just tired.'

He removed the bloodied tissue, held out another into the rain while she protested that he was getting wet. He brought it back again and laid his hand gently against her cut forehead. His cool touch seemed to soothe away the pain.

'That's nice,' she whispered and closed her eyes wearily while Luke settled down at her side and they prepared to sit out the storm.

Sleep came quickly. The wearied, dream-ridden sleep of exhaustion.

The Indian she had seen on the patio was back again. She recognised his shimmering presence at the door of the cave. This time she was unafraid. He leaned over her, touching her head. But she was someone else. She was wearing a long dress. He held her in his arms and told her not to be afraid.

She loved him. Loved him with all her heart, her soul and her body. They were powerless to escape from this love, even knowing that it was to destroy them.

She awoke with a start.

Luke was asleep, curled up on the floor. She heard sounds outside and through the rainsheets, an Indian appeared.

The shadowy substance of that bitter-sweet love still cobwebbed her mind. The dream was reality.

He had returned for her. She cried out to him.

*　　　*　　　*

'Hi, there. It's only me.'

She sat up, rubbing her eyes.

The newcomer was Chay Bowman.

He nodded towards Luke. 'Are you both all right?'

'Yes. We're fine.' And watching him pour coffee from a flask, the dream faded little by little and was gone.

Her normal senses regained, she drank gratefully. 'How did you know where to find us?'

'I saw a red backpack beside the boulder back there. Guessed you must be down here somewhere.'

He didn't add that when he saw the scree he

feared the worst, that he might be finding two badly injured people at its base.

'I didn't know there was a cave,' he said. 'And one with petroglyphs. What a find.'

Luke stirred sleepily as they spoke and sat up, listening to Chay's account of his fortuitous meeting with Mrs Rhodes.

'We were so excited,' said Kate. 'It was all going so well until the storm caught up with us. We found a cultivated garden, like a secret valley. Did you know that there's a house close by?'

The description of the secret valley confirmed what he knew already. That it must be the back of Viejo's house built into one of the original cliff dwellings.

'It looks like a fortress. Guard dogs and all.'

'I guess it is,' said Chay. 'No one ever gets inside.'

'Who's the owner?'

'No one knows for sure.' He was telling her about the millionaire who could afford to excavate a cliffside and build a home remote from the world when Luke tugged at his arm impatiently, wanting to show him the petroglyphs.

Chay grinned. 'I didn't know this place existed. You've probably made a valuable new discovery.'

'We never would have found it, if Luke hadn't fallen down the scree. The boulder hides the entrance. We were lucky. Luke got a few scratches and I fell—'

Kate paused and raised her hand to her forehead.

'What's wrong?'

'Nothing. I cut my forehead. Oh, it's better now. Must have been just a scratch.' She shrugged. 'Not as bad as I thought. Nothing to make a fuss about. It bled a lot though, didn't it, Luke?'

Luke smiled vaguely.

As Kate stared at him, the cold feeling of terror returning, Chay looked from one to the other, aware of something wrong.

Kate smiled apologetically, 'I think I was knocked out cold by the fall and dreamt it.'

'Like you dreamt about a prowler,' said Chay.

When Kate looked surprised, he said, 'Your neighbour told me.'

Kate laughed uneasily. 'Luke was wandering about outside—thought he heard something. Probably just a coyote scavenging, but things sound scary in the middle of the night.'

The rain had stopped and they prepared to leave.

As Chay gathered together jackets and backpacks, Kate pulled back her hair and rubbed her forehead, gently at first. But she could feel no cut. There was no injury on her forehead. Nothing. It was not even sore. If the cut had existed at all then it had healed completely.

She looked down at the neckline of her T-shirt, darkly, heavily stained. Chay followed her startled glance. He had seen enough of that sort of stain in his time not to be mistaken about dried blood . . .

CHAPTER TEN

Magic might begin with a moment of fairly common experience . . . a picture might walk, a tree might speak; an animal might not be an animal; a man might not be a man.

CHARLES WILLIAMS, Witchcraft

Chay said they must get back down to the car before dark. A visit to inspect Kate's secret valley must wait. The light was fading rapidly and, as they followed him down the track, Luke pointed to pinpricks of light in the brush around them.

'Glow-worms,' Kate said to Chay, glancing back up the steep track to the cave. 'How lovely. I always thought glow-worms only came out at night.'

Chay didn't bother to reply intent on the path in front of them. Besides he could only have destroyed her romantic illusions by telling her they were nothing of the sort.

She was surprised to see how quickly all trace of the tropical rainstorm had vanished. The desert cacti looked pleased, greener, fatter and rather more predatory from gobbling down all that water. The air had never smelt so fresh and clean, each deep breath held the fragrance of many scented herbs.

Stretching out her arms, she sighed deeply. 'Divine, isn't it.'

Chay turned, 'Rain is one of nature's many blessings man hasn't succeeded in destroying.' He looked at her anxiously. 'You feeling all right now?'

She touched her forehead and quickly removed her hand.

Chay noticed the gesture, the sudden bewilderment, but her smile was confident as she said, 'I feel wonderful. But I seem to have lost all track of time. As if we had been in that cave all night.'

He grinned. 'I hope not, or some of us might have explaining to do.'

Kate glanced at him. She knew nothing about him after all. Presumably there was a wife or a girlfriend. Most probably the Indian woman she had seen in the car with him. She could imagine him telling her in bed that night about this crazy white woman who obviously needed a man to look after her. Kate pictured the scene a little enviously. How they would laugh softly together and the woman too sure of her man to be jealous, would snuggle into him.

'Sunset comes early in the canyons,' Chay was saying. 'Colours are at their best after a storm. You get the whole spectrum of the rainbow,' he added. 'Look!'

But the first evening star that blazed in the firmament was suddenly a steel lance, the rocks running blood, there were human cries that shattered the stillness . . .

Kate blinked rapidly and the scene returned to normal. What on earth had made her feel that something terrible had happened in this peaceful spot. Something that the rocks remembered, its echoes still reverberating from the canyon walls.

Suddenly she was tired again, so deadly exhausted in body and mind she could hardly drag one foot after the other. She remembered the long distance ahead of them, the way they had come and the thought was like death to her. No longer aware of Chay marching steadily forward, all she wanted to do was cry out, fall weeping to the ground, bury her head in her arms. Close her eyes and sleep. Sleep for ever.

Turning, she saw that Luke was flagging too. She wanted them both to be home and safe again, no longer enchanted by the sunset's fleeting beauty as the dying day wrapped shroud-like around them.

Already the warmth had gone and the air stirred to cool gentle breezes, rustling chaparal

148

and sycamore trees. She was dimly aware that the shadows had deepened into mysterious dark pools near the stark silhouettes of tall rock spires, the twilight blocked by towering cliffs and buttes.

Only their footfalls hitting rock and the hum of cicadas broke the silence. Suddenly high above them, the clear-throated sound of birds winging homeward. Unseen the land stirred in dark and secret places where the creatures whose home was this deserted canyon prepared for another night's foraging beneath the rising moon.

A sharp cry pierced the still air, halting Kate and Luke in their tracks.

Chay turned and smiled reassuringly. 'Take it easy. Only the quail.'

They halted for a moment, listening to the haunting sound bouncing eerily off the canyon walls far below.

Above them the sky was aflame with brilliant colours so intense that it seemed the whole world must be dyed crimson. The vegetation was thicker now and care was needed for paths almost obliterated, vanishing completely in the gathering twilight. The scarlet changed, turned to bright orange, and subsided into a glow of gold and rose.

Their descent was slower now and they stopped frequently as Chay made a careful study of the ground to pick up some animal track that they might follow.

With the safety of the road in sight and the distant prospect of Chay's car, Kate's spirits revived.

No one could long be immune to this vast amphitheatre of nature with its kaleidoscope of changing colours whose disappearance left a sadness, an empty feeling that magic had died and life might never be quite the same again. From the canyon floor twilight crept up rocks, brushing them from blue into deepest purple. The creek was suddenly visible, a glittering crimson ribbon, the lofty buttes majestic black sentinels of the coming night. The evening sky had diminished into a backdrop of ghostly mauves and lingering shades of blue. All that remained of the sunset were drifting ribbons of cloud, like a tired child's party streamers at the end of a long day.

Chay drove swiftly, silently down Main Street where neon signs glittered with the temptations of hamburger places and softly lit restaurants. The faint beat of pop music urged the night world to wake up again. Down the narrow twisting road through cottonwoods and sycamores lay Blackhawk Creek, where pine and sage blended with a hundred other scents to which Kate could give no name, brought by the rain into a brief, tantalising existence.

It felt good to be back again at the end of what had been planned as a pleasant walk and had turned into a scaring adventure. And Kate laughed out loud, a happy sound of relief, as the tiny square with its flagpole came into view.

'Safe home again, Luke.'

As Chay jumped down and came to her side, she heard the neighbourhood dogs in full cry. What a din! She was consoled by the knowledge that one and all seemed to take their duties seriously once darkness fell. Reassuringly it made nonsense of any prowler and of her reaction to what had been a weird dream.

Chay took the key from her, opened the front door, shouted 'Goodnight' to Luke, who smiled broadly and dashed in. They heard the television switched on, sounds of laughter and music.

Chay's expression was invisible in the gloom. Kate looked up at him and held out her hand. He had rescued her twice, as remote as she could imagine from a white knight in shining armour, or the US cavalry whose movie treatment of Indians she had so despised.

He turned, a dark shadow against the gently swaying trees.

'I expect you've both had enough excitement for one day. Too late to take you to see grandfather tonight. How about tomorrow?'

'Oh, yes, fine. If you can be bothered.'

'If it was a bother, I wouldn't ask.'

She knew it was true. Here was a man who made decisions and stayed with them. She was grateful that he had found them in the cave and for the way he had negotiated the treacherous

151

downhill climb with a tracker's instinct inherited from his ancestors, as if he had been rescuing stranded tourists every day of his life.

Watching him head back towards the patrol car, she liked that gliding easy walk, the kind that no white man ever quite achieved.

Suddenly he came back, reached into his pocket and taking her hand put something in it and made it into a fist. Opening it, the porch light revealed two small turquoise beads.

'Found them on the path near the cave.'

She laughed. 'I have two already. Luke found them in the cave. Someone must have been there before us and broken a necklace.'

He smiled. 'A long time ago. Anyway, my two makes four and four is the sacred number of the Navajo. The turquoise brings good luck and they will protect you.' He paused and then added, 'Keep those glow-worms at a distance.'

'Glow-worms,' she laughed to his retreating back, 'surely they're harmless enough?'

Standing by the car, he raised an admonishing finger. 'They weren't glow-worms. They were eyes—the eyes of small animals, watching us.'

'Why on earth should they do that?'

He came back to her and stood very still just a few steps away. His tone when he spoke was urgent. 'Take care, lady. It occurs to me that you and the boy should take great care— exercise caution at all times. And if you want to wander off into these canyons, get someone

152

reliable to go with you.'

Rubbing his chin thoughtfully, he added as if to himself. 'There's something wrong about all this, makes me wonder which is hunter and which is hunted.'

He looked at her directly as if reluctant to say any more and without waiting for a reply, he returned swiftly to the car. The engine roared into life, drowning out her question. A second later, he was gone without even a backward glance.

In the sitting room Luke was stretched out in front of the television having first raided the refrigerator for Coke and cookies.

As she went into the kitchen to prepare supper, she considered Chay's parting words. The idea of those tiny animals watching them was quite absurd. There was another, simpler, explanation. Animals were curious and had been attracted by the alien presence of humans where the right of way down those steep inaccessible paths belonged alone to the predators among them. It was so logical, so obvious, she couldn't understand why it hadn't occurred to Chay. Unless he knew it perfectly well and was merely chiding her for the trouble she had caused him, trying to scare her by this teasing thought.

Thinking about that, she frowned and had to conclude that such a facetious side to his nature was not immediately evident from the little of his character she had observed so far.

Smiling, she decided that her theory would make an interesting topic for discussion and argument when they met tomorrow.

She was glad she would be seeing him again and Luke was so looking forward to meeting his ex-movie star grandfather.

In the sitting room, Luke was asleep on the floor, with the television blazing. The programme had changed to a panel of speakers and, about to switch off, the words 'Red Rock' caught her attention. A strong, virile-looking man in his early forties with film star good looks was speaking.

'A vortex is a high concentration of energy, a sort of supercharged whirlpool, surrounded by grids where ley lines share a common point of intersection.'

The camera scanned the perplexed faces around the table.

'It's easier if you translate into human body terms which we can more readily understand and think of the vortex areas as the acupressure points. The vortices which form a sacred geometric pattern across its surfaces are grids, behaving in much the same way as our nervous systems. Where these are concentrated, as in Red Rock here, things happen at these points. On the earth's body as well as our own. Those of us fortunate enough to recognise such things, like the Indians, have long regarded the earth as a living planet.'

Pausing he smiled and Kate felt the almost

hypnotic quality of his beautiful voice, his charisma upon the other members of the panel.

'This is the only place on earth to contain four major vortexes in a few square miles. And these link up with other worldwide major electrical vortexes—Mount Everest, Ararat and McKinley. Cathedral Rock connects with the major vortex of Glastonbury Tor in Britain, the legendary home of King Arthur and the Holy Grail. A place long recognised as a site of regeneration.'

And turning to the man on his right who was wearing a dark suit and a ministerial collar, he said, 'Isn't that right, Reverend?'

The minister nodded enthusiastically. 'It is indeed. And this is not merely a pagan theory,' he added sternly. 'We know that the early Christian churches were sited along the flow of the ley lines with the greatest source of energy located directly beneath the tower where it was believed to produce the strongest link between heaven and earth.

'When I was a missionary in China many years ago, I learned about the Dragon Currents which mark all sacred paths.'

Smiling he looked at the main speaker. 'These currents are divided into yin and yang, positive and negative forces. The powerful dragon pulse was at its peak where yin, the female force, typified by gently undulating country met yang, the male force, sharp peaks and rocks. Country very similar to this, in fact.'

'Meredith Wills has referred to a positive vortex,' interrupted the interviewer turning in his direction. 'Can you explain this to our audience?'

'I can tell them that upon entering the vibrational field, you become charged emotionally and physically,' said Wills. 'The energy stimulates and elevates consciousness, the combination of electrical and magnetic energy is wonderful for eliminating depression and for stimulating past life memory.'

'Have you any examples of this, Mr Wills?' asked the doubting interviewer.

'I certainly have. I have been experimenting for some years and we have had phenomenal experiences, you'll find many in my books on the subject,' he added reproachfully as if the interviewer should have done his homework first.

'Can you be a little more specific?'

'Of course,' was the patient response. 'Experiences have ranged from intensely spiritual visions, waking dreams, some even religious, to direct contact with spirit entities who remain here.'

'Ghosts, do you mean?' The interviewer strived to keep the mockery out of his voice.

Wills laughed, made a deprecating gesture. 'We don't call them anything as crude. Let us just say, spirits who have remained on earth for their own particular reasons. My students have reported vivid impressions of what has taken

156

place in these canyons in times past, in many cases experiences which have been shared by two or three. Most remarkable of all, the canyon has remarkable powers of healing, as the Reverend here can tell us.'

The minister now revealed that he had been diagnosed as having terminal cancer. Remembering he had long ago visited Red Rock and had always sworn to return some day, he had decided it would be a good place to spend his remaining months. But having come ready to face death, he had instead discovered life, with all traces of malignancy healed.

'Thank you, gentlemen. If you are interested . . .' An address followed.

Kate switched off and went into the bathroom.

In the mirror she saw for the first time the heavily blood-stiffened neck of her T-shirt. She pulled back her hair and frantically searched for the deep cut on her forehead that had bled so profusely in the cave.

There was no wound. The skin was smooth and it was not even painful to touch.

She sat down weakly on the edge of the bath.

It was all starting again. She should never have brought Luke here.

CHAPTER ELEVEN

The barb in the arrow of childhood suffering is this; its intense loneliness, its intense ignorance.

OLIVE SCHREINER,
The Story of an African Farm

On the following morning, Chay found unexpected visitors in his office.

Rita met him in the hallway and hissed, 'Kid claims he was kidnapped.'

Opening the door he saw a handsome Navajo boy, aged about thirteen. Unharmed but unhappy looking he was sitting at the desk opposite a scowling, pock-marked, older youth well known to Chay.

At seventeen Tibey already had an established police record. He had been in and out of the juvenile courts for the past six years, a petty criminal who broke into houses and sold mescalin to tourists as well. As well as trafficking in drugs, he now pimped for prostitutes and rentboys.

Addressing Chay in Navajo, he indicated the younger boy. Beno, he claimed, had been kidnapped. And Beno was his cousin.

Chay sighed wearily. There were always

cousins in plenty to be produced when there might be possible monetary rewards in the offing.

Tibey pointed at the boy. 'Tell him what happened. How you escaped.'

The boy shuddered and shook his head.

'Tell him, Beno. All right, I will tell him. It was a few weeks ago. We were riding our car away from the highway. We had to meet some Anglos.'

At Chay's questioning glance, he said quickly, 'To do some business. This car was following us. It stopped. We thought it was our customer.'

He paused, uncertain how to proceed. 'I went across, but they signalled me away. It was Beno they wanted. He talked with them. I waited. I thought some deal was made and he got in the car with them. I came home.'

'Why didn't you wait for him?' demanded Chay sharply.

Tibey smiled slyly. 'It was nothing to do with me.'

'Was it not? Even when he didn't return?' Rita put in indignantly. 'He's just a young boy. You say he was in your care. What about his parents?'

Tibey regarded her coldly. 'There are none. He has only me. I look after his interests. Sometimes his interests take him away for a while. No questions are asked. It is his business entirely,' he repeated firmly.

The significance of his remark brought a stifled exclamation from Rita, as the youth turned to Beno and said, 'You tell them the rest. What happened to you. Go on.'

The boy seemed to shrink further into his chair. 'The man drove for a long distance. It was getting dark and I could only see occasional lights. I wasn't worried until we started climbing into the canyon on a lonely road. The man stopped the car and blindfolded me. He stuck something in my arm—' He rubbed it thoughtfully. 'I fell asleep,' he added innocently as if he'd never heard of drugs. 'When I wakened up I was in a big empty room with a bed and a table. There was food—good food— and this man who had brought me said I wasn't needed at the moment, I could rest for a while.

'I asked him about money. He said there would be as much as I wanted. I was pleased. There were comic books, a television in the room. It was a lot better than what I had left,' he added with a venomous look in Tibey's direction. 'Although the door to the rest of the house was locked, there was a garden outside with a swimming pool. The servant said I could swim there but I needn't wear anything in the pool.'

Aware of the significance of what he had just said and what he imagined were disapproving glances, he shrugged. 'When nothing happened for a few days, with no action, except that my meals were served on time, I was curious about what was out there beyond the garden which was surrounded by a high wall. I couldn't see

160

over the top of it, but I got the feeling I was in some rich Anglo's house.

'I asked the man who had brought me how long I would be staying. He was one of us, but he was only a servant. He said that his employer would be needing my services soon. Was I not content with all that had been provided for me? Was there anything else I wanted more than I had at the moment? When I said what about the money, he said not to worry as the reward would be worth the wait.

'I was getting bored so I went outside when there was no one around and I managed to see through a crack in the fence. I decided I could find footholds and climb over. I fancied some exploring, but there were four great big black dogs and I didn't like the look of them.'

'Could you see anything else?' asked Chay eagerly. The description of the dogs fitted Kate's story. Maybe this was the break he was looking for.

The boy thought for a while. 'There was a high red rock cliff about a hundred yards away across the garden. When the dogs weren't roaming around I thought I could go that way if I was desperate. Then I noticed the electrified fence at the base of the cliff, like they have in prison. I didn't fancy being fried, so I gave up the idea.'

He paused and looked quickly at Tibey. 'Besides, I had no money yet and I didn't want to leave empty handed. I wanted a look around the house first, see what these rich people might have.'

'You mean pick up a few mementoes,' said Chay.

Beno smiled engagingly. 'Only something they wouldn't miss, to make it worth my time and trouble. After all, we have to live and it seemed the Anglo who owned this house had more than enough—'

'How long were you there?' Chay interrupted sharply.

'Four—five days, maybe. I was happy enough, this was a better life than the hogan Tibey lets me sleep in. I began to think this Anglo life was a good thing. I was in no hurry, I wasn't going anywhere, then one morning, the servant came in and said I was to go with him.

'He put the blindfold on me and, although I protested about that, he led me through long corridors. I thought I was being taken to another room in the house, but instead I was outside again. He pushed me into the back of a car. We drove a long way downhill over twisting roads, then he opened the car, took off the blindfold—' He stopped and looked at them helplessly. 'He threw out a plastic carrier, pointed towards Highway 89. I could hear the traffic straight ahead. I asked about the money. He laughed and said, too bad as I hadn't done anything to earn it and my services were no longer required.'

Remembering made him furious. He

thumped his fists together. 'I cursed him by every god I could remember as he drove away. He'd left me a bag with food and a bottle of wine, but no money.

'I got lost, several times before I hit the highway. Then a car stopped.' Beno looked away. 'It was an Anglo. I did business with him. He took me to a motel.' He shrugged. 'When I got back to Tibey, he beat me and took that money,' he added angrily.

'He deserved a beating,' said Tibey smoothly. 'There was no money or anything from the Anglo's house. He is not with me to enjoy his pleasures without the money.'

'Get to the point,' said Chay stifling his disgust. 'Are you making a charge of kidnapping, or what?'

As he spoke, he realised how little hope there would be of Tibey and the boy's charge being taken seriously, a charge that would never have been made in the first place except as revenge on the mysterious wealthy Anglo. As known juvenile criminals their story, without proof, would be swiftly kicked aside by any harassed law officer wearied by the activities of rent boys.

'Why do you come to me with this information? What makes you think I can help you?' He nodded towards Beno. 'Seeing that he went with them of his own free will and wasn't harmed in any way, quite the contrary, it could hardly be called kidnapping. And if it

163

was, then such matters are for the Anglo cops, not for a private investigator.'

Tibey studied his fingernails. 'We thought you would be interested since you are one of our people and Beno is a cousin of the Begays. What he's telling you about happened around the time they were killed by the cougar.'

'So why has it taken all this time to come to me about it?' Chay asked sharply. 'What's the connection, anyway?' he added casually.

Tibey was only momentarily deflated. He had one more ace to play.

'Tell them, Beno.'

Beno sighed. 'The servant at the Anglo house, as I told you was one of us and he had a tattoo on his upper arm. A Kokopele. We all know that is the sign of the Anasazi and the Magic Men.'

The same tattoo that had been found on the dead man, Lopez.

Chay and Rita exchanged glances and Tibey knew he had their interest. 'We thought there should be a reward for this information. For our trouble, expenses and so on,' he added hopefully.

Chay shook his head. 'I cannot give rewards. That is not my business, but you can try telling the cops all this if you like, see what they'll do for you.'

Tibey scowled, knowing all too well there was only one possible reaction the Anglo cops would have, show them the door quickly before they were put in jail once again.

*   *   *

Going over that unsavoury story, Chay wondered if he should be grateful to them for a possible link with the Begay brothers. Was it significant that all these boys were loners, dubious characters from backgrounds where they had been involved with juvenile crime and their testimonies therefore unlikely to be given a second glance by police investigators? He remembered Rudd's disclosures about the boy killed by Viejo's pet cougar whose foster-parents were well paid to keep silent.

For whatever reason Beno had been released unharmed. Had he been extremely fortunate not to have met the same fate as the Begay boys? Or was this much more serious? Was he on the threshold of discovering a revival of the ritual sacrifice of young boys according to the ancient law of the Atalos–Anasazi?

*   *   *

Kate and Luke were ready when he came for them and they set off to visit Redfeather.

'Tell me about him,' said Kate. 'You mentioned that he was an old movie star. Would I have known him?'

'Before your time, I guess. He took the name

Ramon Fury. Stunt rider in fifties westerns. Married a beautiful Irish girl, a bit player, and, after Pa was born, she ran off with a movie producer who promised he was going to turn her into a glamour queen.

'Grandfather made a decent job of bringing Pa up. Taught him everything he knew about the stuntman's business of riding horses and driving cars. My mother was part Mexican.'

Kate noticed the slight hesitation. This was an admission Chay made to few people. He liked to be thought of as pure Navajo.

'I never knew her. She was killed in a car Pa was driving when I was two. Pa blamed himself and volunteered for the white man's war. He died in Vietnam and Grandfather never got over losing his only son.

'I guess he had a death wish that kept him on stunt riding long after he should have packed it in. A back injury finished his career for good. It was a stupid, unnecessary accident, he knew better than to take chances but he always drank too much. I reckon it's something in our genes from the bad old days. We never could resist the white man's whisky.

'Pa's wish had always been that I follow the white man's way, so I went to the Army Serviceman's School for war orphans. Then I got a scholarship to the university in Flagstaff. Got a master's degree in economics, became a Tribal Ranger, then a policeman.'

Kate had never heard him talk so much

about himself.

'That's about all there is.' He decided to omit the San Francisco incident. 'You'll meet Jake at the ranch. He's my son.'

'You're married?'

'Was. She died.' And before she could do more than murmur sympathy he asked, 'What about you?'

'No.'

'Ever?'

'Never.'

He jerked his head towards the back seat. 'The boy's father.'

'He's dead. He never knew of Luke's existence.'

He looked at her face, the tight closed expression told him there was no further information forthcoming on that subject.

'No ill effects from yesterday?' he asked.

'None. I slept for nearly ten hours. I feel great.' She looked at him. 'Thank you for coming to our rescue. It really was very scary in that cave.'

'Flash floods destroy everything, rivers and creeks can change their course. One moment, everything is peaceful and serene, looks like it will stay that way for ever, next minute houses, trees, everything in the water's path is smashed into matchwood.

'Guess it's nature's way of getting back at man the conqueror.'

Kate agreed. 'We think of ourselves as a

167

superior, indestructible species, don't we? But all it needs is a flood, a volcanic eruption somewhere or an earthquake to make us realise that mankind is very transient.'

'True. And our time is nearly up in the scheme of things, if you believe as we do that planet earth is a living organism with its own laws and that we evolved to love the landscape, hold it sacred. That love is encoded in our genes and we destroy it at our peril.'

'And if we go, what next?' said Kate. 'Do you think there's another species waiting in the wings and being groomed by nature for the ultimate takeover bid?'

'Sure I do. But then I'm not a superior white man. I don't believe that I was created in God's image to hold dominion over the earth and all things in it. We believe that man's place on earth depends on his ability to live in harmony with nature and that every creature's life is sacred and must be respected. They were given to us to eat so that we might live, as they in turn must eat weaker creatures to survive. When we kill to eat, we beg the animal spirit's forgiveness. But we don't make gods of pets and we don't understand bunnies in tweed jackets.'

He looked ahead. They had come a long way from the creek, to the very base of the towering red rocks. The way ahead lay through an estate of handsome mansions, a fair expanse of land between each one ensuring privacy.

Chay drove off the well-made road on to a bumpy track leading between posts on to a flat expanse with a scattering of hogans, which, he explained, were the traditional eight-sided Navajo houses.

Luke laughed delightedly, clapped his hands. This was his idea of how Indians lived. He gave an ill-suppressed groan of disappointment when Chay turned up a steep drive leading to a handsome white adobe house. Relatively modern in appearance Kate realised it must have predated the suburban estate by thirty years.

'Here we are,' said Chay, switching off the engine. And as Kate got out of the car, he said idly, 'By the way, I wouldn't mention your adventure yesterday. Anasazi Canyon is still a taboo place for him.'

She looked at him quickly and he nodded.

'You were aware of some presence. I guessed that. We believe that the spirits of our dead people live on. They're not like Christians who die and go up to heaven and sprout angel's wings. They stay around. And even in these enlightened days we carefully avoid the chindi—the ghosts of our ancestors.'

As he was speaking a good-looking young man with a striking resemblance to Chay appeared from the terrace, ran over and embraced him. They greeted each other in Navajo.

This must be Jake, and Kate was aware of an

appreciative glance in her direction, but as Chay glanced towards Luke he said something that caused a fleeting look of concern on his son's face.

The next moment introductions were being exchanged.

As they spoke, a horse neighed from a paddock nearby. It trotted eagerly over to the railing. Chay put an arm around its neck while it nuzzled his shoulder and snorted into his ear.

'Meet Storm Cloud,' he said. 'He's older than Jake here.'

Luke was delighted, his face bright with excitement, patting the horse and smiling shyly at Jake, who said, 'I'll look after him, show him the sights while you folks talk,' he added, nodding towards the man who had emerged from the house and was waiting on the terrace.

Kate's heart thudded. She blinked in dismay. This was the leader of the Magic Men, who had tried to kidnap her when her car broke down.

Redfeather, Chay Bowman's grandfather.

CHAPTER TWELVE

Our people possessed remarkable powers of concentration and abstraction . . . such nearness to nature keeps the spirit sensitive to impressions not commonly felt and in touch with the unseen powers.

CHARLES EASTMAN,
Santee Dakota Indian Boyhood

'This is Redfeather.'

At second glance, relief flooded through Kate.

She had been mistaken. The tall Indian with his long grey hair in two plaits certainly bore a resemblance to the leader of the Magic Men who had tried to abduct her, strong enough for her to suspect that they might be related. But despite western clothes, white polo shirt and jeans, Redfeather remained the more imposing of the two.

At ninety, his back was still ramrod straight and, as a young man, he must have been outstandingly handsome with finely cut features and high cheekbones that could also have passed for Mexican, Mediterranean or Celtic Highlander.

She thought of Sean Doe's wild gypsy looks.

171

How well they would have fitted into this Indian world.

Redfeather and Chay led the way into the house. Following, Kate saw that the interior was completely modern western, its walls heavy with the mementoes of his Hollywood days. Peace pipes, Navajo rugs and a huge feathered war bonnet.

But between Chay and his grandfather who had taken him aside, she was aware of conflict. There could be little doubt that the old Navajo was not pleased to see her and she suspected that Chay had not warned him. Her visit was an unexpected and unpleasant surprise as, eyeing her coldly, he turned his back and began what sounded like an ill-natured harangue with his grandson.

Although both men remained poker-faced, betraying none of the emotions expressed by what sounded like a heated exchange of grunts and snarls in their own peculiar language, Kate guessed that she was the subject under discussion, especially when Chay paused occasionally to glance nervously in her direction.

Embarrassed she turned her attention to the signed photographs on walls and shelves. Redfeather with various Presidents—Nixon, Carter, Reagan—and with movie stars—Errol Flynn, Gary Cooper, John Wayne, Jeff Chandler. There were stills from films too and she realised then that she had seen him on

172

screen many times.

Trying to look as inconspicuous as possible, she wandered over to the magnificent white grand piano. Was it a mere status symbol or did anyone ever play it? There was no sheet music in evidence but many photographs, mainly family this time. A uniformed marine, Chay's father. A much younger Chay, and a pretty Indian girl proudly holding a baby, presumably Jake.

There were other photos of Redfeather, one with costumed Indians which Kate took particular note of since one of the groups looked remarkably like the Magic Men.

Suddenly she realised she understood what was being said behind her.

'My grandfather bids you welcome,' said Chay. 'Unfortunately this was not a convenient time for us to visit with him. I would have telephoned, of course,' he said darting the old man an angry look, 'if he did not consider all such instruments as invasions of his privacy. He will have to leave us soon, he's addressing a conservation meeting.'

At ninety, thought Kate. That was something.

Indicating the photographs, she smiled. 'I recognise you now. We've seen most of your early westerns in Britain.

They're very popular on our television.'

That pleased him. She detected a distinct thawing as he said proudly, 'My clan fought at the side of the great chief Cochise. The war bonnet hanging on the wall,' he pointed, 'was worn by my father at the real battle with the white soldiers at Apache Pass.'

He named films, told her which roles he had played in them, the famous movie star good guys who were in real life just plain bad guys.

He shook his head sadly. 'Many led lives their most devoted fans would not even wish to know about, or believe what they heard.'

As he talked a pretty young Indian woman brought coffee which she set before them and silently glided away. Neither Redfeather nor Chay even glanced in her direction and, thanking her with a gracious smile, Kate shot an angry look at the two men, so discourteous. It appeared that she had supposed wrongly, that Indian women now shared an equal role with their men.

Redfeather had done with movies and was telling her that it was no longer fighting between Indians and Anglos that was of any importance.

Chay exchanged a wry I-told-you-so glance with Kate as his grandfather continued, 'The final battle is to save the very earth we once fought over. All mankind must now unite, work together, if we are to save earth and all the living creatures from extinction. My ancestors warned the first white men that earth belongs to no man and that as they look at the mysterious ruins the Anasazi left, so one day another race will look at the ruins of the white man's civilisation. In neither case will there be any records left to tell what happened, why they suddenly vanished without trace—'

An apologetic cough from Chay's direction drew Redfeather's attention. Without looking at him he smiled at Kate.

'I apologise. My grandson was weaned on such tales. No doubt you have heard some already. That bad cough says I must not bore visitors. More coffee?'

'I'm not bored,' said Kate. 'I love the earth. And I have a son.'

'So I am told. That is good.' And, stretching out his hands, he took hers and held them tightly as if they might say something to him. 'You are not like other women,' he said softly. 'You have psychic powers. But you know that already.'

Kate withdrew her hands rather hastily and he nodded.

'It is the truth I speak, but you run from it. For many years now you have been running away from your destiny. But you cannot escape, it is waiting for you. Forever yours.'

At her startled expression he said, 'But you are obstinate too,' as if that somehow pleased him. In that accompanying slow smile she recognised that the charisma, the sex appeal he must have had at his grandson's age was undiminished and that the Indian girl was most probably wife or mistress.

At that moment the door opened. Luke came in and Redfeather did a strange thing. He stood up, walked across and took Luke's hands and held them in much the same way he had taken Kate's. He leaned over and briefly addressed Luke in Navajo. What was surprising was that Luke looked deep into the old man's eyes and smiled. He appeared to understand every word.

For what seemed like a long while as Chay helped Kate to more coffee and Jake who had joined them talked about college, Redfeather and Luke remained apart.

Watching them Kate realised that something significant had taken place. From the moment Luke entered the room, the whole atmosphere had changed, become electrified, supercharged. As if this was no longer a mere social visit, but something long planned and preordained.

At last Luke and Redfeather rejoined them. The old man, his hand on the boy's shoulder, said, 'I am taking him to see our proper homes.'

'Would you to like to see them?' Chay asked Kate politely.

'Yes, of course.'

They walked across the terrace and Redfeather, still leaning on Luke, led the way to the hogan nearest the house.

'That one belongs to grandfather,' Chay

176

explained to her. 'There's nothing exceptional about it, it's the kind you'll find on all our reservations.'

The hogan was built of logs cut by adze, stacked up in eight walls. The outside was completely plastered in dried mud, and it looked for all the world like a huge dome of earth thrusting out of the ground and inside, corbelled into a vaulted ceiling. There were no windows. The door faced east. The interior was lit by a single naked lightbulb run in on a wire from some unseen source. The floor was hard-packed dirt. A stack of mattresses lay against one wall, and what the Navajos had long used for cooking and warmth occupied the centre of the floor—a massive oil drum cut in half with a stovepipe running out through a hole in the roof.

It was cool inside, probably well insulated against all extremes of hot and cold. A few ancient posters decorated the walls and from the roof hung clumps of dried herbs, their scent lingering with that of smoked clay.

The overall effect was unexpectedly cosy, but seeing Kate's expression of amazement as she looked at his grandfather, Chay thought uncomfortably that she was making the usual Anglo comparison with the comfort and luxury of the adobe house.

'Grandfather comes here to meditate,' he said defensively.

Redfeather overheard. 'This is how I was

brought up, how our people lived and how I lived before I went into the white man's world.'

He turned to Kate. 'What you see here are my roots, here I get close to the Great Spirit who created all of us. And here one day soon, I will be carried when I die. And this hogan will be burnt, so that my chindi will have peace.'

He looked at his elegant and expensive wristwatch.

'I must leave you now, it is time for my meeting,' he said to Chay and with a nod in Kate's direction, 'Bring them to me again soon, grandson. Next time we will eat together.'

Opening the door of Chay's car, he did a strange thing. He touched Luke's head and closed his eyes for a moment as if in benediction before walking away, his gliding steps swift for an old man.

From the porch he watched them leave, Jake at his side. Kate and Luke, waving to him, turned back as the car braked violently and Chay made way for a pick-up truck coming at great speed along the drive towards them. With a screech of brakes, it swerved past, heading fast towards Redfeather's house.

'The Magic Men!' said Kate. 'Chay, did you see them?'

Chay didn't answer, concentrating on getting a wheel off the grass verge.

Looking round, Kate was in time to see Redfeather and an old Indian greeting one another. And this time she knew she was not mistaken. The old man embracing Redfeather, she was certain, was her attempted kidnapper and she no longer had any doubts that the photograph she had seen was of Redfeather in the midst of the Magic Men.

'That man visiting your grandfather was one of them,' she gasped.

'I didn't see him. I expect it was his cousin, Tomas.'

Kate sat back in her seat. So Chay had known him as she suspected that night when he rescued her. Vividly she remembered them talking together, the old man putting his hand on Chay's shoulder.

Feeling betrayed and angry, she demanded, 'Is Redfeather one of them?'

'Is he one of what?' said Chay casually, his attention on the steep road ahead.

'Is he one of the Magic Men?'

Chay shrugged. 'I don't know his business and neither do you. And the friendships my grandfather chooses have nothing to do with me. Or with you either,' he added sternly.

Seeing her expression he said gently. 'The Magic Men are only spokes in the great wheel of things. Sometimes those spokes converge with what Grandfather also believes. But that does not mean he approves of everything they do.'

'They tried to kidnap me. I'm not likely to forget that!'

'You can't be sure. You could be putting a

sinister interpretation on their natural courtesy towards a woman in distress.'

Kate snorted. From what she'd seen of the way the servant, or whoever she was, had been totally ignored, there wasn't much natural courtesy towards females in evidence.

'Believe what you want to,' said Chay. 'But you have me to protect you. And grandfather likes you and he likes Luke. You are safe with us.'

Kate was too angry and upset by her discovery to make further conversation. He did not seem to mind but drove in silence.

When they reached the main street, Luke touched her shoulder mouthing that he seriously needed to go to the toilet.

Kate explained to Chay. 'He can't wait until we get back. It was all that Coke he drank.'

'He can go at my place,' said Chay. 'We're almost there.'

Rita wasn't in the office which was a relief to Chay since seeing the Anglo woman again would have put her in a black mood.

'I'll wait,' said Kate. But curiosity decided her to follow them inside.

In the hallway she hesitated. From the open door upstairs she heard music, someone singing, 'Forever Yours'. Unmistakeably Sean Doe's voice, with the song that had made him famous.

The unexpectedness of hearing it in Chay's office shook her considerably. Luke raced downstairs again, followed by Chay, but the singing continued.

'You've left your radio on,' she said.

'It's a tape deck. I never switch it off, I guess.'

'It's Sean Doe.'

Chay seemed surprised. 'You know his songs?'

'Yes.'

He was pleased. Here was something else they had in common. 'I've got his whole collection. I'll lend you some while you're here. He was one of the greats.'

'I know,' said Kate sadly.

'Forever yours', hummed Chay happily on the short run back to the creek. At his side Kate was silent, staring at the road ahead. Once he looked at her and thought she looked pale and tired, even a bit unhappy.

Outside the house he said, 'I'll call you later this week. Say Friday.' He would have liked to make it earlier, but didn't want her to think he was monopolising her, maybe scare her off.

'That's fine,' she said. 'I've promised to take Luke to see some of the canyons.'

'I have some maps. Here! These should be useful.'

As she was thanking him Chay gestured towards the car in the drive-in. 'You'll be OK this time.'

She nodded absently and suddenly he thought he knew the reason for her distress.

Taking her hand, he said, 'Look, don't you worry about the Magic Men. You are absolutely safe with us.'

But Kate watching him go, wondered. Safe could sound ominous too in the wrong context.

As ominous as hearing Sean Doe's voice on Chay's tapes.

*   *   *

Warren Rhodes's invitation could not have come at a more opportune moment for Kate, for the bitter-sweet memories of 'Forever Yours' threatened to stay with her. Despite all attempts to banish it with a television quiz programme, Sean Doe's voice remained a persistent whisper at the back of her mind.

Luke did not want to go to the Rhodes. There were two John Wayne films on the movie channel.

The Rhodes house was tastefully furnished with antiques, the walls decorated with original western watercolours. It had none of the transience that mobile homes suggested either.

Offered a drink, she opted for coffee instead, guessing that alcohol would only intensify her nervous state and doubtless induce restless, dream-haunted slumber.

Warren was eager to proceed with the business in hand and produced his file of yellowed papers and letters, further enlightenment on the vague story Kate had

182

heard of the minister's daughter who had been abducted and forcibly married to the chief of Los Atalos.

Tessa settled herself comfortably in a chair and brought out her tapestry. 'Don't mind me not giving you my full attention, honey. I've heard it all before,' she added with a martyred expression. 'He's always threatening to write a book about it. Unfortunately golf seems to come in the way.'

Ignoring her, Warren smiled at Kate. 'I expect Tessa told you that my grandmother was a school friend of Janet Glencaird, the minister's daughter who lived here. That was my original fascination with the place, why we came here when I retired, because my father left me, among the family papers, some letters that Janet wrote to Grandma Rhodes.

'To fill you in. They were both schoolgirls in San Francisco. Janet was Scottish. I'm not sure what brought her father over here, apart from missionary zeal, but from what I've read about the times, it was traditional for younger sons of lairds who had no chance of inheriting the title, to go into the Army or the Church. That was the way my grandmother—she lived to be nearly a hundred—told it to my father when he was a young lad.

'There may have been some deeper reason that we'll never know about. Arizona was a wild place in the last decades of the nineteenth century with the Indians fighting every inch of the way to hold on to what was rightfully theirs, despite swarms of go-west pioneers and US cavalry. This was the age of the great Apache warriors, Geronimo and Cochise and the end of the Atalos–Anasazi tribe, who Reverend Glencaird had in mind to convert.

'His wife came with him leaving their daughter in San Francisco to finish her education. Unfortunately Mrs Glencaird got pregnant with a late baby and when she died birthing, Janet, who was about fifteen, decided that her duty lay with her father and came out here to look after him.

'That was when the letters and Janet's own tragedy began. The chief, Atala, was no wild savage such as you might see depicted in Hollywood movies. He was a clever young man who had become the minister's protégé, educated by him, as well as being his adopted son.'

Warren frowned. 'Did I say young? Perhaps that was a misstatement. He certainly must have looked young, and Janet thought so, according to her letters. But there was a mystery about Atala, something that even the minister turned his face away from. You see, Atala had inherited the secret of immortality from his Anasazi ancestors.'

He paused and Kate said, 'How fascinating.'

Warren looked at her. 'Fascinating?' He shook his head. 'No. I believe sinister rather than fascinating. Before I go any further, I

184

should add that the Atalos had only recently been "discovered" by white settlers. Like many early Indian tribes, such as the Navajo, who believe that the earth is for all men to share, they were prepared to be friendly, to tolerate the white minister and even regard Atala's apparent conversion to Christianity as merely a polite sign of goodwill.

'Perhaps they even believed in the miracle that their legends had promised. That a white god had returned to them. The Anasazi were at one time linked to the same ancient civilisation as the Aztecs and Mayas who believed that their deity, Quetzalcoatl or Feathered Serpent, came from "the land of the Rising Sun". According to the legends he wore a long white robe and had a beard. A saviour to his people, he taught them crafts and laid down wise laws. He taught them the mysteries of communication by building great roads and architectural wonders of great temples.

'His empire flourished. The ears of corn were as long as men are tall and he made the cotton plants bear bolls of coloured cotton. But for some reason he suddenly had to leave and, taking his laws, his writings, his songs, he went away down the same road he had come.

'Some say a ship came for him and he sailed away back to his own people. Others say he went to the seashore and raising his arms to the sky he cried out and when he began to weep, he vanished in a cloud of fire and his heart reappeared as the morning star.

'But all the legends of Quetzalcoatl agree on one thing. His promise to come again. There has even been one suggestion that he was actually one of the Apostles, St Thomas. And that after the death of the Messiah these early Christians spread themselves through the world carrying the message of Christ crucified.

'Legend goes further. That the Apostle Thomas crossed from Europe to the Americas by way of the lost continent of Atlantis, which was then submerged under the ocean.

'But to return to Los Atalos. Seeing other Indians perish and having only recently encountered a caring and genial white man, perhaps they regarded the Reverend Glencaird—a patriarchal figure who could have stepped from the pages of the Old Testament—as their miracle, the promised redeemer.'

Warren indicated a transparent packet containing photographs. 'You'll see for yourself. I often wonder what happened to sour relations between them. Possibly Glencaird discovered that his adopted son, whom he had baptised as a Christian was being kept alive by the annual ritual sacrifice of a young boy. His heart removed by the Atalos priests and given to the chief to be consumed.'

He looked at Kate. 'You shudder, but think about it, most religions have sacrifice at their base. As Christians we symbolically eat the

186

body and drink the blood of Christ at the Mass and thereby are promised eternal life.

'Anyway, we know from Janet's letters that she fell in love with Atala and he with her. That they tried to separate. She went away, took a teaching job in Tucson, it's here in her letters to Grandma. In case you're interested I've taken photocopies for you to keep. Here are the photographs, they are of great historical and sentimental value, but thanks to the miracle of modern copiers, I've had them reproduced.'

He looked at them critically. 'They're not quite as good as the originals, some of the detail is lost, but it gives you an idea of what it was like.'

Blackhawk Creek, blurred in sepia, but the rocks still standing out majestically. A tall, elderly man in ministerial garb posed proudly in front of a frame house with a cross on its roof: the Mission Church. His shock of white hair and long white beard confirmed Warren's description. Reverend Glencaird looked exactly like an Old Testament prophet from an illustrated Bible that had belonged to Kate's grandfather.

Another photograph, this time with a group of Indians in western dress, Los Atalos.

'Which is Atala?'

'He may well be one of them. We don't know,' said Warren. 'The man of mystery. It's doubtful if he would allow his image to be taken. The old suspicion was to regard it as a dangerous procedure which might steal a man's soul.'

But what interested Kate most was the girl in a white dress. She looked about fifteen, a cascade of golden curls and a wide-brimmed hat almost hiding her features.

The doorbell rang. One of the Rhodes's neighbours came in with a petition to be signed against extending street lighting beyond the highway boundary. Invited to have a drink, he sat down. It looked like being a long session and Kate excused herself. It was late and Luke was alone.

As she was leaving Warren said, 'Enjoy your read.'

Following her down the drive Tessa looked up at the star-bright sky and shivered, 'It's all so beautiful here, everything in harmony with nature, makes it hard to believe all that Warren was telling you. About ritual sacrifices.'

She went on, 'I know it's crazy in this day and age but it does make you think. I mean you can't help wondering, can you, whether those two poor Indian boys were killed by a cougar, or whether it was something much nastier. I'd have felt happier, I can tell you if they had found a killer that they could have put behind bars.'

At the gate her smile was calculated to put Kate at her ease again. 'Well, goodnight, honey, I dare say Warren's old papers will soon put you to sleep.'

CHAPTER THIRTEEN

Letters from Janet Glencaird to her best friend, Lily Rhodes née Harkness, circa 1872–5.

Kate had hoped for all manner of revelations about life among the Indians in Blackhawk Creek, and some insight into Reverend Glencaird's character. The first few letters suggested she was in for a disappointment. Largely undated, as often was the case in Victorian times, they were also so lacking in atmosphere or interest that they could equally well have been written from a country parsonage anywhere in Britain.

The earliest consisted of schoolgirl confidences and urgent discussion of the latest materials for gowns, of going to church, of walks and social evenings and worthy books read.

The poor quality ink had faded, the handwriting was hard to read and almost illegible in parts. At best they were a mere glimpse into the restricted life of a Victorian miss and of little interest to anyone but the immediate members of the Rhodes family. Doubtless that was why they had been preserved, thought Kate, stifling a yawn as she laid yet another aside.

Warren had obviously worked hard and, lacking exact dates, had used the contents to number them in some sort of chronological order. After number six Kate decided to read one more before returning them to Warren with some polite remarks.

Suddenly she sat up. At last, here was one worth waiting for.

The Mission House, Blackhawk Creek.
August 14
My dear Lily,

I so enjoyed your visit and I am disappointed that it could not have been longer and that you had so little chance for more than the most superficial acquaintance with A. Dear, dearest Lily, I did so much want you of all my friends to LIKE each other.

I must confess that I am a little surprised—and hurt!—that you do not share my high opinion or even a little of the esteem in which I hold A.

I do not agree with you that he is just a savage Indian, or that he is 'ALIEN despite being a Christian'. After all my confidences and our long friendship, I feel it is quite unnecessary for you to warn me about my FEELINGS for him. I know you have my best interests at heart and you are a year older and engaged to be married, so even as I say all this I most earnestly ask you to believe me that it is not out of any disrespect for your experience of the world, which I fully acknowledge to be much greater than mine.

What you are telling me, dear friend, alas I know all too well already, nor am I likely EVER to forget that anything but the most superficial acquaintance between A. and myself, as you most sincerely advise, is unlikely EVER to take place. Such an association as you are hinting at would break Papa's heart, nor do I think A.'s people would countenance such a union since they regard him as THEIR GOD!!

I was glad you liked Matt Hepple. He is the kindest and best of men and a great friend to Papa and me. I am well aware of his FEELINGS for me, and I am grateful as always for your most friendly advice. However, at present I have not the least wish to encourage his advances . . .

After these gentle reproaches, the remainder of the letter contained queries about samplers, the request for millinery ribbons and an urgent reminder, plus precise instructions, about gown patterns which Lily had offered to send. It was signed, 'Forever your friend, Janet'.

The next letter was almost illegible in parts written at high speed, obviously in great agitation and desperation.

Hollands Hotel, Arroyo Street, Tucson.
October 24
My dear Lily,

I expect you are feeling anxious at not hearing from me sooner. I was so sorry I was unable to come to Monterey for your engagement party last month. I left in plenty of time and as Papa was certain a storm was coming he asked A. to escort me on horseback through the canyon behind the house. (The Anasazi Canyon; you will remember we walked there together.) It is the short way to the stage depot and although rough going, it cuts off several miles.

All went well until the storm broke over our heads with terrible ferocity. We took refuge in a bear's cave but the beast returned. A. fought it off bravely with only a knife. It ran off but his arm was mauled.

Dearest Lily, I have never been more afraid in my whole life. I thought we would both die and in that moment, yes, I CONFESS it TRULY, I knew I LOVED him more than life itself!! I would have taken on that savage beast single handed as I tore up my best petticoat to bandage his arm.

I cannot tell, nor even whisper to you, my dearest friend, the wonder of our love for each other we discovered that night in the cave. I have NEVER hated dawn as I did that dawn breaking, knowing we must part and FOREVER.

You do not have to tell me, dearest Lily, for I know all too well the consequences of my behaviour and that I can NEVER be his wife. I must NEVER return to Blackhawk. I am quite resolved about that and my prayers have been answered for I have been offered a teaching post in a kindergarten school around the corner through the kind couple who own this hotel.

I have taken heart that this may not be for very long since Papa has been so poorly lately. Quite suddenly he has grown thin and old and I have persuaded him that we should both return to Scotland, that some younger minister be found to take over his charge.

I cannot begin to tell you how his dear eyes light up at the mention of his beloved homeland. Meanwhile I teach little girls about what is good and honest and upright and how they must love Jesus while my heart is far away with the man I shall always love and who can never be mine. I have nothing of his now. I lost the turquoise bead necklace you so admired—on that blissful God-given night together, somehow it got broken.

In closing, dearest Lily, please write to me at the hotel here. I beg you do not show this letter to anyone. Please DESTROY it immediately and try to forgive and pray for

her who is
Forever your friend, Janet.

Lily did not keep her promise. The following March saw Janet back in the Mission House at Blackhawk Creek.

My dear Lily,

I deeply regret that I must decline the honour of being bridesmaid at your forthcoming marriage to James Warren Rhodes. It grieves me deeply to write this letter as I know how sad and disappointed you will be and I can only hope that when you know the circumstances you will feel it in your heart to forgive me for breaking the promise we exchanged long ago, and which was renewed when you became engaged to Mr Rhodes.

Alas, dear friend, if I had a heart left unbroken it would do so now. I have a further piece of news, I am to be married within the month to Matt Hepple, who you will recall as the ardent suitor whose advances I have rejected many times.

You will doubtless be almost as astonished as I am myself. But there is a reason for this speedy marriage. I am with child. Not by Matt alas, although he knows of my condition and still wishes to marry me in spite of it. Such love will earn my undying gratitude, although I will never be able to return it. The father of my child is known to you already, he whom my whole being worships and adores, and who is forbidden to me by his people and mine. Such knowledge would break poor Papa's heart. He basks in the happy thought that I have chosen well in Matt as a husband. A wise choice he keeps on saying, the one he would have made for me. God will surely bless our union with little ones.

It breaks my heart to listen to him.

The remaining page or pages of this letter were missing. There was only one more, written from San Francisco, undated, but presumably some time later.

My dear Lily,

I am writing to apologise, knowing you must have waited in vain for my visit. Since our escape from Blackhawk Creek, the child and I have sought refuge in many strange places. I know you would have gladly given us sanctuary, but in your own delicate condition I did not feel it right or wise to expose you to the danger we bring to those who try to help us.

God help us, and God rest my dear Papa whom I do not doubt is in paradise. I weep for him constantly and for that one I love more than my own life. For his dear sake our child, his gift to me, must be saved. Those who pursue us so cruelly and relentlessly would not hesitate to murder me and to steal A.'s child.

As I write I seem to hear the pursuit is near. It is never far off. They gain upon us each day as we flee, hoping for some miracle that will get us across the sea to safe harbour.

I fear we will never meet again in this life, dearest Lily, so pray for me and do not forget she who is

Forever Yours, Janet.

Kate replaced the documents in the file. There were so many tantalising gaps, so many questions posed that could never now be answered.

Had Atala died? It sounded as if both he and Janet's father were dead. What had become of Matt Hepple who had behaved more nobly than any of them, loving her and knowing she cared only for Atala and was carrying his child.

In an effort to see the photographs more clearly, Kate remembered the magnifying glass that Luke kept for studying, small insects and flowers. It was on his bedside table and, holding it to the group with Reverend Glencaird, she searched each of the Atalos faces minutely.

She shivered. How like the Magic Men they looked. The western dress imposed on them by enforced civilisation resulting in an appearance that seemed indefinably more savage, seen against those dark alien countenances.

She wondered if that was Atala standing by the minister's side. If so, the photograph did him an injustice according to Janet's account of her handsome, dynamic lover.

The shrill ring of a bell shattered the silence, sent her heart racing.

It was no spectre from the past. Chay stood on the doorstep.

She was heartily glad to see him and hardly listened as he explained that he had to go to Phoenix on business to see a client and might not be back in time to take them to see Redfeather.

'Sorry for coming so late. I tried calling you and when there was no reply I was going to slip a note in the door.'

Kate shook her head. 'Luke was in but he doesn't answer telephones. Won't you come in?'

Chay hesitated. He was tempted but it was almost midnight. 'Thanks but no. I have an early start in the morning.'

'Some other time, then.' Her mind elsewhere, her response was automatic. 'Before you go, I have something for you.'

She darted back into the living room and returned with a bunch of papers clipped together.

'I was visiting my neighbour across the way. You should meet Mr Rhodes, he's a retired

197

historian and his grandmother was a friend of the girl who lived here, the minister's daughter. The early letters are the usual schoolgirl stuff, but these ones are really worth reading when you have a moment.'

She watched him go, wishing he had stayed. Restless, she didn't feel like going to bed and knew she was unlikely to sleep much that night.

The turquoise beads that Luke and Chay had found at the bear's cave were in a little glass bowl on the windowsill. Was she holding the remains of the necklace Atala had given Janet long ago, or was it some strange telepathy that had made her identify with the lovers in the cave and their first meeting in the stagecoach.

She turned the magnifying glass on the girl in her white dress and had her first shock. The sense of familiarity increased as she picked up the family portraits she had brought with her from Edinburgh and realised that fifty years later, her grandmother Jetta Alexander in the absurd fairy frock, might have been mistaken for Janet Glencaird.

She would never know for certain. It was too much to expect life to neatly round off situations and provide solutions to questions doomed to be forever unanswered.

Forever yours.

A chill went through her and although the night was warm and calm, the glass doors seemed to rattle in a sudden draught.

Forever yours.

How Janet had signed her last letter to Lily took on a deadlier significance.

The song from which she could never entirely escape. A song that haunted her. Sean Doe's 'Forever Yours'.

CHAPTER FOURTEEN

Breathe on me, Breath of God
Fill me with life anew . . .

HYMN NO. 103

Chay was on the road at dawn. The contents of Janet Glencaird's letters to her friend Lily had created a vivid picture he was unlikely to forget.

His chief concern was not for Blackhawk's tragic past but for the present and in particular for Kate Fenner and the boy, Luke. Like some monstrous cloud of suspicion forever building up at the back of his mind, he was surer than ever that there was something distinctly sinister about the non-appearance of Mr Wilderbrand and the bizarre conditions of the prize the boy had won.

Why hadn't his mother made more careful enquiries before leaving Britain. Could she be that naive?

199

He thought of Lopez who had been involved and had almost certainly been murdered. He now gave particular consideration to the Magic Men and Kate's insistence that they were trying to kidnap her.

Had she been right? Had he dismissed too lightly a woman's instinct for such dangers?

As he drove fast along the almost empty highway, he was aware that his compact disc was playing Sean Doe again. He switched it off.

Kate's reaction to hearing his voice had been more than sentimental interest. Her face had gone white and she looked as if she might faint. Her reaction to the long-dead pop star puzzled him.

Sean Doe had prided himself on being a man of mystery. Where had he come from, what were his origins?

From the days of his first hit recording and his meteoric rise to fame until his untimely death, he had remained an enigma. And it wasn't through lack of trying on the part of the media. Fan magazines, interviewers, or anyone 'trying to get something on him' had come up against a brick wall. Such reticence hinted at very obscure origins, Chay suspected, maybe even criminal associations which he had been very anxious not to make public.

Come to think of it, Chay realised he knew precious little about Kate Fenner's background either for a man whose job was investigation.

His thoughts drifted to Janet Glencaird's

pursuers in her flight with Atala's child. Were they the predecessors of the Magic Men and why was their quarry so important? Had they eventually escaped?

Returning to the present, he once again thrust aside the Magic Men and any possibility of some connection with his grandfather. He was certain now that the Begay brothers, Beno's kidnapping and the death of the first Navajo boy two years earlier, were links in a sinister chain of events, which meant there was still a killer on the loose, preparing to strike again.

But instead of the excitement and triumph of solving a mystery, Chay had only a feeling of despair, a premonition of disaster that he was involved in a deadly race against time.

All the signs pointed in the direction of Luke Fenner, as the next victim.

*   *   *

On the sunny terrace above the creek, Luke's zoo grew daily more overcrowded.

'You are just about the best meal ticket that has ever come their way,' said Kate, 'but that's the last slice of toast till we go to the supermarket.'

She smiled indulgently at the scene before her. Feeding one hungry boy plus the five thousand meant that one loaf didn't go very far these days.

Her thoughts turned to gloomier things. Still wrapped about by the nightmare hours of a sleepless night, she was giving serious consideration to how she might cut short the holiday and return home. Never had Edinburgh seemed more attractive. She thought constantly about the Victorian house in Newington, how good it was to live an uncomplicated emotional life bounded by the often dull routine of running a guest house.

At four that morning, she had been ready to negotiate the flight home, whatever the cost or inconvenience. Now watching Luke, she knew she could not do it. Seeing him so settled in a climate that suited him, he looked fitter, more carefree and far happier than she had ever seen him back at school in Edinburgh. Especially since Toggers's death. She shook her head in a deliberate effort to cast out that tragic memory.

The thought of finding another school threw a deep cloud of doubt and misery over her. She envied Luke's childlike absorption in the present joy and excitement he had found in Blackhawk. She sighed and turned away, knowing she could not find it in her heart to lie to him with some fittingly plausible reason for going back to Britain that would make his disappointment bearable.

She wished she could see Chay, sure that he would confirm that she was being unfair, taking her neuroses out on Luke.

The Merc was in the drive. She was used to

handling it on the short scenic trips Luke enjoyed, which brought his poster of **Red Rock Crossing** to life. However, she was cautious about leaving the beaten track after their first experience, afraid they would get lost again, or break down, or encounter a flash flood, unbelievable looking at the azure sky, but according to Chay, the weather was still unreliable. Spring could be a treacherous illusion, a temperature in the seventies followed next day by a heavy fall of snow.

Breathing deeply, filling her lungs with the wine-clear air, she thrust the trauma of Blackhawk Creek's unhappy past behind her. That was something she could never change.

For Luke's sake, she resolved to be sensible and enjoy the rest of the holiday, glorying in the beauty all around her that had seen man and woman come and go. The short span of human lives, their joys and sorrows alike were nothing to the red rocks which overshadowed them. Soon they too would be gone, a mere shrug in the passing of a century. Only the rocks would remain, timeless, unchangeable, a philosophic lesson to be well heeded.

*　　　*　　　*

Luke was looking forward to seeing Redfeather again, he kept asking her how long—when do we leave?

Chay had called from Phoenix. Thanks to his

early rising he would collect them at four o'clock.

He arrived at three and Kate knew by his expression that it was bad news.

'Grandfather's had an accident. He's in hospital. With concussion. It looks bad.'

'What happened?'

'His bicycle was hit by a car.'

'A bike—at his age?'

'Yeah, claims he likes the exercise, now that he's too arthritic to ride Storm Cloud. He was coming home from Dinsdale, on the other side of the canyon. Jake said he'd remembered an Atalos from his Hollywood days and thought he'd call on him. That this old guy might have some information.'

He paused. 'Information for you about Blackhawk in the old days. Anyway, it was after midnight on a side road. He had no tail light on the bike either and a car tipped him off turning a corner.'

The thought of anyone riding a bicycle on roads off the main highways in pitch black sounded suicidal to Kate. And for a ninety-year-old, what hope of survival?

'Grandfather's nothing if not a man of impulse. This old guy he was visiting with hasn't a phone either, he abandoned the white man's way and went back to his roots long ago. I thought I'd let you know. I'm on my way to the hospital.'

Luke was pressing Kate's hand urgently.

'We'll come with you, if we may. Luke wants to see him.'

Chay looked in amazement at the boy's eager, anxious face staring up at him.

On the way he filled in the details. 'The bike was just touched by the car or he'd have been killed. Fortunately the driver was a local guy, so he gathered him up, took him into Casualty and stayed with him till they found out from the Tribal Police who he was. Nothing on him for identification, of course, but he's well known for his conservation protest meetings and suchlike.'

'This happened last night, you say,' Kate interrupted, 'surely the family were anxious when he didn't return.'

Chay shrugged. 'He comes and he goes, time means nothing to him. If he's having a good time with friends and heavy on the whiskey, he'll stay out all night. No one bothers. No way would he tolerate even his own family checking up on him.'

The hospital was large, white and cheerfully well scrubbed but still the lingering odours that typify illness refused to be banished and a feeling of death emanated from the walls and ceilings, resistant to all known sweet-smelling detergents.

Their footsteps sounded unnaturally loud on the long corridors, but as they reached the ward they heard chanting, a man's voice.

Chay put a hand on Kate's arm. 'Wait! That's

grandfather.'

'He's singing,' said Kate hopefully.

'Yeah. Singing his death song.'

'Oh, no!'

'I guess we're too late.'

Through the glass panel looking into the tiny ward, Redfeather was sitting up cross-legged leaning against the bedrest, his bandaged head bowed as he chanted.

For the first time, Chay thought he looked incredibly old. He went in and spoke to him gently. But if he heard, he gave no acknowledgement of his grandson's presence.

'We might as well leave him in peace,' said Chay bowing to the inevitable. And at Kate's protest he said, 'Look—he's dying. He's almost gone already.'

'Can't you do something?' said Kate wildly.

Chay looked at her. 'Like what? His mind is made up.'

'Just like that! I was taught that while there's life there's hope.' Kate began to cry and Chay put his arm around her shoulder.

'He's had a long life. It's almost over and this is the way he wants to go, making his peace, preparing himself to meet the Great Spirit.'

From the bag he had brought containing Redfeather's toilet articles Chay extracted an eagle's feather. Placing it between his grandfather's clasped hands he leaned forward and gently kissed his forehead in a gesture of farewell.

The old man didn't move, the slow dirge continued fainter now but uninterrupted.

'The eagle's feather will guide him on his long journey,' Chay explained as Kate took hold of Luke's hand.

'Come along, dear,' she said softly.

The boy was swaying slightly, as if in harmony to the chanting, his face dead white as he leaned against the door, his eyes never leaving the old man's face.

Suddenly the chanting stopped. Redfeather's head dropped forward onto his chest. He slumped sideways on the bed.

He was dead.

They stood aside as nurses bustled forward, pushing them out of the ward. Chay stood by the glass panel, watching as a doctor took his pulse, waiting for the final confirmation, and at last they laid him back on the bed, covering his face with the sheet.

The doctor came out. 'Sorry, Mr Bowman. There's nothing we could do. If you'd like to come to the office, we'll make the necessary arrangements.'

Kate was drying her tears, the scene blurring in front of her. Chay's arm was around her.

'I'll put you both in the car first,' he whispered.

'Luke,' said Kate.

They had momentarily forgotten him and looking through the glass panel, they saw he had slipped back into the ward and had pulled the sheet away from Redfeather's face. He stood looking down at the old man, whose face was serene, the heavy lines of age already beginning to dissolve under the peace of death.

Chay found the scene touching. Not a man to cry easily he felt the tears rising behind his eyes. He gripped Kate's hand as she prepared to call to Luke.

'They had a great bond, the kind the very old have with the very young,' he whispered.

'Wait!' said Kate.

Luke had gone forward. He lightly touched the hands folded over the eagle's feather. Leaning over the dead man, he stretched his thin arms across his chest so that their faces touched.

Chay was deeply moved by Luke's devotion, this last act of salutation, tears coursing unbidden down his cheeks.

About to enter the ward again, Kate's restraining hand held him back.

'No. Not yet.'

The silence of death was broken by Luke's breathing, heavy and unnatural.

Chay stared at Kate, frowning. What was going on?

But before he could speak, Redfeather's body jerked under the sheet. His eyelids twitched open. He stared at the ceiling.

Chay rushed forward.

'What has happened?' Redfeather demanded in Navajo. 'Have I been sick? What am I doing in this place? This is a hospital.'

The disgust in his voice was evident. He had never been in such a place in his long life.

Looking round, he said 'I've been asleep. Get me something to drink, grandson, I'm thirsty,' he added crossly, struggling to prop himself up on one elbow.

A nurse stared through the glass panel, saw the group around the bed and, with one startled look at Redfeather, she rushed out again, returning with the doctor. Chay, Kate and Luke were thrust outside once more and screens pulled quickly around the bed.

'He wasn't dead,' said Chay. 'Jesus, he wasn't dead at all.'

Kate went to the window where Luke was staring up at the sunset clouds gathering beyond the hills. She drew him to her, and with a sigh he rested his head against her shoulder. They stood close together motionless, looking out into the night.

At last the doctor emerged smiling and said to Chay, 'You may go in now. Just a few moments.'

'How is he?' demanded Chay. 'Is he going to be all right?'

The doctor eyed him pityingly. 'As much as any man of ninety can be all right after a road accident. He's had a great shock, but I'm glad to say he seems to be making an amazing recovery.'

The complacent smile that accompanied his

remarks made it sound as if the hospital and indeed, he himself might be responsible for this miracle of resurrection.

'Wait a moment,' said Chay. 'You pronounced him dead. His heart had stopped beating. I watched you. We were standing here—we saw it all.'

The doctor exchanged glances with the nurse by his side. Their anxiety was obvious, indicating that they hoped they hadn't another hysterical relative on their hands who was going to be a problem. The last thing they were prepared to admit was that they might have made a mistake and pronounced a living man as dead. Fortunately they had a ready answer to that one.

'In a man so old,' said the doctor smoothly, 'the heartbeat can be erratic, very weak. He was in a coma simulating termination.' He put a hand on Chay's arm. 'Just be thankful that he survived at all, Mr Bowman. We'll keep him in a few days for observation and let you know when he's ready to go home. I presume he has people to take care of him.'

*　　　*　　　*

Chay drove Kate and Luke home. It was a silent journey.

When they reached the house, Luke was already fast asleep in the back of the car, curled up on the seat.

Chay put a hand on Kate's arm. 'Don't wake him, I'll carry him inside. Come on, young fellow,' he whispered softly.

Luke's eyes opened once sleepily and closed again.

Chay waited while Kate undressed him and tucked him into bed. 'Sleep tight, lambie,' she said.

He smiled and then turned on his side with a sigh. A moment later, he was breathing deeply.

Kate closed the door quietly. 'Thanks for all your help, Chay. Now, can I get you something to drink?'

Chay followed her into the kitchen and put a delaying hand on her arm as she switched on the kettle.

'Something stronger,' he said firmly, 'like white man's whiskey.' He managed a shaky grin.

'What a good idea. I brought some from the duty free.'

As they carried their drinks into the living room and sat down on the sofa, he said, 'That's a very remarkable child.' And taking a deep drink, he added quietly, 'Isn't there something you should be telling me about him?'

Idly studying her glass, she said, 'I don't know what you mean.'

He seized her wrist. 'I think you do, Kate. Look, I was there. I saw what happened. And I suspect from your reaction that it has happened before. Right?'

She looked at him sharply and he grinned. 'Mothers whose sons raise people from the dead for the first time might at least be expected to say—or do something. Faint or laugh, or scream. But you did nothing, you behaved as if it happened every day.'

She still didn't reply and he continued. 'And what about your scalp wound that healed so miraculously in the cave? You said it bled profusely, I believe you, but the only blood was on the neck of your T-shirt.'

'Stubbornly silent, she looked at him.

'And you never did tell me me why he doesn't talk. He wasn't born mute, so what happened?'

Kate's breath came out in a deep sigh, as if she had been holding it back. 'At school. An accident. Shock, they said; but they told me there's nothing wrong with his vocal chords and that his voice will come back some time.'

Leaning back comfortably, drink in hand, Chay said gently, 'So why not start at the beginning?'

CHAPTER FIFTEEN

Strange friend, past, present and to be;
Loved deeplier, darklier understood;
Behold, I dream a dream of good,
And mingle all the world with thee.

ALFRED, LORD TENNYSON,
In Memoriam

Chay felt like a cross-examining defence lawyer, eyeing her intently, willing her to start talking.

'Who was Luke's father, if that isn't too indelicate a question?'

'Sean Doe.'

Her reply was so faint, almost a whisper, and so totally unexpected that Chay wasn't sure he had heard correctly.

'Sean Doe? You mean, our Sean Doe, the pop star?'

She smiled sadly and Chay's eyes widened.

'I get it now. So that's why your reaction was so goddamned odd when you heard my tape. It must have been a shock for you. That plane crash put an end to a great performer.'

He waited for her to continue.

'He never knew about Luke. Not that I ever pretended that it would have made any

213

difference if he had known. I was a young student in my first year at Edinburgh University, studying literature. I was infatuated—crazy about him, like thousands of other girls, long before I met him.'

Chay held up his hand and shook his head, not wanting to hear any more, knowing he was jealous enough for any further details of their intimacy to offend him. He had enough imagination for that.

'I get the picture,' he said hastily. 'When you found out about the kid—what then?'

'Sean was already dead. As I've said, I never pretended it would have made any difference. I was one of many, but I had my moment—I had his child.'

Chay considered this and said as tactfully as he could. 'There were plenty of paternity suits—the usual scandals. I seem to remember the tabloids loved them. But none were ever proved—something about an almost unique blood group. Lucky for him.'

Kate looked at him. 'Luke has it too. And it isn't lucky for him. It's been a major worry that if he ever needed a blood transfusion we'd have terrible problems.'

So Luke's father was Sean Doe. It was almost incredible, thought Chay completely bowled over by Kate's revelation. The pop star who never courted publicity and got it despite all his attempts at avoidance. He was American and that was about all anyone knew. If he was

Mexican or South American as rumour interpreted his exotic good looks, then he had a whiter skin than most, and quite remarkable eyes. Amber and luminous. His child had inherited them.

'Luke and I were always very close,' Kate said. 'Right from the start, we seemed to be telepathic. I thought probably all mums were to an extent, but this was different, far more intense, far more than mere motherlove could account for.'

She glanced towards the photographs on the windowsill.

'I never knew my mother. I was illegitimate, child of a bigamous marriage, and she went off to Australia when I was a baby, left me for my step-grandmother to bring up. I adored Gran but she used to shake her head and say we were an odd family. All-female descent she used to claim, until Luke came along.'

'What did she mean by odd, were you all psychic?'

'What makes you say that?'

'Because Redfeather knew.' Chay rubbed his chin thoughtfully. 'About you and about Luke. And he's never wrong about recognising that sort of thing. He just knows.'

'I had strange experiences as a little girl,' Kate admitted, 'what Gran called slipping off the time circle—finding myself for a split second in a different world, at a different time. I never made much of it. *Déjà vu* is a common

215

experience with most people at sometime in their lives, the feeling that we've been here before and experienced this situation exactly, the same people, the same conversation.'

She laughed shakily. 'I thought I had outgrown it until I came here and—thought—I was in a stagecoach, riding across the valley. There were Indians. I fell in love with one of them. It was very vivid and if I believed in reincarnation, in having myself regressed, then I think I'd find that I had been married to him.'

She regarded Chay helplessly. 'But it wasn't really me, not the person I am now. I can't explain, it just happened that way.'

How impassive and disbelieving he looks, she thought as she added apologetically, 'I'm not making much sense of this, am I? I dismissed it quite sensibly I thought, as having seen too many movies and perhaps I dozed off for a while and dreamed it all.'

'You think this psychic thing maybe ties up with Luke?'

'What you really want to know is—is this the first time he's displayed the Lazarus syndrome.'

'A good description. Yes.'

Kate looked out towards the window; a full moon was rising. Across the road, noise and laughter from the Rhodes', Raj's barking indicated visitors were leaving. They seemed to belong to another age.

She took a long drink before continuing. 'As I've told you, we have a guest house in

216

Edinburgh. I had to leave university when I was pregnant. I never even considered putting Sean's child out for adoption. He was too precious a gift for that. Gran was wonderful. She'd already brought up my mother and me and she said she would stick by the baby too. So I took a secretarial course, took temping jobs—there are always plenty of them in Edinburgh—and helped her in the guest house during the busy season. It all worked out fine, Luke was a lovely baby, a normal, happy, carefree child.

'Luke was about six, the first time it happened. Gran had a pet linnet who had lived to a great age. This was long before keeping wild birds in cages was forbidden. Pippy sang joyfully every day of his life just to prove, she said, how happy and grateful he was for captivity, for decent birdseed and water, instead of foraging for mucky worms and taking his life in his hands every day with the neighbourhood cats.

'She came downstairs early one morning and there was poor Pippy lying on the bottom of the cage, his legs stiff, his claws curled up. He was cold and quite dead.

'We had a good weep together and decided we should get him safely out of the way, bury him in the garden, before Luke or any of the boarders appeared. But that morning Luke, normally the world's worst riser, was down before eight o'clock. Hearing him on the stairs, Gran threw the cover over the cage, winked at me and when he came in, said that Pippy had died, during the night, explaining that he was very old and he had gone to heaven to be with the angels.

'Luke didn't believe a word of it. He stood looking at her very sternly and said, "I want to see Pippy." He opened the door of the cage and, despite Gran's protests, he took the little bird out and held him against his cheek. Then he placed his mouth on the tiny beak.

'Gran shouted to him, "Don't do that, dear! We don't know what he died of. You tell him, Kate. He mustn't kiss dead things. He could catch anything." But even as she spoke, Pippy began to twitch in Luke's outstretched hand. He tried to roll over and then, flapping his wings feebly at first, he squawked indignantly.

'Luke set him back on his perch and we both watched as he shook his feathers out several times before rushing to the water bowl. After a few sips, much to our amazement, the little bird who had been cold and dead for hours started whistling happily again.

'We tried to explain it all away, that the poor old bird had just taken a fit. But we knew we were fooling ourselves. There is absolutely no mistaking a cold, dead bundle of feathers for a living bird. And while Gran was gloomily prepared for his return to life being short, he's still alive and singing like mad.

'I'll never forget Gran standing there, staring into the cage clutching my arm and in an awed whisper saying, "Lass, it's like he's been reborn."'

She looked across at Chay and said, 'Luke was just an ordinary little boy, but clever enough to win a scholarship to a boy's private school in Edinburgh. I still couldn't have afforded the fees but Gran was determined. She had a win on the premium bonds and she said that if she died before his education was completed, then her insurance would see him all right. Her dearest wish was that he'd go on to university. Make something of himself, she called it.

'The only problem was that he wasn't happy at a school where the emphasis was on games and was highly competitive. The first thing you set eyes on in the hall was an imposing glass case of shining cups and shields dating from about 1860 just to prove the school's excellence. But such things have never interested Luke in the slightest. Apart from his own computer games on the Internet, he loves dungeons and dragons, but as for cricket, well—he hated that worst of all and his aversion was regarded by teachers as bordering on perversion. They never cease to din into pupils and parents alike the importance of the competitive killer instinct. Kindergarten is not considered too soon to fortify a chap for facing the rigors of public school and the ultimate traumas of a successful career in politics or merchant banking.

'Luke was rated an odd child, his reports said "Bright but needs concentration". But he was prepared to work hard for Gran's sake, and mine. Make us proud of him. He was always thoughtful and considerate. He never tried to manipulate us or thought that parents were merely to be tolerated, put on earth simply for the comfort and convenience of their young, without any lives of their own.'

She looked at him. 'You have no idea what snob schools are like in Britain. Classmates whose backgrounds don't rate chauffeur-driven cars force parents to motor four hundred miles and back, delivering and collecting, despising the railway station ten minutes away from the school as something limited to the lower classes. Any form of public transport is a lowering of their social status. They would be a laughing stock.

'Until Luke encountered other small boys, I'm sure he hadn't the slightest idea that his consideration for grown-ups was totally unchildlike.'

She was silent for a moment. 'Sometimes I looked at him and felt that inside that small childish frame, as he played with bricks and did jigsaws, there was another person who was a wise old soul, directing operations. I know that sounds stupid but it's the nearest I can get to explaining it.

'Like all young children he asked where his daddy was. When I told him about the plane crash before he was born, he cried inconsolably, as a child would cry for a beloved parent who had just died. Never having had two parents I wondered how he would react to ever having to share me with someone else.'

'Was that on the cards?' Chay asked, relieved when she shook her head.

'Never. Not that I wasn't hopeful, but I haven't met the right man.' Smiling, she stared into her glass. 'Not so far, that is. Anyway, I thought it wouldn't be a good idea when he told me how boys from what the teachers called broken homes, mostly despised their newly acquired stepparent or the new aunt or uncle, but knew at the same time how such feelings could be best turned to their own advantage. In addition to class teams in healthy competition on the sports field, Luke pointed out on the sidelines parents being played off against each other, not for cups or shields but for extra pocket money or expensive gifts. And that did leave me thinking how he would react if I ever met the man I wanted to marry.'

She went on hurriedly. 'We have always been close and by the time Luke was eight, we could talk to each other on the same adult level. Not like some parents I used to encounter as a baby-sitter, whose treatment of their offspring lay somewhere between superior domestic pets or a species of sub-humans.'

She stopped, took another drink and replaced the glass somewhat shakily on the table.

'Now we come to Toggers. Toggers was Luke's great friend, the school's idol, the most promising athlete and all rounder. What's more, he had rescued Luke from the school bully. That was curious too.'

'In what way?'

'Well, when Toggers intervened, Luke apparently told this bully that he would be sorry. Next day the lad slipped running downstairs, broke his arm and was carted off to Casualty.'

She glanced at Chay as if expecting him to make a comment.

He smiled. 'Coincidence I would call it, rather than divine retribution.'

'Yes, of course.' Then with a sigh she continued, 'Like all mums, I had to go to sports day. For Luke this was even more important, because Toggers was the star of the cricket team and I had to see him. It was a beautiful, cloudless summer's day, the kind we dream about for cricket matches in Edinburgh, and so rarely see.

'I was enjoying every moment, Toggers was batting and doing very well when Luke suddenly seized my arm. "Look, Mum! See that great black bird that's landed on Toggers's shoulder." I couldn't see anything, but Luke said frantically, "You must be needing specs, Mum. It's like a raven, huge and black." I looked round. Did anyone else see a bird on

Toggers's shoulder? It certainly didn't stop him. He was scoring like mad, everyone cheering. "That bird. Mum, it has a human face! Golly, it must be an angel! That's a good omen, isn't it?"

'I suddenly felt very cold despite the heat. The cheering had turned to a horrified gasp. Toggers was lying on the ground. People rushed forward and he was carried off the field.

'He died that night. Meningitis. Sudden inescapable death.' Kate buried her face in her hands. 'Oh, God, it was terrible. Terrible.'

Chay came over to the sofa and took her in his arms. When she seemed more composed, he said consolingly, 'So his best friend died, surely that wasn't enough to deprive him of his voice.'

'He did see a bird with a human face, I'm sure of that, but none of the rest of us did. And, don't you see, that bird was the angel of death.'

'And you think that was enough to strike him dumb?'

'No. Not that. What happened later,' she whispered. 'That was worse. They sent everyone home and put Toggers's body into the sick bay until his parents who were abroad could be notified.

'But Luke was seen sneaking back. The door was locked but he climbed through an open window. The janitor heard him and alerted the headmaster. They found him lying on top of Toggers weeping and trying to force his mouth open, trying to breathe life into him again. As the masters tried to drag Luke off, a fire started in the office next door. No one knew how or why, but the masters and Luke narrowly escaped with their lives. The fire spread rapidly to the sick bay, consumed everything. Including poor Toggers's body.

'They brought Luke home without telling us all the details. We put him to bed. He seemed all right physically, but he couldn't tell us what had happened. He couldn't speak. The doctors say it was shock from the fire and that it'll come back in time. He isn't permanently dumb, he does try to talk to me, but not very often. Fortunately I know everything he is trying to say. The benefits of telepathy,' she added with a sad smile.

'Did he ever try to tell you about what happened?'

'He wrote on a piece of paper, "I did nothing wrong, I just tried to breathe life into him. Like I did Pippy. Remember, Mum?"'

CHAPTER SIXTEEN

The strange and buried men will come again in flesh and leaf.

THOMAS WOLFE, Look Homeward, Angel

Jake had told Rita about Redfeather's accident.

224

She had been very upset at the time, but when Chay told her there was no need for panic, that he was making a good recovery, she said, 'That's incredible! At his age. What a constitution he must have. It's a miracle he survived.'

Chay considered telling her about Luke's part in it. He had a desperate need to confide in someone like practical Rita who would soothe him with a hard-hitting sceptical interpretation. He hesitated. At that precise moment he could not bear one solitary glance, one disbelieving, questioning look that would reflect even indirectly on Kate.

He sighed. These were changed days. Rita, who had never shown any interest in his female clients except in a joky kind of way, was showing unmistakeable signs of jealousy regarding his concern for the Anglo woman and her son. And if he told her what he had seen with his own eyes in the hospital, she would laugh at his gullibility, prepared to put the worst possible interpretation on anything or anyone connected with Kate Fenner.

Trouble was Rita knew him too well to hide many things from her and she was acutely aware that he was directed by more than mere kindness of heart, his feelings far beyond those for a business client. Each day he waited guiltily for her to point out that he was neglecting what little business might be coming their way.

225

On his way to the hospital, he called at the ranch to collect Jake. And there was Redfeather. Far from lying prostrate in the recovery ward, he met Chay fully dressed, his manner very aggressive and behaving as if the accident had never happened.

Dismissing Chay's anxious question, he snorted. 'I signed myself out, prevailed upon one of the orderlies—one of us—to get me a cab. I could have saved the money and walked,' he added with a glance that defied Chay to comment on his health. 'What's all the fuss about?' he snapped. 'I feel fine, never felt better. So here I am. When are you bringing the boy and his mother to see me again?'

'Whenever you want.'

'Good. Soon then. I got a lot of information from my visit with Joe Shalwaaw at Dinsdale.'

*　　　*　　　*

Kate was surprised to get Chay's phone call. Yes, they would be delighted to go and see Redfeather.

'How's Luke this morning?' he asked.

'Oh, he's fine. Really looking forward to this outing.'

As if by tacit agreement there was no mention between them of the extraordinary events at the hospital. At his side, Kate seemed shy and a little distant, in the manner of one who has revealed more of her past than she ever intended. After his mother's strange revelations, for the first time, Chay felt awkward with Luke.

Jake was waiting for them, accompanied by a group of children, who were doubtless cousins. There were several boys of Luke's age and Jake said to him, 'Maybe you would like to come with us. We're going to walk Storm Cloud over to meet his great-grandson's new foal.'

Luke looked wistfully at Kate.

'You're not too tired?' she said trying to conceal her anxiety.

He shook his head vigorously.

'We'll take good care of him,' said Jake.

Following Chay inside the house, Kate was taken aback at the difference in Redfeather's appearance since she had last seen him. Far from being on the brink of death, he looked defiantly fit and youthful, as if he had shed thirty years.

'I am very well, Miss.' He made a dismissive gesture. 'But I asked you here to tell you about my meeting with an old comrade. It was most useful. We had not seen each other for twenty years but he still lives on the reservation in the same hogan. Apart from a score of grandchildren he seems little changed.'

Touching his long plaits, he smiled. 'The hair of course grows white, the limbs are stiffer. But we go on, being young inside. I remember well,

227

he was younger than me, a daredevil—'

An apologetic cough from Chay's direction received an indignant glare before he went on, 'But you are not here to listen to tales of my youth. There are many, many . . .' he sighed wistfully. 'Perhaps some other time you would like to hear them?'

'I would love to.'

'So you shall. Joe Shalwaaw is a medicine man, one of the few survivors of Los Atalos. In general, they appeared to be an ordinary tribe, although one of two were gifted with supernatural powers inherited from their ancestors, the Anasazi. The chief, Atala was regarded as a god by his people, part human, part divine.'

He paused. 'Like your Jesus Christ. The Great Spirit had given him the secret of immortality as long as he carried this recognition of his divinity.'

Again he hesitated, looked across at Chay and said some words in Navajo.

Chay said, 'Grandfather finds it difficult to translate into your language. The nearest I can describe would be like the Christian Holy Grail, a sort of Talisman, which carried the essence and sanctity of life itself.'

Redfeather nodded. 'All religions have such sacred emblems. In the case of Los Atalos, they had proof that he was sacred and immortal because no one ever saw him die.'

He laughed. 'If primitive men had been

movie-makers who could create magical images with a camera lurking in their cliff dwellings, then it would have appeared that through the passing centuries Atala remained the same man. It was a trick of course.'

'A trick? You mean he wasn't divine?' Kate interrupted.

'Not at all. Periodically, every quarter century they sacrificed a young boy and Atala was given his heart.'

'But that isn't possible. Heart transplants are twentieth-century discoveries, and not always successful,' said Kate.

'True, but there are other methods of transferring organs from one to another. We consume the flesh and blood of other creatures, for instance. In less enlightened days, many human societies believed that by eating the heart of an enemy, warriors were renewed with their strength.'

Kate realised that this was another version of the story Warren Rhodes had told her.

Redfeather glanced at her face. 'I can see that you are shocked and revolted by such a practice. Such things were thought little of in days gone by and by people who were revered. Not only those the white man dismissed as savages,' he reminded her gently. 'There are stories in your Bible. Abraham about to sacrifice his son. Jesus Christ who was born to be a sacrifice. There was magic involved too, this renewal brought the strengthening and recharging of living tissues. The breath of life, you might say.'

His words touched a chord and chilled Kate with the memory of Luke in the hospital ward and Redfeather's buoyant appearance.

'Atala was immortal as long as he retained this holy spirit and this included the ability to work magic, to give life, to even raise the dead. But there was a price to pay, each time he used what we might call the breath of life it weakened his own immortality.

'In all other respects he was a human being, but his powers did not include procreation. To beget a human child was the ultimate blasphemy, by passing the Spirit to his offspring.

'According to Joe Shalwaaw, Atala fell in love with the missionary's daughter, impregnated her and, by wishing to marry her, he signed his own death warrant. Instead of being consumed by the fire magic, the equivalent of your hellfire, the thunderbolt that waited for such blasphemy, he would have been hurled to his doom from the Temple of the Sun God.'

'Has your friend ever seen this temple?' Kate asked.

'No one has. But according to legend it is in the sacred rocks, where the white millionaire, the one they call Viejo, has blasphemed by building his home.

'After the massacre at Blackhawk Creek,

230

Atala, who had forsaken his right to divinity, disappeared—most probably killed by a white soldier's bullet or the high priest's ritual slaughter. No one will ever know. But his death also signalled the end of the Atalos. The few who were lucky enough to survive became known as the Magic Men and professed, among their many strange abilities, to have telepathic powers. What one knew, they all knew.'

Chay had told her that.

'They still believe such things?' she asked.

Redfeather laughed. 'Oh, yes. And I have witnessed remarkable examples of their powers. Like many others in this troubled world of ours, they still search for their lost prophet, that elusive second coming. They believe that they have had signs that Atala's seed still lives on—somewhere on earth, and that is their quest, to find and reinstate their god and by his magic save the planet Earth from destruction.'

He sighed, suddenly weary, Kate thought. He is not quite as fit as he would like us to believe.

'Shalwaaw's grandfather was one of the original medicine men, the guardians who set off in search of Atala's child, by the Anglo woman. Apparently after Atala died, she fled and decided to take the child and make her way back to her own country far across the sea, on the other side of the world.

'They followed her trail for many moons—years passed in fact before they arrived in the great city beyond the Sacred Mountains of the San Francisco Peaks. They had her almost in their grasp, they were only minutes too late—in time to watch her sail away in a great ship across the horizon which they believed marked the end of the world. Many of the guardians who set out had died on the long trail through the white man's towns and settlements where, with their strange dress and fierce looks, they were regarded as hostiles and killed on sight. The few who returned with heavy hearts, their mission unfilled, were broken men.

'But there have been signs, omens, of late. Many of the present-day guardians are clever men in other walks of life and they have found a way, the possibility that through the intervention of modern science they may be able to trace the descendant of Atala's child who carries the Talisman.'

His voice was weaker, he coughed a little and fell silent, staring out of the window as if no longer aware of their presence. Suddenly he was an old man again and Chay signalled to Kate that they should leave.

She stood up and he took her hands. She was surprised to find them warm and strong, despite the bones showing through the paper-thin transparent skin.

He fluttered a hand in a gesture of weariness. 'Come again. You and yours are

232

welcome in my home and we will talk together some more.'

He did not shake off Chay's supporting arm as they walked through the house. Outside, Luke sat on the wall watching the boys playing baseball.

Jake came over. 'He's just dropped out. We've taught him the rudiments, but I think he was getting a little tired.'

But when he realised that Kate and Chay were heading towards the car, Luke jumped down, his face clouded with disappointment. He left the others and went over to Redfeather, staring up into his face.

He did look pale, diminished somehow, Chay thought. Poor little kid. But his expression insisted that he was having such a great time. Must he go back? His wistful glance towards the shouting, yelling baseball players said it all.

Redfeather turned to Kate. 'Let him stay, if he's enjoying himself so much. It's good for him to be with children of his own age. We will take good care of him.'

Jake came over. 'I'll drive him back later.'

Luke seized her hand eagerly. Its pressure said, Please, Mum—please.

As they drove towards the town, Chay was unusually silent. He guessed looking at Kate's face that she was worried about Luke.

Picking up the mobile phone he called the office.

'OK, Rita. I'll be there.'

Turning to Kate, he said, 'I was hoping we could spend the rest of the day together. On our own. I thought I might take you to another magic place, Boynton Canyon. However, it seems I have a client coming.' He sighed deeply and added with a grin, 'The divorce market hasn't been flourishing lately. Could it be another miracle, that couples are learning how to live together and work out their differences?' With a shake of his head he continued. 'Bad for the poor private investigator's business.'

He left her at the house by the creek. He didn't trust himself to take her hand and leave it at that. So the kiss she was hoping for never came and she felt cold and unhappy watching him drive away without one backward look.

Tessa came to the door and seeing her alone said, 'We're partying again. Having a few neighbours in for a drink. Like to come?'

Kate accepted gratefully. She was never really comfortable or at ease here alone without Luke. His presence filled the house and kept her mind away from those dark worrying regions she had little desire to explore.

Deciding it was dress-up time, she was regarding her more elegant reflection with some satisfaction and thinking that a suntan did much for the simple white dress, when the telephone rang.

It was Jake. The kids were having a barbeque, could Luke possibly stay the night. He was having a great time.

What could she say but, Of course.

She hoped her cheerful acceptance concealed her nagging fears, but by the time she returned from the Rhodes', she was wine-happy and sleepy. On a high too, having met a bewildering number of couples who had said nice things to her. They were mostly from the golf club with names she could never hope to remember, but with faces she hoped she would recognise again when they met in some different context, like the supermarket.

As she showered she felt happy in the house which had seemed more welcoming, with its lights glowing in the dusk. She was glad too that Luke had found friends of his own age. After all, he was a growing boy, it wasn't healthy or wise to expect to have him by her side for ever.

As she was closing her eyes, Redfeather's face appeared before her, again she heard his words of greeting, 'I feel great, better than I've felt in years. I seem to have shed quite a few of them.' And how as they parted on the steps, he pointed to the severely mangled bicycle frame. 'And to think I have not one single bruise anywhere,' he said proudly. 'I thought I'd be black and blue all over,' and frowning, he rubbed his leg. 'My knee too, I thought it was badly cut—would need stitches. But it seems to have healed completely. I feel great,' he repeated. 'I guess I was just lucky.'

Perhaps as a result of that chilling remembrance of Luke's part in Redfeather's recovery and of the coincidental tale of Atala's magic powers, Kate had a vivid, waking dream.

A faint rattle awakened her and she saw in the full moonlight the four turquoise beads on her bedside table had rolled off and were spinning along the floor. She stared at them in horror and then realised that she had probably thrown a hand against the table as she dreamed, and that was what had awakened her.

Come back—come back—

The words from her dream remained an echoing resonance all around her. She turned on her side, facing the window with the shadowy red rocks pale in moonglow.

There was someone there, out on the terrace.

An Indian was staring in at her. He had warpaint on his face. The palms of his hands were pressed against the glass as if he was trying to force open the door. His lips were moving.

Come—come back—

She sat up in bed. It was one of the Magic Men. Something had happened to Luke. She ran to the window, heedless of any danger to herself. But as she opened the glass door, the Indian seemed to shimmer and fade but his words remained, echoing upon the night air, filling the room, filling her head.

Come back—back. Come back.

She thrust her hands against her ears trying to drown out the words. The dream had been real—the ghostly visitor was Atala.

Come back—come back—

She began to sob in fright and at that moment, the front doorbell shrilled through her cries. Once, twice—there was no doubt about its urgency.

Running through the house, she opened the door and Luke fell into her arms.

Jake was saying, 'Sorry to wake you, but Luke had a nightmare, he wrote down that he had to come home. That you needed him.'

CHAPTER SEVENTEEN

INTERLUDE

I am Atala

She must leave Blackhawk Creek and her sick old father in Atala's care. Los Atalos had medicines to cure every ailment and the minister, who regarded Atala as his son, would be in safe keeping until the brain fever, the result of his wanderings in the red rock canyons, had abated and his mind and memory cleared once more.

As for Atala, she wasn't afraid of him any

more. He was, she told herself, just a man after all. She had decided to accept Matt Hepple who loved her and wanted her so badly. Once she was a married woman, she would see Atala as just an ordinary Indian who had been befriended by her father. She resolved to keep only the kinder memories, the gentle smile which transformed his face usually so immobile it sometimes reminded her of an exquisite carved mask with the angel eyes of a primitive icon.

There was a thrill of pleasurable excitement at the prospect of a new life in Tucson with Matt, already asking for a transfer to the Sheriff's office. There would be new friends, other married couples, new dreams to weave. And Matt would help her persuade Papa to come and live with them.

She smiled at the possibility of long careless days free of the emotions that had torn her apart for so long here in Blackhawk Creek. The secret anguish of a love forever forbidden.

She must escape forever, she thought, saddling up Dainty. She would ride up to Atala's camp, tell him about Papa, and catch the Tucson stage.

As always, she had no difficulty in finding Atala. He seemed to be waiting for her, anticipating her arrival and she wondered if his heart ever threatened to leap from his breast as hers did now.

'Your father is sick? In what way?' he asked.

She shook her head, 'We don't know. He has a fever. It comes and goes.'

As she was explaining why she must leave to go to Tucson and describing his symptoms, he didn't seem to be listening, watching the sky above them and frowning.

'Nausea, vomiting, and sunburn—very painful. In some places his skin has peeled off.'

'That is not unusual with white men. In a short while—'

Janet shook her head stubbornly. 'I agree. If I get sunburned it is gone in a week. But this is different. His hair is falling out. And his gums bleed. Perhaps you can help. They say you are a healer,' she added desperately.

'We call it a shaman.'

'Medicine man, shaman, or whatever. He will listen to you. Please get him to listen to you. I hate having to leave him like this.'

'I will take care of him.'

'You will?'

'Of course. But you are going to miss the stage. You should be sitting on it right now.'

'How do you know that?' she asked. There were no clocks in Atala's camp.

'We have our own clocks, rather more reliable than the ones I've encountered in civilisation. The level of the sun in the sky and how it relates to the angle of the earth, that is the most predictable timepiece. It is all we need. It means a time to sleep, time to eat, time to feed a child. Even a time to die,' he added sadly.

He looked at the sky again and thought for a moment. 'There is a quick way through the canyon. I can get you to the other side to join the stage for Tuscon.' He smiled. 'I will see that your horse is returned safely. Don't worry about her.'

As she followed him along the narrow track, she shivered. It was colder as they climbed. He noticed her discomfort and handed her a blanket to drape across her shoulders.

'There is snow in the air. Too soon this year. Let us hope it will be many hours before it falls,' he said with a reassurance he did not feel.

It was more than cold which caused Janet to shiver now. It was a sudden awareness of danger and she wondered if the canyon made Atala's people extra sensitive. Was there something in the old legends of this being sacred ground, the burial place of their ancestors?

Would she ever know what had happened to her father during his wanderings? When he first returned with a raging fever, she had listened to his ravings, none of which made sense. Expecting him to talk of God, here was the delirium of a mad scientist. There was a log book with drawings she did not understand. What had he found during those weeks when he was lost?

She thought of the old cliff dwellings, silent, watchful, as they had stood unchanged for nearly a thousand years. The Indian's way of life had hardly altered either. The Atalos–Anasazis had enjoyed the days of their great civilisation while her people in Scotland were just emerging from their mud huts.

At that moment, she wished with all her heart, she could halt time and spare them any further contact with the white man's world. A world that spelt their destruction, a world where man's sense of values was gross materialism, the god he worshipped was no longer the giver of life of Papa's sermons, nor even the Indians' Great Spirit, but greed for gold and the evils in its train.

Atala's urgent voice broke into her thoughts. 'We must make haste or the storm will catch us before we leave the canyon.'

They took an upward track, steep and wild, overgrown with sage, their horses baulked and their flanks trembled as they clattered among the rocks, dislodging boulders and sending the echoes of bouncing rocks and frightened birds far below. The air was heavy with the scent of sandstone pulverised by the horses' hooves.

'Come along. You must hurry,' he shouted back to Janet whose horse was less skilled at picking its way. At that moment the storm overtook them. In seconds the sun was quenched and they were blinded by sleet needles, their clothes drenched. Ice froze on their eyelashes. Breathing became an agony and the horses, too, added their neighs of protest.

Atala spoke soothingly to them, held blankets over their heads to protect them from blindness.

'Back to the canyon,' he panted. 'We must find shelter.'

'But I'll lose the stage.'

'Better than losing your life. And the horses,' said Atala, seizing their bridles and ignoring her protests.

The sleet whirled around them, stinging their eyes, biting their throats. In this maelstrom of whirling ice, Janet felt her legs and arm grow numb, paralysed with weakness.

'I can't go on.' She sank down onto the snow, buried her face in her arms. 'I must rest.'

Atala stood looking down at her. 'Rest and you'll die. You'll freeze to death in minutes. Look, there's a cave, somewhere near here. I've seen it many times.'

'I don't see anything. You're just trying to make me go on.'

'Stop arguing, woman,' shouted Atala above the storm. 'Look! That overhang of rock. The cave is there, I tell you. Hold tightly to the reins.' As he led the horses through the storm Janet did as she was told, trying to protect her eyes against the icy sleet.

Suffocating ice forming on her breath, at last they reached the shelter of the rock.

'See? I was right.'

There was a cave. Small and foul-smelling,

Janet greeted it like some enchanted palace sprung from a fairytale. Inside she fought to get breath into her agonised lungs, and lay panting on dry ground while Atala tethered the horses.

'What's that smell?' she asked sniffing the air.

'Bear,' was the brief reply.

And by the foetid strength of it, the cave had been used as its den very recently. There was a proverb in the white man's language which Atala had learned about beggars not being choosers, which he thought applied aptly. Hoping this woman would not observe the agitated behaviour of the horses, he also hoped that he was wrong and that the bear wasn't about to shamble back any moment. If they were put off by the smell of bear perhaps bear, in his turn, would be put off by the smell of humans. But if that bear was female, with cubs, it might be a very different story.

He quietened the horses, talking to them gently.

'What's scaring them now?' asked Janet.

'Just the smell of bear and the storm.'

Shaking the snow off her soaked cloak while Atala inspected the darker interior of the cave, she stared dismally out into the storm. If she didn't leave soon she would miss the stage to Tuscon and then it would be several days before she got there. Term would already be started.

Atala came back. There was no evidence of

cubs. He hoped they would be safe enough for an hour or two.

Janet was adjusting the hood of her cape. 'I must go,' she said. 'The storm seems to be abating. But it will take me all my time—'

'Are you out of your senses? This storm may last all night.'

She swung round to face him. 'I must go, I tell you. We are almost clear of the canyon. I could see the path leading out. You know it's there. We both saw it before the storm—'

'You will never keep to it. The sleet could come again—'

'I will. I will. Heavens, I've been caught in many a mountain blizzard in the glen at home in Scotland, when I was just a child. I know what I'm doing. I can look after myself. And Dainty will look after me.'

He watched her go out, taking the horse's rein. She turned to face him. 'Thank you for helping me. Look after Papa for me.'

He seized her arm and she looked down at his hand, as if its presence on her arm mesmerised her. 'I must go,' she said in a tiny voice. 'Please, please, don't try to stop me.'

Without releasing her arm, he said. 'There will be other stages, a day or two won't make all that difference.'

She didn't answer, staring stubbornly past him.

'What is it you're scared of? Me? Am I worse than the storm?' he asked gently.

There was still no answer, only a small tightening of her mouth and he shouted angrily, 'Do you not trust me? Do you think I couldn't stay here all night with you and not make love to you? Do you think I am just a savage who would take any woman—'

Avoiding his eyes, Janet shook her head. 'That isn't what I'm thinking at all. I just know I can't stay here. I have to go. Take my chance.'

He stared at her tight-lipped. 'Then do. But don't play the hypocrite with me. At least be honest with yourself. Would you rush out if it were your father—or Matt Hepple?'

Angry now, he gripped her hand. She looked at it in wonder, as its stealthy warmth invaded her body. With a sense of shock she realised that this was a new sensation, flesh touching flesh. Atala who never before had touched her. Not so much as a finger could she recall or the brush of a bare arm against her own. Even when it was her birthday and he had given her the string of turqouise beads she wore always, he had laid them down on the table between them for her to pick up.

For they both were aware of the consequences. Time spent in each other's company left them in little doubt of what lay in store. They were held apart by the most gossamer of threads. Even the most minute of moves between them could break that frail thread of restraint, hurling down barriers that kept flesh from flesh. Flesh that would be transformed into a raging torrent of desire, ripping them apart, dissolving all vows made to God and man, destroying them.

Without one backward glance, she ran out and away from him. Mounting Dainty, she turned her head into the storm. With the full fury of the sleet's icy needles on her face, she heard him calling.

'Come back—come back—'

Shutting out his voice, she rode on and on, gasping for breath. Stumbling, slipping over the uneven terrain, Dainty missed her footing and threw her.

Janet struggled to her feet and tried to remount, but the lamed mare whinnied in protest and she knew her last hope of reaching the stage and safety was gone.

Dazed now, she staggered on until at last the reins slipped from her numbed fingers. Dainty released, whinnied once and turning, hobbled as swiftly as she could back along the track. Janet called after her in vain and with the tears freezing on her face, she knew there was no alternative but to press on alone.

The blizzard had intensified and the snow covered all landmarks, the track that led downward to the stage post had vanished.

Still she stumbled on. As she must until she had no strength left.

The snow was a good clean death, they said. There would be no pain. She would simply fall down and go to sleep. Be at eternal peace with herself and with all the world. And most of all, at peace with Atala. She was tired of life without him, of fighting her love for him.

At last she fell, striking her head hard on some hidden rock. Stunned, she rolled on and on, down and down, and saw the white wilderness around her darkened with her blood. Too weak now, she let the snow embrace her like a lover.

She was going to die. This was death. Death . . . So silent and peaceful. Not a bit of pain at all.

Come back—come back—

The voices in her head faded.

Oh, welcome death.

*   *   *

'Fool of a woman—come back—'

Atala's words were lost in the blizzard that had swallowed her.

What do I care, he said to himself. Furious with her, battling with a pride too great to plead with any woman. He hated her at that moment. Hoped she would marry Matt Hepple—any man to take her out of his life—and never, never show her face in his camp again.

Into his mind's eye came a picture. He saw her vividly, lying at the bottom of a crevasse, her frail body broken, the snow that drifted over her darkened with her blood, almost obliterating her small still shape.

As he ran towards his horse, his heart leaped once, like a vessel suddenly emptied.

She was dead.

He rode out into the blinding storm, the animal rearing beneath him, protesting at this mad rider. Away from the protecting ledge of rock, he was in a solid wall of floating ice flakes where every breath was agony. At each halting step, he expected the horse to drop in its tracks.

'Janet! Janet!'

Knowing she was past hearing, desperately, again and again, he called her name. Stopping to listen he imagined her calling back to him, but knew it was merely the shriek of the storm.

She was dead. He had let her go to her death.

Nothing and certainly no frail woman could go down that mountain and find the track that led out of the canyon. No one could travel on foot for more than a few hundred yards and survive in such conditions.

Against the driving snow, the picture of her lying so still came again. So clearly he saw beyond the wall of ice the small figure in a green travelling cloak, lying motionless.

Then out of that blank wall came the muffled jingle of harness. Her horse Dainty, riderless.

He grabbed the reins. 'Where is she? Where is she?'

But Dainty dropped her head and with a

shudder nuzzled his arm, snorting indignantly as he dragged her round to follow him. Then he noticed she was lame.

Dragging both horses, he slithered down the track, blindly, inch by inch. Time ceased except as a measure of his agony and remorse. As he moved, he called her name against the storm, even though he knew she had lain in the snow already too long.

Suddenly he saw a dark bundle at his feet, and almost fell over her. Face down over the edge of the crevasse, she lay, exactly as his first terrible vision had depicted. Gently he lifted her, cradling her in his arms, trying to restore warmth to her lifeless body, realising as he did so, that he had never, until today, touched even her hand.

But now all that was over. Now it did not matter. There was no danger left. She could not destroy his life, nor he hers.

The snow too had ceased. All around him was a great silence as if the world too held its breath. He made his way back slowly, carefully, through his own fast-fading tracks.

The horses were no longer walking uphill and, through a gleam of sunshine, he saw what he thought was a familiar overhang of rock. Moving a few steps closer, his eyes aching with unblinking concentration, he saw for a split second the outline of the bear's cave. Then the snow began again with renewed vigour, an endless curtain over the landscape.

He looked at Janet's lifeless body in his arms. Only the long red hair was undimmed, living still. Her face already white in death, the snow unmelted on her lifeless mouth, clinging thickly to her eyelashes. Angrily he brushed it aside and his hand came away red from the badly gashed forehead where blood already congealed darkly.

As he stumbled upward and into the cave's shelter he knew that time was against him for what he had to do. The breath of life. That was the gift the Sun God had given Atala. But it could only be used sparingly. Only once before he had used it, on a drowned child. Even then it had diminished him, as if his own spirit had weakened. He had been warned. To use it on his own kind was one thing but to use his power on an alien woman was blasphemy, damning his soul for all eternity.

But he no longer cared. He had to save her even to give her to another man.

There were urgent preparations that must be made. The body must be naked and cleansed. The little Atalos boy with only a breechclout had been easy. But this white woman with her layers and layers of clothes was different. A drenched jacket and skirt, with innumerable buttons, petticoats, linen drawers, stockings. Hook and eyes and ribbon ties that adorned upper and under garments seemed endless as he strove to unfasten them, his fingers fumbling, numbed with cold.

As he laid her naked body down, straightening out arms and legs, he saw that the cut was deep on her brow; perhaps that had been enough to break her skull, kill her outright. Her limbs showed no evidence of broken bones. Her body was still in one piece.

Now they must both be cleansed for the healing ritual. First his own body, then hers. The snow made it easier than he had imagined and as he worked he chanted the healing way.

In the normal course of earth time, he realised she would be far beyond saving but, finally ready, he used the first of his powers to suspend time and then called upon the Great Spirit as he held his arms above her and his body levitated like a cross above her, his breath a shadow that covered her.

At his command a glow of light filled the cave turning its walls into sudden golden crystal. The light engulfed them both, unflickering, cleansing.

How long it lasted, how long he was out of his body, he had no means of telling. When at last he heard her moan and stir as one awakening from sleep, he knew from the weakness in all his limbs, from the sense of all power being removed from him that she would live.

Even as her eyelids flickered open, he wrapped the blankets hastily around her.

'You are safe now.'

He was relieved that her eyes were wide

open. She was shivering with life, even if her teeth chattered with cold.

'You crazy woman,' he said, but his voice was gentle.

It was over. He felt sick and dizzy with exhaustion, like a man who had climbed the highest mountain and he had to summon all his remaining strength to the business of lighting a fire. As he did so, he heard her sudden shocked intake of breath and wondered how he would explain to her how she came to be stark naked.

'Where are my clothes?'

'Over there. They were freezing on you—'

'I see.'

Nakedness was a sin, her contemporaries found it absolutely beyond the pale, even between married people. How would Papa, or her dearest friend Lucy react to such wickedness? But strangely she felt no shame with this man whose hand had never touched hers until a short while ago.

Better be embarrassed than dead. Dead.

Watching him build a fire, she began to remember.

'Atala—I had a strange dream.'

'When was that?'

'Out in the snow.'

'What was this dream about?' His voice seemed muffled, far away, his back towards her.

'I thought—I thought I was dead. That I had died out there. I left my body and I was flying through the air, coming back to the cave to find you.' She laughed uneasily. 'Doesn't that sound silly?'

'I'm glad it was only a dream.' He did not turn round.

'I fell and hurt my head and then I died.' She looked around her. 'But if this is heaven, then it's a very different place from what Papa preached. Very different from what I expected. No angels.'

Except that any place with Atala and those strange eyes would seem like heaven, she thought sadly, remembering how scandalised Papa had been when, as a fourteen-year-old, she first saw Atala and said she guessed that's how the angels looked. Papa had given her quite a long sermon on blasphemy.

Atala had managed to get a fire going. The smoke filled the cave for a moment making her cough.

'Look around you,' said Atala. 'We're still in the bear's cave. And you, I am glad to say, are very much alive.'

Smiling, she sat up, wrapping the blanket around herself modestly.

'So I am.' But she was still bewildered, unconvinced, as if she was hovering between two worlds.

'Do you know, I can hardly believe I've been through all that. Frozen, falling off my Dainty. Where is she? She ran away. She was lame. Oh poor Dainty. I must find her.'

Atala smiled. 'She's outside. Her leg is better. She came back to tell me you were the one who was hurt.'

'Oh Atala.'

'Yes. I followed her tracks and found you.'

'And I thought she had deserted me.'

'No. She saved you.'

Janet tried to sort out her thoughts. It was all very confusing. Those last moments when she was dying—or believed she was dying—'I distinctly remember my head struck a rock when I fell. It was bleeding. Split open.' As she spoke, she touched her forehead gingerly where the blood had been streaming. When her hand came away clean she rubbed, harder this time, but there was no break in the skin, no tenderness.

'I can't understand it,' she said. 'It was so bad, it can't have healed so quickly. I thought I'd be scarred for life—'

But Atala was concentrating on lighting the fire. How could she make him accept what she couldn't understand herself? She sighed. It must have been part of the vivid dream. The blood pouring into the snow, turning it red as she died.

'How odd.'

'You were mistaken,' he said gruffly. Crouching, with his back towards her he went about blowing the fire into life.

When at last it glowed, and flames lit up the dark comers of the cave, he said, 'As well there is plenty of brushwood about. The bear's winter bed. But we have nothing to eat.'

'I don't mind. I feel wonderful.' She touched her neck. 'The turquoise beads you gave me— I wear them always. Oh, Atala. They broke when I fell.'

'I will get you other beads.'

She smiled, 'I feel very good, Atala. As if— as if I've been—reborn. As if I've just ended a long, sad, terrible journey. And I'm safe home at last. Papa would say that angels were watching over me.'

'Yes. He would say that. Now sleep. It will be dark soon.'

They lay silently with the glowing fire fading between them. Soon it was ashes as outside the storm raged, died and raged again.

Atala slept lightly, with the wide-awake awareness of those whose lives are walked in constant danger. He sat up suddenly. A small snuffling sound. And for one terrible moment he thought the bear had returned. Then he realised it was Janet. She was crying.

He went over and knelt by her side.

Was there something in the ritual he had overlooked? Had he done it wrong? Were there other internal injuries?

'What is wrong? Where do you hurt?' he demanded.

'I don't hurt anywhere. I feel marvellous. But I'm—so—cold.'

He touched her cheek, her hands. They were

255

icy and she clung to his arms. 'How lovely and warm you are.'

Pulling free of her, he felt her drying clothes, propped up on sticks before the dead fire. They would make her worse if she tried to sleep in them, give her a chill. He took his deerskin jacket and put it round her.

'There. Is that better?'

She nodded. 'The fire was lovely—can't you relight it?' she asked, teeth chattering.

'I'll see if I can find anything to burn.'

His search brought a handful of brushwood. Facing him across its glow, Janet saw that he was huddled in the one remaining blanket.

'Here, take one of mine. I have them all.'

'I'm not cold.' He lied, for the effects of the ritual had seriously diminished his body heat.

'Take it. The fire has warmed me. I'll sleep now. Goodnight.' And she threw the blanket across to him, then curled up with her back to the fire.

The firelight soon faded and far to the east the first streak of dawn lay several hours away when Atala awakened a second time.

There was an old saying among his people that no man sleeps in a bear's cave unarmed. Now it took on new significance as, alert to danger, his hand sought the rifle he had concealed from Janet, and felt the reassurance of the knife he always carried.

For a moment he listened. The storm had gone. That was why everything was so quiet.

Janet seemed to be sleeping peacefully but when he crawled across to where she lay, her eyelids sprang open.

'Why aren't you sleeping?' he asked.

'I'm cold again,' she said and stretched out her arms to him like a little child.

He sprang back from her touch and stood looking down at her angrily. Then seizing his blanket he lay down beside her.

'Turn your back to me,' he commanded.

'Atala,' she whispered.

'Do as I tell you. Turn your back. Let us sleep.'

And gathering her in his arms, blanket and all, he lay with his chin resting on the top of her head, his arms clasped around her waist.

'Now go to sleep,' and he wondered as he lay there if he would ever sleep again, trying to ignore the crazed beat of his own heart as all his anguished longing for this woman was denied him.

'Warmer now?' he asked.

There was no response and he knew from her deeper breathing that she slept. That was good. The healing process would be completed by morning. She would remember nothing. Only the dream.

When he opened his eyes again, it was because the cave smelt abominably of bear.

Slowly he turned his head and the bear was there, its huge bulk filling the door of the cave, cutting off their exit and the bright streaks of dawn. The bear sniffed the air, peering short-sightedly into the darkness. Then with a series of angry grunts it charged this alien presence in its lair.

Atala leaped across the cave, grabbed his rifle and fired. The sound shot Janet out of sleep. She jumped up, bewildered. The bear grazed by the bullet, roared with pain, adding to her scream of fear.

Lurching towards the man, the bear's outstretched paw struck the rifle out of his hand and sent it spinning across the tiny cave to where Janet crouched in terror.

In the open Atala, armed with a knife, light on his feet, might have stood a chance. Cramped by the small space he stepped aside, stumbled and felt something hot and sharp tear down his shoulder.

The whole world had turned into bear as the huge animal cornered him. He raised his arm, struck, struck out again, but nothing seemed to matter to that monstrous shadow of fur lurching towards him, its paws flailing the air.

He heard Janet scream again, then the cave was filled with the thunder of rifle fire. The bear grunted once and rolled over at his feet.

He turned and saw Janet kneeling, holding the still smoking rifle. She dropped it and, naked, leapt to her feet and into his arms. Sobbing hysterically, her cries of terror filled the cave. He struck her hard across the face with one hand and still clinging to him, her cries became a wail, a whimper, then stopped.

Slowly he lifted her face to his, no longer feeling the pain of his ripped shoulder or the blood that streamed from it. Then his hands ceased to be those of a saviour protecting, placating. They were the hands of a lover, questing, caressing, demanding.

Janet responded with a moan of pleasure, her arms around his neck, they stood close, their lips bound. Limbs mingled, their feet touched the bed of blankets and they dropped down onto it as one body. Roughly, without tenderness, to satisfy his terrible need of her that was beyond the laws of Sun Gods or men, Atala took her and as she cried with the pain of fulfilment, the first pale light of morning filled the cave.

Still bound to her by lips and arms, Atala gently freed himself from her embrace and walked over to the mouth of the cave. A few moments later he was aware of her by his side.

'You are hurt, my darling,' she whispered, touching his shoulder where the blood had caked. 'You should have told me.'

'You didn't ask.'

She looked up at him, drowsily, her face transformed by love. 'You look very beautiful with the golden rays of the sun on your face, my Atala.' And half-closing her eyes, said, 'Are you really the Sun God as men say? From where I stand you could be.'

He looked away from her across the canyon.

She sighed, 'I'm glad you're just a man, after all. I've always been rather scared of you. As if you might really be a god, some kind of supernatural being—'

Suddenly aware that he was no longer listening, she looked up into his face, kissed the pulse throbbing at his neck. 'Dearest—'

Roughly, he shook her off. 'No, Janet!' His voice was harsh. 'No.'

'What's wrong? Atala? Please look at me.'

He turned slowly and with eyes that were tinged with the amber gold of morning, he shook his head and placed his fingers over her lips.

'No. Don't say it. It's better to remain unsaid. Get dressed and go now. Go to Tucson. Nothing will stop you. The storm is over.' His voice was hoarse with pain, 'Go now, please, before I change my mind and keep you here— and destroy us both.'

At that she smiled up at him, shaking her long red hair back from her naked shoulders. 'All right, I'll go now, as you ask me to. But not before I tell you what you must know already— after all this.'

Stroking his face she said, 'I love you. Love you so much I don't know exactly where it began, I think it was in a garden when I was fourteen and you were on your way to be married. I seem to have been fighting it ever since. Now I'm beyond caring how it will end. For some women love lasts a lifetime, perhaps for others, like me, it lasts a few hours in the arms of the man I love. The man who is, and always will be, my whole life.'

Still he did not speak and with a sigh, she picked up her clothes, testing them one by one to see if they were dry.

'If I go now and never see you again, you're still my man Atala, the only one I'll ever love. And that's final. Don't think you're the only one who is fighting either. I've lived with this love for you so long now I feel as if I'm living two lives.'

She shrugged. 'One me is virtuous, hardworking, God-fearing—the minister's daughter waiting patiently for some dull good man, like Matt Hepple, to marry me.' She clutched the bundle of clothes to her breast. 'The other half of me sleeps at night with you in your camp. Your woman, Atala, neither wife nor mistress. Only your lover, until I die. Forever yours.'

The sun had risen. It streamed into the cave, into Atala's eyes. Blinded, he could not turn from its accusing rays knowing the enormity of what he had let happen that night. Doubly he had betrayed his god. He had betrayed this woman and he had betrayed all those whose survival depended on him.

'For your own god's sake and for mine, go now,' he said. 'These things can never be between us. I tell you so.'

'Oh, yes, they can. We can make them

happen. If we love each other, nothing is stronger than love. Neither gods nor men can touch us.'

And throwing the bundle of clothes aside, she stretched up on tiptoe, pressed her clasped hands behind his head and brought down his lips to meet hers. Lips that were cold and dead, like kissing a marble statue of an ancient god.

'Kiss me back, damn you,' she sobbed. 'I don't care about tomorrow. I don't want to see tomorrow. Tomorrow I'll be on my way to Tucson, the respectable schoolteacher, and you'll be somewhere back in these mountains. All I want, all I ask for, is one day with you. This day. It belongs to us, my darling, we've waited for it, we've earned these hours and neither your gods nor mine can take them from us. Today we can make our own time. Don't you see that?'

When he didn't answer, she rested her head against his shoulder and whispered, 'I'll never love anybody but you. I never have. I can't, I won't let you just walk out of my life. These few hours are ours forever. I want you. Your body and soul. I want to belong to you so completely that wherever I go for the rest of my life, I'll be taking you with me.'

Atala put his hand over her lips. 'Hush. Hush then. No more.' Gently he stroked the long red hair back from her face. 'I do love you. But I have no right to give myself in love. You don't understand, you can't. I am not as other

262

men, free to love. I belong to my people, to my gods. I must be prepared to live for them, die for them when the time comes. And no one, especially a woman, must be allowed to change my destiny.'

Gently he drew her close, his lips resting against her soft hair. 'You're not listening, my Janet. But this is important. This you must remember. Some day, it may be important to think of my words. At this moment all of me belongs to you. There is only one thing stronger. The vows I made when I became Atala. Nothing mortal, not even you can make me break them. Not even you,' he repeated slowly, 'with your heart and your life twisted so close around mine.'

'I'm only asking for a few hours,' she whispered. 'Then we both go back to our worlds. Nobody but us will ever know of this day we shared. Now stop talking and kiss me.'

Atala did as she asked. Then again, their bodies moved as if of one accord. Bound together they lay in each other's arms, and this time there was no breaking away as the waves swept over them and their wild delight carried them beyond the brink where gods command and reason waits to have its still small voice. Beyond the barrier of fear, beyond judgement, to that shore where neither world nor time exist.

Cocooned in that web of enchantment, they slept in each other's arms. Slept and loved and

263

slept again. Until the morning came.

CHAPTER EIGHTEEN

*Before talking of holy things, we prepare
ourselves by offerings . . . one will fill a pipe
and hand it to the other . . .*

MATO-KUWAPI, Santee-Yanktonai Sioux

Chay was a very bewildered man. After what
Kate had told him about Luke and what he had
witnessed in the hospital ward, he would have
believed anything and although Shalwaaw's
account of the Atala tragedy might be an
overworked legend, he could still see some very
modern repercussions.

Like the three murders. He still couldn't
shake off the idea, running like a snowball
gathering momentum down a steep hill, that
the Begay brothers had been slaughtered by a
human agency. And Shashtso's confidential
report about the first murder two years earlier
which had been so smoothly swept under the
carpet, confirmed what was already a certainty
in his own mind that this was the work of a
serial killer.

Except that serial killers like to get on with
the job while the adrenalin is high. Once they
have started nailing victims, they get a taste for

blood, and it's unusual for them to sit back and relax for a couple of years until the next victim comes along.

That theory didn't fit the pattern. And that pattern, Chay decided was far more grisly and closer to his family. These showed the mark of ritualistic killings. The first boy, then Gerry Begay and for some reason his brother had got in the way and had also been murdered. The final confirmation that he was right came with the kidnapping story Beno had told him.

It all fitted in except the reason why they let him go.

As for the Temple of the Sun God and its situation among the red rocks, a link could exist there with the reclusive millionaire known as Viejo. Perhaps it had given up its secrets to him and was the source of his fortune.

Was he behind these killings? And if so why?

Was he mad—or just plain bad?

These were all matters that would bear careful investigation. Difficult enough because labelled as 'fatal accidents' the files were officially closed. But Chay was determined that anything touching Kate Fenner and her strange son that might also involve his grandfather, however indirectly, was of the utmost concern.

Even without Shalwaaw's account, he had a gut feeling that Kate and the boy had become involved with some kind of supernatural force beyond his powers to protect them.

He had the evidence of his own eyes that

something was wrong. First, Kate maintained that she had cut her forehead badly outside the bear's cave. But although the neck of her T-shirt was deeply stained with dried blood, an hour later no trace of scar or wound remained. Second, Redfeather had escaped unscathed from the car accident which had demolished his bicycle. The badly cut knee and bruises he claimed to have sustained had all vanished within twenty-four hours.

Unhappily aware of sinister events outside his usual line of business, Chay lay sleepless that night and decided to take a few days off. He would go to Flagstaff, see what his old friend Inspector Rudd Shashtso could produce in the way of a confidential dossier on the millionaire Viejo and perhaps be in time to avert another tragedy.

*   *   *

Redfeather had had a visitor the previous evening and the two old men sat together in the hogan beside the grand adobe house.

Tomas had his own reasons for serving in the House of Anasazi Fire while secretly manipulating its owner for his own purposes. Even though Redfeather was a cousin, and famed for his hospitality to the whole clan, Tomas had remained true to his roots and his beliefs and, as though afraid of contamination, he preferred superstitiously that they talk in the traditional manner, sitting cross-legged on the hogan floor smoking the Navajo pipe.

Twilight was gathering across the now silent pasture, empty of the children who had filled the air with their laughter a short while ago.

Inside the hogan Redfeather had just related his point of death experience to the old shaman. They had grown up together, had been close as young men, but Redfeather never indicated he knew that Tomas was also the leader of the Magic Men.

Tomas had been very interested in his cousin's strange experience, asking him to repeat every detail, especially about the Anglo boy Luke's part in it. At the end, the shaman's eyes glittered with excitement and he was obviously impatient to leave.

Watching him being driven away in the old pick-up truck, Redfeather had his first misgivings. Maybe he should not have told him so much. He was guiltily aware that by exaggerating the account of his miraculous recovery just a little, he might have put the boy in danger. And he did not want such a thing on his conscience, especially as it was already overburdened by knowing a great deal more about the deaths of the Begay boys than he would have willingly admitted to his grandson or the cops in Phoenix.

Redfeather was a man with deep problems, part Navajo, part Atalos–Anasazi, torn between two worlds, his aims for the future of the planet and for their tribe were in sympathy with the Magic Men, but the ritual sacrifice of a child was something he preferred not to consider too closely, especially those two boys who were of his own clan. Deliberately he had thrust aside thoughts of all his own grand-nephews and how he might have reacted had any of them been chosen by the Magic Men. Until now he had appeased his conscience that this was a tribal matter. As Tomas pointed out the future of their Atalos–Anasazi clan depended on such things, that the least must be sacrificed for the greatest good to the clan.

Tomas had further pointed out that living with the Anglos had made Redfeather squeamish. Were not such sacrifices part of their tradition? Had they any right to question the sacred inheritance from their ancestors?

'We are not as the white man,' he further reminded Redfeather. 'We do not take any life lightly or for sport. It is part of our code that we kill only where it is strictly necessary to survive, and that includes the smallest animal that we eat. Or a human life,' he added grimly, 'if such is considered necessary.'

Waiting for a reaction that was not forthcoming, for Redfeather continued to smoke his pipe slowly, thoughtfully, as if it required his full attention, Tomas regarded him sternly.

'You cannot deny that this is a case of survival not only of our people but, maybe ultimately, of all life on earth. Think of the Navajo nation. Have I to remind you that when we die out then the earth itself is also going to die without the ceremonies being performed to keep it in balance? You know what will happen, it will fall apart, destroy itself. There will be earthquakes, the ground beneath our feet will split open, great floods will sweep across the planet as they did when the red rocks were formed and once more there will be no human survivors.'

Redfeather guessed it was already happening, since he watched the television and read the newspapers.

Tomas went on, 'This destruction to the environment is the fault of the Anglos. Their civilisation, not ours, brought about the pollution of the atmosphere that is slowly killing us all. They cannot stop it with all their clever scientists, but we can. We have the power. The Anglo government in Washington should come to the reservations, hire all the medicine men and have one big healing ceremony for the earth, right across the States. Only then will the hole in the ozone layer close and only then will the earth heal itself.'

Redfeather smiled wryly and shook his head. Tomas glared at him. 'I know what you're thinking—that it would be too expensive for them to consider, but it isn't one fraction as much as they spend on arms to kill each other.'

He leaned forward earnestly. 'We are old

friends as well as cousins and, as such, I have no reason to be telling you what you know already, what you were born knowing. This is our land. This is what we dreamed and it happened like this,' he made a gesture towards the open door. 'This land outside was shaped by a dream. It was dreamed by us, by our gods and they helped us to make it happen. All they asked was our respect, our belief and sometimes a sacrifice.'

He paused and Redfeather looked across at him. 'Are you sure—about the sacrifice, I mean?'

Tomas nodded. 'If the gods demand it, yes.' He sighed. 'We have failed before but this male child has remarkable powers. The Great Spirit directed him here so that he might ensure our leader's immortality.'

'Aren't you forgetting something? The boy is white.'

Tomas looked at him. 'Long ago, far back in our history we were promised another white god, another Quetzalcoatl. Perhaps it is he who has come to redeem us in the shape of a child.' He shrugged. 'When I was a child long ago at the Mission School they taught us their Bible, how their great prophet Elijah came back to earth in the shape of Jesus Christ, as a child born to woman, a child born for sacrifice.'

Again Redfeather said nothing and Tomas gave him an angry glance. He would have liked a more enthusiastic response to his argument.

That he had none, confirmed that the years with the white men had contaminated his cousin.

'Whatever the colour of his skin and however he came by it makes no difference. From what you have just told me, he carries the Talisman, the spirit power.'

Redfeather had secret doubts. He could not believe quite as wholeheartedly as the Magic Men in their road to immortality. 'How can you be so sure?'

Tomas frowned. 'If you need further proof, then remember he was sent to us, but he came of his own free will. He is here because he wished to come, the Talisman directed his vibrations onto the magic machine, the one they call Internet. Its secrets are known to some of our people here.'

Redfeather shook his head. He would have nothing to do with cars or telephones and knew nothing of magic machines by which he was told the world carried on its business. Machines even more complex than the telephone wires which let people speak to each other on opposite sides of the world.

He knew that Rita, who was once Chay's woman, had a machine with a television screen, but she laughed and said that her fax machine, which would spew out printed messages and letters from friends and business colleagues, was a very primitive form of this frightening new instrument she longed to possess and which Tomas called the Internet.

Even in the glory of his Hollywood days, Redfeather could not be persuaded that telephones were not connected with witchcraft. He shuddered at the monstrous tasks Rita's machine was capable of and regarded Tomas with awe and respect for his knowledge. He only tolerated a television set in his house for the secret reason that there was a movie channel which often showed the westerns he had appeared in long ago. This indulgence was a great and moving experience to be shared with no one, for Redfeather, who seldom cried, shed tears at the camera's magic in turning back the years, transforming an old man of ninety once again into a handsome, virile, black-haired youth.

Such was his own immortality readily to hand, but he had seen enough of the world to know the dangers of fanaticism and Tomas's departure left him, once again, torn between the ancient loyalty to his tribe and concern for his grandson Chay. But most important of all, loyalty and protection for the Anglo boy, Luke, who he knew had breathed life into him and, when he had already set foot into the unknown, brought him back through the darkness into the light of the world.

He sighed. He owed Chay a warning, for he suspected that his grandson loved the boy's mother and although Redfeather would rather have seen him settle down with Rita, who was one of his own people, he had a grudging respect and a little liking for the woman Kate, even if she belonged to the same race as his despised ex-wife who had betrayed him and broken his heart.

* * *

Chay was preparing to leave for Flagstaff when Jake looked in.

'Grandfather wants to see you—urgently. I tried to get through on the phone but your fax must be in operation—'

'Is he ill again?' asked Chay anxiously.

'No. Nothing like that. We had quite a night of it though with young Luke.'

And he told him of the boy's nighmare and how he had had to rise from his bed in the middle of the night and take him back home.

Jake grinned. 'He wanted his mother, just like a little boy. Mother needs me, he wrote down. She was mighty glad to see him, real scared at being awakened in the middle of the night, I guess. Of all the nonsense,' he added rather scornfully, 'if he'd been mine I would have slapped him, put him back to bed and told him to go to sleep again.'

The incident increased Chay's unease. He phoned Kate from his mobile on the way to Redfeather but there was no reply. He'd just have to keep trying.

*　　*　　*

At the ranch, he had not expected his grandfather's solemn words that the woman and child must leave immediately. That there was maybe a plot to kill Kate and steal the boy away to fulfil the Atalas–Anasazi prophecy.

'How do you know all this?' he demanded.

Redfeather shrugged. 'I cannot tell you. But believe me I know what I am talking about.'

Chay had to ask, 'Is there some connection with the two boys who have been killed?'

Redfeather looked away from him.

It was no comfort to know that he had been right all along. There was no triumph for him when he asked, 'Are the Magic Men behind these killings?'

That Redfeather did not answer was enough. His sudden agitation was all the confirmation needed for, although the old man shook his head stubbornly, he refused to meet Chay's eyes.

'I cannot tell you, grandson.'

'Then you are deliberately concealing information and that is being an accessory to a murder attempt. You know all this, grandfather,' Chay added angrily.

'Then arrest me. I do not care, I have lived a long time, grandson, and I have never broken my word. I will not do so now. I am just warning you about what I think might happen. I have a feeling about it, so get the woman and her son

274

away from here.'

'And how do you think I am going to do that?' said Chay desperately. 'This holiday was a prize, there were restrictions, I imagine, on travel arrangements tied in with it.'

'You have been a policeman, you can think of some excuse,' Redfeather said sarcastically.

*　　　*　　　*

Chay faced the dilemma Redfeather's disclosures had put before him. His duty was to inform the FBI, since he was almost certain that the Magic Men had been involved in the murder of the two boys, that there was no wild animal, no human serial killer at large, and that the brutal slayings were a throwback to the days of ritual sacrifice among his people. In modern language, seen through twentieth-century eyes in the white man's world, it remained a case of homicide.

But if he obeyed the law as he should, then his grandfather would suffer. He knew he must deal with this on his own. Go to Kate and invent some reason why she and Luke should leave Blackhawk right away.

He could see the problems that would raise. Even if she could be persuaded that they were in mortal danger, the business of changing flight tickets could be difficult without a substantial loss of dollars which she might not be willing or able to meet.

Walking past the travel agents next door to his office, he saw a notice in the window. And there was his answer. A coach tour on which their movements would be monitored by a reliable guide and they would be safely surrounded by other tourists. A subtler method which would keep them out of harm's way until he returned from Flagstaff, by which time he should have worked out some other scheme ensuring their safety until the plane left Phoenix bound for Britain.

Kate was delighted when he called her to say that he had picked up a bargain four-day tour to the Grand Canyon and New Mexico.

'We'd love that. Thank you for thinking of us. How much did it cost?' He noted the apprehension in her voice.

'I've paid the deposit,' and cutting short her protests, he lied about the price. 'You can pay me back later. There were only two places left, sharing a room. They go fast with all these tourists in town. It leaves tomorrow morning at ten—'

She repeated the directions to see she had got it right.

'Luke will be so thrilled, Chay. He's always wanted to go to the Grand Canyon and I've put it off. It's such a long drive.'

He heard the doorbell. 'Hang on.' A moment later she said, 'It's my neighbour.' And hastily: 'Thanks again, Chay. You're so kind.'

He replaced the phone with a sigh. All these

heroics, all these efforts to get her out of the country were hardly calculated to further his own interests. He knew that he wanted Kate badly and had been guilty of imagining some kind of future for them both.

One more hurdle before he left. He had better inform Rita of his plans. At best she would ask no questions, and although she would be furious with him for wasting more money, she would be glad to be rid of the woman she seriously considered her rival. At worst, knowing the shrewd workings of Rita's mind, she would ask questions about this surprising trend of events. Why all the rush when Miz Fenner's vacation was half over anyway? And if he told her the truth, could he persuade her not to inform the cops? By withholding information on a homicide case, they were liable to prosecution and he would lose his private investigator's licence.

Would she co-operate he thought anxiously? Even if they no longer slept together on a regular basis, just being around all day, working together, had seemed to be enough for her . . . If only he could be sure of that.

It was only then he noticed a written message from her stuck up on his desk. She'd gone to see her mother, rushed to hospital with a suspected heart attack. And there was a new client who suspected his office accounts were being laundered. Delicate family matters were involved.

Chay called the businessman in Flagstaff to say that he would be in the area and a hotel was arranged for a discreet first meeting.

He sped off in the car deciding things were shaping out well, feeling almost light-hearted in the knowledge that he had arranged for Kate and Luke to be safe in his absence.

He was only away for a couple of days, so what could go wrong?

What indeed? As always he had bargained without Fate's malign interference with man's well-laid plans.

CHAPTER NINETEEN

Danger and delight grow on one stalk.

ENGLISH PROVERB

Kate and Tessa were having coffee on the terrace when the telephone rang again and, answering it, Tessa heard Kate's voice rising in excitement.

She came out laughing. 'Can you imagine! At long last! That was Mr Wilderbrand. I thought he'd forgotten all about us. Remember I told you, he was supposed to meet us when we first arrived. Well, apparently he had to go to Hawaii on urgent business. He sent a message—he was quite upset when I said that I

278

never got it.'

'The mail is hopeless here,' sighed Tessa. 'Everyone seems to rely on their fax machines these days.'

Kate nodded. 'What a relief to hear from him. I've been so worried in case something awful happened. I've had nightmares that instead of the prize money, we would be suddenly presented with a huge bill for staying here.'

She looked at Tessa earnestly. 'I haven't a clue about the workings of the Internet but I've never let Mr Wilderbrand's letter out of my sight, since the day it arrived. You hear about such things being hoaxes, don't you? Even if they are on the level, it's scary coming to a strange country and not knowing anyone.'

She stretched out her hand to Tessa. 'But you've all been brilliant.'

Tessa smiled politely. Warren had been very suspicious, full of gloomy forebodings, but then he always thought the worst of all so-called charitable deeds and would not allow her to enter prize draws for thousands of dollars and fabulous holidays.

'It's all a racket,' he said. 'A giant con.'

She would be pleased to tell him that he was wrong for once. And, to give Warren his due, he liked Kate. He had a big soft heart and although he considered babies outside marriage the sign of a decaying society, he was sorry for this good-looking intelligent girl from a decent background. She had brought up a handicapped boy on her own and made a good job of it too.

'I sure hope someone isn't making a monkey of her with this prize holiday,' he told Tessa. 'If there is, you can bet your bottom dollar, honey, that I'll make it my business to see they're exposed and put in jail. Nice kid like that.'

Kate had drained her coffee and was looking at her watch surreptitiously. 'Mr Wilderbrand's sending a car for me right away, to take us to lunch at the Desert Oasis. He's staying there. Do you know it?'

Tessa's eyes widened. 'Sure do. It's the best—and most expensive hotel around here.' Warren would be relieved at this indication of Mr Wilderbrand's authenticity.

'Oh good,' said Kate, with another quick glance at the time.

Tessa took the hint. 'I'll be going then, honey.'

Kate stood up and smiled cheerfully, running a hand through her long hair. 'Better make myself look presentable. And Luke, too.'

'He can come across to me if this is just a business lunch,' said Tessa remembering how her two kids would have loathed such a grown-up occasion, branding it dead boring and the pits.

Kate shook her head. 'That's very kind, Tessa, but Mr Wilderbrand especially wants to meet Luke, seeing that he won the prize and so forth.'

* * *

Chay's Flagstaff investigation concerned a wealthy businessman who had reason to suspect his company was being defrauded of considerable sums of money. He was afraid that his chief accountant, who was also his son, with whom he had a somewhat abrasive relationship, might be at the root of it. As delicate family matters were involved he had no wish to bring in the police and the possibility of making it public. Much to his relief, Chay's probings uncovered one of the minor clerks who, by an unexpected stroke of luck, Chay had encountered during his days with the San Francisco Police. He had turned up again, using a false name; an ex-con who was working a scam for a rival firm.

Three days later he met up with Rudd Shashtso who had some interesting and disturbing information about the recluse millionaire of the House of Anasazi Fire.

'This Viejo's real name is Heinrick Wilderbrand, an ex-patriate Dutchman, born in Maastricht in 1916 of a wealthy arms dealing family who made their fortunes selling guns to both sides in practically every conflict in Europe and Africa from the Second World War onwards. Never married, he was a suspected homosexual when such activities were still criminal, and a paedophile too. However this didn't stop him becoming a US citizen in 1948.'

'With a reputation like that? Hardly squeaky clean, is it?' said Chay.

Shashtso shrugged. 'The dirt was revealed by the McCarthy regime, but I guess very big money changed hands and toned down any of the red faces that had admitted him into the country. He had a very low profile from then on, very few records until he reappeared in the sixties as an entrepreneur, high in the art business, an expert whose opinion was sought by the President as well as minor African countries who wanted to make a cultured impression on visiting heads of state.'

As Chay listened his feelings of triumph battled with a growing element of disquiet. Wilderbrand's early life as a known paedophile suggested that, although evidence of his role in the Begay boys' deaths was circumstantial, he might well be the man behind Beno's strange abduction.

Most disturbing of all was the heart attack that had ended the career of the detective in charge of the Begay investigation.

Shashtso looked grim. 'In the light of what I've unearthed on Wilderbrand, I'm wondering whether it really was a coronary or one simulated by a substantial payment to drop the enquiry.'

'Have you some reason for thinking that he could be bribed?' Chay asked.

'Sure. I knew the guy and never liked him much. When we were both young cops in Phoenix he was implicated in a drugs case and a suspected cop killing. He managed to squeeze his way out—but only just. I sure wasn't surprised to hear he had been transferred to a quieter manor on health grounds. When I mentioned that early bad record, the authorities were scandalised. Did I not know he was a Vietnam hero, beyond reproach? They sure gave him one hell of a send-off, a massive funeral in 'Frisco with all the top brass in attendance.'

Shashtso's disclosures left a nasty taste in the mouth and Chay drove back to Blackhawk with the unhappy thought that this might not be just a backwater for lame or lamed cops but might also have deeper darker secrets that would not bear close investigation, mouths that could be closed, if not by blackmail, then by a more permanent method. Such as the road accident which had written Lopez out of the scenario.

Kate was never absent from his thoughts, and after Shashtso's revelations regarding Wilderbrand aka Viejo, he congratulated himself on his foresight in having sent her and Luke away to temporary safety at the Grand Canyon. The next step would be to see them safely on a plane back to Britain. That needed considerable thought and delicate planning, but knowing Viejo's real identity was an ace in his hand although he had not yet worked out how best to play it.

Eager to get back in time to welcome Kate and Luke off the returning coach tour, he discovered that his office door was locked. Of Rita there was no sign, only frantic messages that he must get his mobile phone fixed. She had tried to get through several times to tell him she was taking the morning off to get her mother out of hospital.

He walked quickly along to the travel office where the girl in reception said, 'You've just missed them. The tour came in half an hour ago—while I was out at lunch.'

Chay drove fast down the hill to the creek and into the square. Kate's car was in the drive. A few moments and he would be with her again. His heart rejoiced at the thought.

As he rang the doorbell he smiled, thinking of how much he had missed her in the few days absence.

*　　　*　　　*

There was no welcome sound of footsteps in the hall. He rang again and, guessing that they were outside on the deck and hadn't heard him, he climbed the wall.

The garden was deserted, the glass back door locked.

He stared in at the window. The house seemed empty. Telling himself that they had most probably decided to stay on in town for lunch and he had maybe missed them by minutes, he was about to drive away when Tessa ran down her path.

'Looking for Miss Fenner? She's away.'

'I know, I thought she might be back by now.'

He looked so anxious, Tessa decided his visit must be urgent.

'I haven't seen her since Monday. They were taking a trip to the Grand Canyon.'

'Sure. The tour's just back. I guess I missed her on the road down. Did they get away all right?'

Tessa looked puzzled. 'I never saw her after she came back from her lunch date on Monday—after you called to say you'd got tickets for them. I offered to take them to the tour place next morning but they never showed up.' She looked a little hurt. 'Well, maybe she got a better offer. You know how it is—meeting someone and so forth. She's just a young woman—'

'This lunch date—where was she going?'

'She didn't say. It was just after your call. She had to meet someone—a man—at the Desert Oasis.'

At least the most popular and expensive hotel in town ruled out the Magic Men, Chay decided.

Tessa was smiling, he had already rated her as a lady who enjoyed gossip and might readily supply any required information.

'Did she say who she was meeting?'

'Oh yes. A Mr Will-something. A funny name.'

'Wilderbrand? Was that his name?'

'That's right, the man who arranged her visit here. He was staying at the Oasis.'

Why should Wilderbrand who owned the House of Anasazi Fire stay at a hotel just a few miles away? Chay's sinking sense of disaster left him like a drowning man gasping for air.

'Did you see them leave?'

'Oh yes. He sent a car for her. With a chauffeur. A limo.'

He could hardly ask if she noticed the number.

She watched him drive off, his questions as strange as his rapid departure. She would have plenty to tell Warren, their talk over lunch was either of golf or non-existent, but not today.

*   *   *

At the travel agents, he learned that Kate and Luke Fenner had failed to show up. The tour had left without them.

His worst fears realised, Chay headed straight for the Desert Oasis, where 'Police' got some respect from the doorman. Parking in front of the hotel, he ran up the steps to reception. His arrival coincided with a bus party of foreign tourists and he had some difficulty getting the clerk's attention without being mowed down by a bevy of strident ladies intent on getting to their allocated rooms. Murmuring excuses, he showed his badge and pushed to the front of the queue.

'Mr Wilderbrand, please. He's staying here.'

The computer was consulted, keys were tapped. The girl shook her head. 'No one of that name is registered. When was he to check in?'

'Three or four days ago.'

'A moment please.' More keys clicked. 'Sorry, officer, there's no one of that name this week.'

'What about lunches? Do you have a record of back bookings.'

'I guess the head waiter might have. Hey, Cosmo—' she signalled to the man bustling past and repeated the question.

'No, sir, we don't keep records. How can I help you?'

The waiter obviously thought this an odd request but as the cops were involved and you never knew when a good word might be useful, he was prepared to co-operate.

'Do you recall an elderly man, Mr Wilderbrand, who made a booking for lunch, with a woman with long fair hair, young, thirtyish, striking-looking, about four days ago.'

Cosmo smiled wryly. 'Sorry, sir, the name doesn't ring any bells and as for the description, well, it's that sort of hotel—we get dozens in like that every day. Old guys tryin' to

287

make it with young chicks—'

But Chay was already on his way out to his car.

Back in the office he told Rita about Shashtso and about his visit to the Desert Oasis and the non-existent Wilderbrand.

'So what? Maybe he likes staying in hotels for a change. I guess he can afford the best suite.'

'But he wasn't there.'

Seeing his worried expression, Rita said, 'Maybe Miz Fenner's neighbour got it wrong that he was staying and he was just taking her there for lunch. Maybe he couldn't get a table booking, that's all.'

'Come on, Rita. Don't tell me he wouldn't have booked one or he couldn't have used his influence, even if there wasn't one available. They'd have put him in a private room somewhere, dammit, if he had flourished a few dollars.'

'OK. Could be they don't keep records of such transactions.'

'All right. Want me to check all the hotels in town?'

Chay was silent, drumming his fingers on the desk, trying desperately to think.

'What's wrong?' she asked. 'You surely don't imagine something's happened to them, that they've been kidnapped. Even if this Viejo or Wilderbrand hasn't a record as a top-drawer character, maybe age has changed him and he's

288

now a philanthropist giving away big prizes to kids on the Internet.'

Without betraying his grandfather's confidence and relating the extraordinary occurrence in the hospital which had led to it, he said, 'Doesn't this background of his make you think—just a little—that he might have something to do with the killers of the Begay boys. It ties up with Beno too.'

Rita sighed again. 'You're back on that track. I get it. You're thinking we're back to the bad old days of ritual sacrifice and so on. OK. Could be you're right. But this Luke Fenner's an Anglo boy from the other side of the world. From Scotland, for heaven's sake.'

'Is it so ridiculous? You're always telling me the extraordinary things the Internet can achieve. You know it all.'

Rita frowned. 'Only very vaguely as yet.'

'Then don't you agree that there's a possibility we might be on to something. He won a mysterious prize from some competition on the damned thing, a prize to get him over here. Neither that nor the equally mysterious, and from what we now know, sinister, Mr Wilderbrand's part in it has been properly explained. I sure would like some answers to how it was all worked—and why. For what purpose?'

'This is way out stuff, Chay,' Rita interrupted, 'you can't be serious. Surely not!' When he didn't say anything, she continued more gently, 'This doesn't sound like you, with your scientific reasoning for everything.'

But Chay wasn't listening. 'There are just one or two facts, pieces in the puzzle which, put together, fit a bit too well for coincidence. Remember Beno's description of looking through a chink in the wall and seeing guard dogs and a high cliff face.'

'Sure I do.'

'I've been thinking that our reclusive millionaire Viejo aka Wilderbrand has guard dogs at his house, and it's built into a cliff face.'

'Like plenty of others about here. That could refer to a dozen houses in the area. Don't forget we have one or two millionaires in residence and it's nothing for rich Anglos these days to build mansions in the red rock wilderness and have a brace of fierce guard dogs to guard their property.'

When Chay looked at her sharply, she laughed. 'Come on, Chay, you surely don't think Wilderbrand retreated from his world of big deals to set up as a child murderer?'

'He might be a madman.'

'He's more likely to be a visitor from Mars, I'd say.'

Chay ignored that. 'Think about it, Rita. No one has ever set eyes on him. All I've ever seen is his back or the glimpse of a face with dark glasses. An old guy with white hair and a fedora pulled well down over the eyes on his rare visits into the town. And we know from Shashtso that he was gay and had the reputation of being a paedophile.'

He leaned back in his chair. 'What if he is behind all this, a madman who believes he is the saviour of our people, a reincarnation of Quetzalcoatl? Or that he's just a little unhinged, maybe even just gullible enough for some fanatic from our people to persuade him into it. Including the ritual sacrifice bit.'

Rita thought about that. 'You know what is really missing, Chay? Motive, that's what. He must have had some sure big reason for building a retreat from the world in a cliff face at Blackhawk Creek.'

'I'm well ahead of you. My reckoning would be some criminal activity that forced him to spend the rest of his life in hiding. Like running drugs—or homicide. Or both,' he added, picking up his hat.

'Where are you off to?'

'The House of Anasazi Fire, where else?'

'You don't mean that, they'll never let you in without a warrant.'

'Then I'll try some other means.'

'Chay!' she shouted at him. 'Don't be a crazy man.'

'Oh, I won't be. There's enough of them about.'

'When will you be back?' There was panic in her voice now.

'I don't know for sure, but if I don't put in an appearance, or call you, within a couple of days, you'd better get on to the cops and tell them all we know.'

'Chay, don't do it!' she screamed, but he was gone.

CHAPTER TWENTY

Whatsoe'er we perpetrate we do but now, we are steered by Fate

SAMUEL BUTLER, Hudibras

The car from Mr Wilderbrand had arrived for Kate and Luke shortly after Tessa returned home. Kate had barely had time to wash Luke's face and urge him into clean shorts and T-shirt while she exchanged her own informal garb of jeans and sleeveless blouse for a tailored linen dress.

The car was a black limousine, chauffeur-driven with dark windows. They were ushered into the back seat and after a few attempts to make polite conversation with the driver, who made not the slightest indication that he heard or understood, Kate gave up. His dark skin and what she could see of his face from under the peaked cap and dark glasses suggested that he was Indian or Mexican. Perhaps he had little English or was forbidden by his employer to converse with the passengers.

Soon they were cruising along the main street towards the outskirts of the town. She saw the sign for the Desert Oasis Hotel and when he skirted the front entrance, presumed he was going to the car park. She was surprised when he drove past and continued along the road.

She tapped on the glass partition. 'Excuse me, I thought we were going to the hotel to meet Mr Wilderbrand.'

Ignoring her remark, he drove steadily on. Was he deaf or something, she thought desperately. A moment later, with the traffic lights against them, she tried again.

This time he turned his head impatiently. 'I am taking you to Mr Wilderbrand. He is waiting to meet you.'

That at least was a relief. 'He told me we were to meet at the Desert Oasis,' she said lamely.

'I am taking you to him.' The driver's English was perfect and he certainly wasn't deaf.

'We were to have lunch. Has there been a change of plans?'

The driver nodded vaguely and smiled at her for the first time, as if in reassurance, then the lights changed and the car gathered speed.

Kate sat back, the man sounded as if he knew what he was doing. She obviously wasn't going to get any more information out of him. He had his orders and was sticking to them.

Now they were out on the highway, the desert flanked by the sycamore-lined creek of Blackhawk on their right. The car moved fast and when she looked out of the back window she saw how far Red Rock had retreated.

They had travelled some distance when Kate experienced her first feelings of alarm. Was her rather sinister driver lying? Were they being kidnapped? Had something happened to Mr Wilderbrand? Perhaps he was being held to ransom. Frantically, she thought about escaping from the car. On the highway there were plenty of travellers who might be prevailed upon to come to their assistance, although she wasn't too hopeful about that, remembering the night when Mr Lopez's hired car had broken down. But she tried the door handle anyway, and wasn't too surprised to find it was locked; the mechanism obviously worked from the driver's seat.

She didn't want to alarm Luke, who was gazing out of the window. Her anxiety hadn't communicated itself to him but when he turned quickly and looked into her face, she saw that he was also experiencing her fears. He took her hand and squeezed it in a gesture of reassurance, as they turned off the highway to where the red rocks towered far above them. The driver negotiated a steep road which finally petered out in front of massive locked gates.

'Where are we?'

He didn't answer, but held up an electronic device which opened the gates. There was nothing exceptional about such an action, so why should she find it sinister, she thought as they slid through and the gates slowly closed behind them.

There was no house in sight and, looking back, she saw that they were climbing high into the canyon. Suddenly the view was familiar; it was the one she and Luke had seen from the cliff face where they had lain down to look over the edge into the secret valley with its cultivated gardens, its swimming pool and guard dogs.

Was this where Mr Wilderbrand lived? In times of less stress and fear, Kate would have enjoyed the experience as they rode between buttes which wrapped themselves around them. It was a fantasy world of sandstone, a series of tiny private landscapes each complete with rock towers and secret alcoves. As they drove through arches of rock, there were sudden glimpses of cliff dwellings far above their head. The lost city of a lost civilisation.

They appeared to be driving straight into a rock non-stop. The driver suddenly reduced his speed, negotiated round a boulder some eight feet high to emerge into a narrow canyon, so narrow that a car's dimensions would have to be measured very carefully if it was to make the passage unscathed. They were so close to the rock on either side that Kate could have reached out and touched the delicate crossbedded layers of sandstone, the geological calendar of millions of years.

The sun had vanished, the air was cold as if daylight and warmth never touched it. The sudden darkness was intense. It spread over them like a miasma of fear, a living tomb.

'Where are we? What is this place?' she shouted at the driver.

He answered her this time. 'Not to worry, we are almost there. Mr Wilderbrand is waiting for you. See!'

She saw a round O of light, it grew larger, increasing in size until the warmth of the sun took over and they emerged onto the flat expanse of a twisting drive leading to a house shrouded by palms and sycamores, with stone gargoyles spouting water into an elegant man-made fountain. This they skirted and the driver stopped in front of an imposing door of very ancient black oak with carved figures and symbols. It resembled some doorway from an age-old temple.

Kate felt the lock on the door at her side being released. Not waiting for the driver, she jumped out pulling Luke after her.

Before she could do more than look around, the front door opened and an elderly Indian with long grey hair in plaits stepped out of the shadows.

He did not offer his hand, merely bowed and said, 'I am Tomas, my master is waiting.'

Kate's hand flew to her mouth. Instinctively she put a protective arm around Luke as, too late, she recognised the servant. They had both met the man who ushered them into the house. On the day they arrived in Blackhawk. He had tried to drag her onto the pick-up truck; the kidnapping attempt which had been foiled by Chay's arrival.

Fear rose into her throat like bile, for she knew it was this man, Tomas, she had glimpsed greeting Redfeather as they left the ranch on that first meeting. He was the leader of the Magic Men. She was trapped, knowing without the slightest doubt that they were prisoners, of whoever or whatever lay inside the house.

As for Mr Wilderbrand, she realised too late that he had probably never existed.

She had been tricked for some purpose too terrible to contemplate. She had led Luke into a trap.

*   *   *

Four days later, Chay was heading fast towards the House of Anasazi Fire. He owed a certain amount of success in his work to following hunches, and guessed that Kate and Luke had been kidnapped and were being held there as prisoners. His grandfather's warning, the mysterious Mr Wilderbrand, the place of Beno's captivity established by Kate and Luke's descriptions of the cliff garden and the guard

297

dogs, all were doubly confirmed by the results of Shashtso's probe into the secret and confidential files on the man known as Viejo.

As he had said, 'Big mouths that can't be closed by money can be permanently silenced by a bullet.'

Driving swiftly towards the cliff house, Chay was still trying to work out some valid reason why Luke had been lured to Blackhawk. This business about the Talisman was beyond him. His grandfather's gullibility, his faithful interpretation of ancient legends and rituals threw doubts on his reliability. This, Chay was prepared to dismiss as the inevitable normal aging process of a nonogenerian who had never lost his passionate belief in his people's cause.

Beno's experience, and his cousin who was notorious as a pimp for both sexes, suggested that Wilderbrand might be head of a paedophile ring. But why on earth should an eighty-year-old paedophile or child murderer go all the way to Britain to find a victim?

That didn't make any sense. The most likely reason that occurred to him was that the man they called Viejo had murdered the real Wilderbrand and was using that as a lure. Unfortunately that pointed to Kate's fears about the Magic Men being valid and inevitably to Redfeather's involvement with what the FBI would prosecute and swiftly wrap up as a criminal organisation.

No, lawman he might be, but he couldn't go

with that. All he knew and loved of his grandfather refused to accept that Redfeather would countenance child murder, ritualistic or otherwise, particularly of Navajo children of his own clan, like the Begay brothers. Knowing how deeply he cared for children, even those of the despised Anglos he had worked with during his Hollywood years, when he said he often wished the scalping knife or rifle he carried on film was for real.

The old man was impossible. Chay shook his head, allowances must be made for old men. Maybe he was losing his marbles, his sense of the real world.

He groaned, unable to escape from the fact that if he had interpreted Redfeather's oblique warning correctly, Kate might already be murdered and the boy sacrificed to give immortality to the madman who was masquerading in the gruesome role of a centuries-old tribal leader of Los Atalos. Whatever the reasons, he knew that time was running out fast and he tried to thrust aside the agonising thought that he might already be too late; that by the time he confronted the old man in the House of Anasazi Fire, Kate and Luke might be dead.

His only hope lay in the fact that the elements had a part to play in the grim ceremonial. The moon had to be in its right phase for some goddamned shaman's magic to work.

He felt like banging his head against the wall in despair. With most criminals, he had the ability to get inside their minds, walk about a bit, see what made them tick. But how was he to get inside the mind of a madman who was also a millionaire and could use his influence and knowledge to bend ignorance and superstition to his own sinister purposes? A man who could play on the passionate but gullible Atalos–Anasazi in their desperate quest for a redeemer who would turn history back to the golden years before the white man came. A man who promised to save planet earth from destruction.

Driving fast, leaving the highway for the turn-off road marked 'Strictly Private' that led up to the House of Anasazi Fire, he prayed that he would be in time, with a wry thought that a prayer to the Christian God might be more appropriate where Anglos were concerned.

Remembering it had been impossible to interview Viejo, he tried to decide on how to best conduct a deliberate confrontation and escape not only alive, but bringing Kate and Luke back with him through this treacherous terrain where fast driving was an impossibility, the narrow steep roads through tunnels with sharp bends making it suicidal.

He had a gun and he knew he would not hesitate to use it to force his way in and rescue them. He was prepared for a fight. But that must be a last resort. One man with a gun would have little chance against what he suspected was a small army with automatic rifles.

And a dead policeman, however gallant, was of no use to Kate and Luke.

First then, the polite enquiry. Pressing the bell at the gate, he would ask to speak to Viejo. If that was denied him then he'd demand to see Kate and Luke on the pretext that they had told him their destination and if they were being kept by force and he did not return within the hour, then Viejo could expect to see a convoy of police cars screaming up his drive with a search warrant.

But Chay was the one to be surprised. This time there were no gates slammed in his face. They opened smoothly to admit him. Like an expected visitor he proceeded along the drive and reached the front door. It was opened by a servant, one of his own people, a good-looking young man in rather old-fashioned formal attire, who said that his master was at present in a meeting and could not be disturbed.

Pondering on how often he had heard that excuse, Chay said, 'Then may I see Miss Fenner and her son. They told me they were coming to see Mr Wilderbrand.'

He was pleased to see a flicker of doubt touch the mask of inscrutability before him.

'You are to wait here,' said the young butler. He disappeared indoors and Chay could hear the whisper of words on a telephone. A moment later he returned.

'You are to come inside and wait, please.'

Standing in the shadowy hallway, all Chay's senses were on red alert. This might be a trap, these might be his last moments of consciousness. He might be gunned down, used as target practice by unseen armed men. He looked round rapidly feeling intensely vulnerable outlined against the open doorway. Then to his relief footsteps announced the return of the servant, who signed that he was to follow him.

For the first time, feeling only slightly less nervous, Chay took an interest in his surroundings. Larger than life-sized Kachina dolls stared down at him from the walls of the vast echoing hall with its marble floor. There were no windows, the only light came from ceiling level and in the gloom, the Kachinas, with their grotesque masks looked alive, menacing and unnerving.

Still expecting surprise of the fatal variety, he kept his hand on his gun. At last the servant stopped by a large and elaborately carved door, turned, and indicated that Chay was to hand over his gun.

There was no mistaking the gesture.

'Your mobile telephone phone too. Both will be returned to you when you leave.'

That was significant. He was to be cut off from any outside communication. He thought about the odds. In a straight fight, the young butler would have been no match for him, but doubtless his reactions were being carefully monitored from the television screens which he guessed were hidden in every room.

With a sigh, he did as he was told, consoled by the comfort of a second small pistol nestling against the calf of his leg.

A door was thrown open and Chay was admitted to a huge library with one wall of red rock. In it, long narrow windows had been carved through solid stone, throwing light into the room, which he realised had once formed part of an ancient cliff dwelling belonging to the Anasazi.

Although the windows would look like narrow fissures from across the wide valley, the view from inside this room was magnificent. It also revealed that there was no way anyone could approach the house from this angle without being observed. Straight ahead was a flat expanse of ground, beautifully cultivated— the garden Kate had described—and on the far side was the sheer rock face where she and Luke must have stared down into the secret valley.

He guessed that his luck had run out. They were here all right, somewhere in the house, held prisoners. Why he had been allowed inside, he would presently find out. How he was to get them out was another matter.

While he was thinking about it the door opened and to his great surprise and relief,

Kate came in, free and apparently unharmed. He ran towards her, searching her face, waiting for her tale of terror, her sobs of delight at his arrival, once more in the role of rescuer.

*   *   *

Even as Chay prepared to give Kate reassurances he guessed that he might not be able to substantiate, far away in his office in Blackhawk, Rita was receiving a fax from Flagstaff. Its contents were brief but so shocking that she quickly dialled his mobile.

Why didn't he reply? Why hadn't he had the damned machine fixed?

She felt sick inside, sick with anxiety, frantically searching her mind for what on earth she should do next.

Why did he never listen to her! Headstrong fool that he was, Chay had walked straight into a trap.

CHAPTER TWENTY-ONE

Touch might drive the Dream away...

SE-TEWA, Indian Love Letters

Before him, Chay saw neither fear nor terror registered on Kate's face. There were no sobs

304

to console, she was quite calm, smiling politely, as might befit one confronting an unexpected, but not unwelcome caller.

He grasped her hands tightly, reassuringly. 'You're not hurt?'

'No. Why should I be?' Her bewildered look indicated that the question was rather silly. 'But what are you doing here?'

Keeping his voice low in case the place was bugged, he said, 'I've come to get you both out of here. Where's Luke? Can we get to him?' he demanded urgently.

'He's upstairs, playing chess.' Her calm, slightly surprised attitude irritated him profoundly. Did she not realise the boy was in mortal danger?

'You should have stayed with him.'

'But I'd be in the way. I don't play chess.'

What on earth had happened to the woman? Her mind seemed elsewhere. Wait a moment. He considered her carefully. She was behaving like someone in shock. Sedated, or on drugs. Could that be it? Could they have drugged her?

He felt furiously angry. 'I don't know how they tricked you into coming here, or what they've told you, but you are in terrible danger.'

She laughed in his face. 'You must be mad, Chay.'

He regarded her grimly. That was it. They weren't going to harm her yet. They'd told her some convincing pack of lies.

They'd deal with Luke first. Kill her later.

305

He took her arm. 'You shouldn't have left Luke with them. Don't you know what they are going to do with him—and with you?'

She shook her arm free, said sharply, 'Chay, listen, I don't know why you're here, but I assure you we are quite safe. And happy,' she added with a wistful smile, and going over to a drinks cabinet she poured out two glasses and handed one to him, as if this was an ordinary social occasion.

She smiled at his doubtful expression. 'Here, take this. Whiskey. The very best.' She indicated the sofa. 'Let's sit down. I must anyway, my legs are still weak. I still can't believe it. Please, Chay,' she said patting the sofa beside her, 'I feel unnerved when you stare down at me so accusingly.'

'Kate—honey—I'm not accusing you,' he said gently, trying desperately to reach her, to get through this miasma of pleasantries and make her aware of the danger. 'I've been almost out of my mind worrying about you and Luke.'

'Have you?' That seemed to surprise her. 'That was very sweet of you, Chay, but you didn't need to worry about us.'

He tried another tack. 'I gather that you've found Mr Wilderbrand at last.'

She laughed, a trilling sound of delight. 'I have indeed.' She shook her head. 'I don't know where to begin, Chay. It's like some miracle. Like some dream that you think could

306

never come true on this earth. And then quite suddenly, it's all real, it all falls into place and it's happening to you. Until you walked in and brought me back to reality, I had to pinch myself frequently, thinking this is where I wake up. As I told you, Luke is upstairs, playing chess. With his father.'

* * *

It already seemed to belong to another age, that moment four days ago when Kate had stood in this room, trembling with apprehension, her arm protectively around Luke.

The door opened and a tall man entered, his back to the light.

He bowed. 'Welcome to my home, Miss Fenner. You and your son.'

She would have known the voice anywhere. Although the face was badly scarred and his body skeletal, the angel eyes of an ancient icon, strangely luminous as if a light shone behind them, were the same eyes that she looked into every day on her son's face.

Sean Doe. She blinked.

The man walking towards her was undoubtedly Sean Doe, risen from the dead. At first glance Kate thought she was dreaming. The dream long abandoned that had haunted her nights and awakened her with tears during those first years after Luke's birth, that some day a miracle would happen and he would walk into her life again. He would take her hands and say: I love you. I never died. It was all a terrible mistake.

But this was not the dream world, he merely took her hands and said, 'I trust you have had a pleasant stay in Blackhawk Creek and that you both found your accommodation comfortable.'

And she knew that she dreamed alone. He had not the slightest idea who she was.

The once beautiful young man had aged far beyond thirteen years. Neither she nor anyone else, for that matter, had been certain of his real age in his days of fame. It had been a closely guarded secret like everything else about him, but she had guessed that he had been less than thirty. Now he looked ravaged, his face lined. In a curious way he looked as old as Redfeather, but not nearly as fit, she thought.

She knew now why they called him 'Viejo'. Only the remarkable bone structure of his face and those strange amber eyes told her that this was Luke's father.

'You're not Mr Wilderbrand,' she whispered. 'You're Sean Doe.'

Lips tightening grimly, he stepped back, displeased at recognition. Obviously, he had intended keeping up the assumed identity.

'You are mistaken—' he began.

'No.' she interrupted sharply. 'No. We have met before. Thirteen years ago. I heard you sing at the Albert Hall.'

He unbent a little and smiled, relieved and flattered that she wasn't going to make any trouble, that she had been just one of his fans. One of many girls who thought his love song was for them alone, who wept and yelled and threw their underwear onto the stage when he sang. What a coincidence! He straightened his shoulders, raised an eyebrow mockingly, a touch of long abandoned vanity.

'That was a while ago.'

Kate nodded. 'Afterwards you rescued me from under a cab's wheels. I was running across the road and it was raining. Don't you remember?'

He inclined his head, nodded vaguely. He didn't remember and was merely registering polite interest.

'You took me back to your hotel,' she whispered.

His mildly attentive expression froze for a moment and then changed into an apologetic shrug.

'Did I, my dear? Well, well.'

That told her enough, that she had been just one of many girls he had taken back to many hotels after many concerts. The only difference was that she had carried his seed after that lover's night and had borne him a son.

'The Albert Hall, eh?' A deep sigh and he continued, 'That was my most successful tour. And my last,' he added sadly.

He looked across at Luke who, keen to escape this grown-up conversation, was eagerly examining the bookshelves. 'There is a lot to tell. Would you like the boy to stay?'

'Please,' she said, perhaps her sharp tone indicated anxiety, for he smiled again, the slow, lovely smile that had seduced so many other females before and doubtless after her, in the short time he had left before the plane crash.

'There is no need to be afraid, Miss Fenner. My men like to be mysterious and dramatic, it's a game with them. My apologies for allowing them to scare you, but you have my assurances, you are in no danger. You are here in this house as my guests.'

Kate looked at Luke, who had turned towards them, conscious that he was being discussed.

Sean held out a hand. 'I am Mr Wilderbrand, Luke. Congratulations on winning our prize holiday. I hope you are having a very happy time with us, and I'm delighted to have this chance to meet you in person.'

Luke's radiant excitement said that the delight was mutual.

'Are you happy here? Is there anything you need?'

Luke shook his head.

'How would you like to extend your stay? Indefinitely perhaps.'

Luke frowned across at Kate, who said, 'You are very kind, but I don't think that would be possible. I had to get him special absence from his school.'

Looking at him, Sean turned quickly to Kate. 'Can he not speak for himself?'

'No,' said Kate putting an arm about Luke's shoulders. 'There was an accident at the school. A fire. He was terribly shocked. I've been told it will take time for him to get his speech back.'

Sean was silent, his glance, now brooding and intense, held Luke. 'How extraordinary,' he whispered and then turning to Kate, 'it will return, you know, don't worry, for that was exactly what happened to me after the plane crash.'

He sighed and she saw again how tired, how old he was. Or was it the memory that made him look sick and frail. He put his hand on the back of a chair, an old man's gesture for support.

'Shall we sit down, Miss Fenner?'

Kate took the seat opposite and when he remained silent, she said, 'Everyone thought you were dead. Four bodies were found.'

He shook his head. 'I never died. It was all a mistake.'

Kate closed her eyes. The dream again.

(I never died. It was all a mistake. I love you.)

Only the last vital three words belonged to a fantasy and sadly would never be said.

The door opened and the old Indian who had admitted them returned. Sean spoke to

Luke.

'You must be hungry. Tomas will find you something good to eat. And maybe a look at the garden. You'd like that, wouldn't you?' he added with a smile.

Kate's look gave assent. When the door closed on them Sean went to a cabinet, poured two drinks and handed one to Kate. 'It is only tequila and tonic, is that all right?'

As he handed her the glass, she again recalled vividly that first drink they had shared in his hotel as she emerged from the shower, shivering still, wearing his bathrobe.

(Gin and tonic, is that all right?)

Trying to sound sophisticated she had accepted it, unused to a half tumbler of almost undiluted gin which took her breath away and made her head spin. She would never know if Sean Doe had already planned his seduction by first getting her tipsy.

He sat down beside her and held up the glass. 'Cheers, Miss Fenner. Welcome to the House of Anasazi Fire.'

And, twisting the stem in his hand he said, 'About the plane crash. We took on an extra passenger who told us he was one of a film crew and had to get to Arizona quickly. Would we take him with us? When we were airborne he hijacked the plane and held a gun to the pilot's head. We discovered his real destination was Mexico.

'We ran into a terrific electrical storm over

New Mexico and were struck by lightning. I remember thinking "this is the end" as we hurtled down out of the sky, and as we hit the ground my door burst open and I was flung free. I was knocked out,' he touched his scarred face, 'my head bleeding but I was still alive. No bones broken.

'When I ran to the plane and tried to drag the others out, I yelled and shouted at them to hurry. But no one heard me and I knew they were all dead.

'There was a terrific explosion which threw me into the air but again, I escaped death by some miracle. I was knocked out, concussed, but still alive. When I came too, there was only the burning wreckage and, lying a few yards away, the briefcase the man had carried. I had no idea who I was and had a vague notion it might belong to me.

'When I opened it the four million dollars it contained weren't much help at that moment, lost, alone and injured in some wild place near a red rock canyon.

'My cheek had been ripped open—it hurt so badly—and there was no shade from the blazing sun. I must have passed out again because the next thing I knew I was being carried on a travois by Indians in warpaint.'

He looked at Kate and shook his head. 'You have no idea how terrifying it was. I seemed to have floated back in time. While I had been out of my head—delirious—they told me my body

313

had been taken over by an Indian chief who had disappeared a hundred years ago.

'I was too weak and ill to care and they took me to one of their hogans and nursed me back to health. All kinds of herbs, sand paintings, healing ceremonies—God knows what went on—but it did the trick. My body recovered, although I still had no memory and I was dumb.'

Again he stopped and glanced across at Kate. 'Like your son, shock had made me speechless. I had another shock in store when I discovered that they regarded me as their lost god, their chief Atala who was immortal and had promised he would return from the skies. And not only had I done that but I'd apparently talked to them in their own language while I was delirious, telling them I had come back to save their people.

'I was grateful to them for helping me, but I wanted to get back to civilisation as quickly as possible. Naturally I had no memory of the bit about being their lost god either, but it seemed that the conclusive proof they needed was the tattoo on my upper arm.'

He rolled up his sleeve. 'Here, look.'

Kate remembered that too from the night they had spent naked in each other's arms. Like a child's drawing of a man playing a flute.

'It's Kokopele, the flute player. From a petroglyph in the Anasazi caves, they told me. I knew I had little hope of escaping; that they'd

314

never let me go. I was quite a prize, so I was resigned to believing their story about Atala. After all, that tattoo was a birthmark, and now I knew what it was and who I was—their god returned. I had no other memory to contradict their story.

'Most important of all, as far as I was concerned, I had in my possession four million dollars which would need some explaining away if and when I reappeared. They never touched it, you know. Money was of no interest to them. Or maybe they thought the gods had sent them that as a present, along with me.

'Anyway, my memory began to come back as I recovered, bit by bit, and then pretty well everything about Sean Doe. However, with no voice, a badly scarred face—their stitching left a lot to be desired—my career was over. I got my voice back too, but it's only a whisper of what it once was. I can hardly sing one blasted note on key. I decided that Sean Doe should stay dead. I must confess I became quite fascinated by the idea of Atala, and the life and lost times of the Anasazi. Another drink?'

Handing him her glass, Kate said, 'Are you Indian then? There were just the usual pop magazine and media interviews. But no one seemed to know for sure.'

He laughed. 'Precisely. Because I didn't know either. I might well be one of their lost tribe, the Atalos–Anasazi were scattered like chaff to the winds after the massacre.

'However, my earliest recollection is a Catholic orphanage in Brazil. I was about six years old, picked up off the street. One of numerous kids begging—and stealing, when they got older—for a living. Even in those days, children disappeared mysteriously. Perhaps the police had started killing them.

'I was one of the lucky ones. I was educated by the priests and in due course I became a choirboy. They discovered I had an astonishing voice and, when it broke, my tenor voice was even more remarkable. It gave me ideas that had nothing to do with going into the priesthood and Christianising poor heathen Indians. Good works were not included in my manifesto. So I left the orphanage to seek my fortune. I went to San Francisco.

'For a few years I scraped a living here and there. Somehow. Then I met by chance a man who became my—benefactor. Let us say,' he added wryly, 'that he adopted me for his own purposes. I was a valuable asset and he had me make a record. Almost overnight I was famous.

'My benefactor's name was Hank Wilderbrand, an emigré Dutchman. He had a jealous lover who didn't care for the young protégé, however. They quarrelled and poor Mr Wilderbrand was stabbed to death.'

He stopped and looked at Kate, to observe the effect of this on her. She could think of nothing to say and he smiled.

'You know all about my meteoric career. I won't bore you with details. But five years ago I bought this house half completed by a millionaire who went out of business. It was everything I wanted.

'But I was still intrigued with this idea that Atala had taken over my body while I was unconscious. I wanted to know more about him. I've learned a lot from my Indians. Their attitude to survival, for instance and to the landscape we live in. How it reminds us every day that nature will not bend to our will. As I was taught, the Bible tells us that man was given dominion over all the earth, but the passing centuries have proved only his folly, his misuse of what he was given.

'To the Atalos–Anasazi, the land is sacred, to be revered, it cherishes and enriches them, while to us it is a place to be subdued and conquered and broken. The sacredness of the land we live on is not some nebulous religious idea. It is encoded in our genes and it has helped us to survive. We don't love it by accident, we evolved to love it.'

Kate looked at him. Chay Bowman had said exactly those words.

'I thought for a while I had made the most wonderful discovery in the universe. I had found myself, my time and my reason for being,' he said, and listening to him, Kate thought how Redfeather would love this man.

His face had clouded. 'If only it were so. But

life's like that. You think you have it all in your hands that you are writing the scenario, then suddenly without warning, the scene changes.'

He was silent so long, Kate felt that he had forgotten her presence.

A tap on the door heralded Luke's return. As Tomas said some words in his own language to Sean, Luke ran over to Kate and took her hand. His eyes were bright, excited. He was having a great time.

'Luke wants to see the animals. It is a rule that Tomas has to get my permission first.'

'Are they dangerous?' Kate asked anxiously.

Sean shook his head. 'Not really. But for safety's sake let's say, some of the less domesticated ones are kept in cages. It is nothing really, no danger, but we have to take precautions.'

Sean watched Luke wave to his mother at the door, then with a sigh he turned again to Kate.

'That's a fine son you have.' And then curiously. 'Are you married—divorced?'

'Neither. I have only Luke.'

'I envy you. That is something I can never have.'

Mistaking his expression for regret, Kate said, 'You are mistaken. I have brought you something. Luke is your son.'

CHAPTER TWENTY-TWO

Sometimes within the brain's old ghostly
* house,*
I hear far off at some forgotten door,
A music and an eerie faint carouse,
And stir of echoes from the creaking floor.

ARCHIBALD MACLEISH,
Chambers of Imagery

Anger, disbelief—the emotions that flickered across Sean's face at Kate's announcement were many and varied. But joy was not one of them. Doubt was the most in evidence.

'Wait a minute. You are telling me—that one night . . .' he stared at her.

'It was my first time. I wasn't prepared,' she whispered, aware that she was blushing.

He raised an eyebrow. 'A virgin, eh. That must have taken me by surprise,' he added mockingly.

She looked away, embarrassed by his gaze and not knowing what to say. The dream was never like this. Everything was sweetness and understanding, a rapturous reunion blessed with tears.

When he spoke it was in the manner of one who had given considerable thought to his words. 'I don't doubt that your intentions are good, Miss Fenner, but I'm afraid your story just isn't credible,' he said coldly.

She had never imagined that he would react in this way as she withered under his intense gaze. Her eyes filled with tears and for a moment he relented.

He laughed uneasily. 'I can only conclude that you have been mistaken.'

'I know what you're thinking, but I'm not lying. I'm speaking the truth,' she cried indignantly.

'And so am I. Paternity claims were not unknown in my short and varied career, but none were ever proved,' he added grimly and continued with a shrug. 'You see, it so happens that even legitimately I would have had difficulty in producing a child.'

Such a confession obviously didn't come easily. 'It was just another of the well-kept secrets that my reluctance to marry any of the women with whom I had relationships was because I had an abysmally low sperm count. Without going into the sordid details, the medical verdict suggested it was possibly the result of child abuse during my early years on the streets. Not that I had any ambitions then to be a family man. I'd seen enough babies and young children used and abused first hand not to yearn to add any more to the human race.'

He looked at her for a moment and his laugh was a little hollow as he continued, 'In fact, such knowledge was a boon and a blessing, a

God-given gift to the kind of life I enjoyed. An inbuilt form of contraception, if you like. However it was hardly good for the pop star's macho image.'

Again he paused, looking at her intently. 'I'm only telling you all this to prove that it made nonsense of those paternity claims. And I'm afraid that goes for you too, my dear.'

There was silence between them as, grim-faced, he waited for her response.

But there was nothing Kate could say. Whatever he believed, Luke had been conceived by him. She certainly was not going to deny that just to please him.

He was frowning, biting his lip. Her attitude was unexpected, he had imagined a demand for money would follow this startling announcement. There was something about this woman, incredible as it seemed, as if for a moment he remembered the night in the rain, the hotel room. Yes, she took a shower, wore his bathrobe. She was so young, innocent. And she had worshipped him.

'You say, that it happened only once and I made you pregnant . . .' he began cautiously.

'We made love several times,' Kate whispered, 'during the night.'

'Did we now?' He brightened. 'And was my performance satisfactory? No problems?' he added a trifle anxiously.

'It was wonderful,' she said softly, not wanting to go into details but remembering how ecstatic she had been.

Painfully aware of his brooding gaze, she wondered what thoughts, what doubts were filling his mind. Was he considering her confession as yet another scheming woman's attempt to trick him, to get money from him. Fighting against her sense of outrage at this injustice, Kate realised that he had to be naturally suspicious having gone through this scenario with many other short-term lovers in his years of fame. What right had she to expect one insignificant incident in his life was enough for him to believe her story?

He went and poured himself another drink without offering to refill her glass. Perhaps he thought she'd had more than enough already.

Coming back across the room, he stood looking down at her.

'Well, well. Strange fate that all unknowing I should have brought you out here,' he said, rubbing his chin in a gesture she remembered. 'You see, we can prove that you're telling the truth.'

He gave her a moment to digest the significance of that before asking, 'What is your son's blood group?'

She told him, adding, 'It's very rare, I'm told.'

He sat down heavily. 'Very, very rare,' he repeated. 'And it is one we both share. Does he know it?'

'He does indeed. It has been a constant nightmare all his life that if he had some

322

accident he might not be able to get a blood transfusion.'

'And, of course, that is how my Indians reached him. They believe they can prove that there are only a handful left on earth who share it. A group who are the only surviving ancestors of the Atalos–Anasazi and those who are related to them by blood. It is unique to them, unknown in your western world.'

It was obvious from Kate's puzzled expression that she hadn't a clue what he was talking about.

'Tell me about your forebears,' he added curiously. 'Did any of them travel in this part of the globe?'

'My great-grandfather was a sea captain from Scotland,' said Kate. 'From one of his voyages to North America, he came home with a so-called Spanish child bride—'

'Which part of America?'

'He'd been taking emigrants to San Francisco.'

'Ah,' said Sean. 'Go on.'

'His marriage caused quite a family rift—he was a widower with grown-up sons and according to family hearsay she couldn't speak a word of Spanish or a word of any kind, for that matter. The rumour was that she was dumb. She never got a chance to prove them wrong as she died in childbirth—with my grandmother—a few months later.'

'So she was a mute, too.'

323

Kate gave him a quick look. He apparently thought that important while she had never given it much significance until now. Perhaps there might be some inherited weakness or sensitivity in the vocal chords.

'I wonder if this so-called Spanish bride could in fact have been the child of Atala and the Anglo minister's daughter.'

'I have their wedding photograph. Taken in Scotland. It's poor quality and she's rather out of focus. She doesn't look particularly Indian.'

'If you mean like the ones you see in movies, neither did Atala, from what I hear he looked more Aztec than Apache.'

'You'd probably be very interested in the letters my neighbour at the creek gave me. They were written by Janet Glencaird to his grandmother, Lily Rhodes. They mention Atala.'

Kate dug into her capacious bag that held tickets, brochures, notes, pills. 'I have them here.' She had been carrying a copy to show to Mr Wilderbrand, guessing that he would be interested.

Sean held out his hand eagerly. It didn't take long for him to read them and Kate realised that for her nothing had changed.

Watching that down-bent head, so altered from the vibrant young man of the past, she knew she still loved him and always would. Every man she had met and liked and tried to love, to efface the memory of him, had been like faint shadows in the sun. The only exception might have been Chay Bowman if fate hadn't thrown Sean Doe across her path once more.

'Forever yours'. She thought of the song and was afraid to close her eyes, to look ahead and lose these precious moments with him. Afraid to think of the vast greyness that would sum up her life after he sent her back to Blackhawk Creek and she returned to Edinburgh, to the lonely, empty years stretching ahead without him. She knew that nothing so precious as these hours would come in her life again or would ever exist beyond the walls of the House of Anasazi Fire.

'Forever yours. Forever yours.' The words seemed to echo around her, from some other forgotten time and place she had known and only dimly remembered, but whose poignancy was inescapable.

'Forever yours.' The words of his song.

'Forever yours.' The words Janet Glencaird had used to sign her letters. Her heart raced. Could there be some connection? She was thinking rapidly, about to tell him, when he looked up at her, smiling.

'This is fascinating stuff. It all makes sense from what I have heard. The minister, Janet's father, refused to marry them and Atala killed him at the altar. That was the beginning of the end, the death of the Atalos tribe.'

Handing her back the papers, he said, 'There

is an odd coincidence here. Atala was brought up to believe that his immortality lacked the powers of reproduction. In every other way he seemed human, but no one ever saw him die. He had apparently been alive for hundreds of years.'

'But that is impossible, surely,' said Kate.

'So we are led to believe from our understanding of the human life span, but according to legend, as soon as he began to show signs of aging, every thirty years or so, he underwent some kind of ancient magic, or ritual sacrifice. They gave him the heart of a young boy. Someone the age of Luke,' he added casually.

Kate's own heart began to beat wildly. She was beginning to see what all this was about, the pattern was taking shape. The horror of her situation and Luke's danger began to dawn. Tessa had told her two boys had been killed by an escaped cougar; one had had his chest ripped open.

Dear God, what did they keep in that garden zoo, locked in cages? And what if the killings had not been a beast's claws but a man with a sacrificial knife?

The door opened and Tomas appeared alone bearing two glasses on a tray.

'Where is Luke?' she demanded.

'Ah, refreshments,' said Sean, handing her a glass as if he hadn't heard her question. 'Drink this. It is very special. You will never have had drink like it. Nectar made from the rare flowers that grow in our canyon garden. Flowers that are now extinct elsewhere in the world.'

'Where's Luke?' she demanded again.

'Luke's just fine. Come on, drink, while it's cool.'

Obediently she took a sip, expecting it to be excessively sweet. It was not. This was like champagne, the best champagne anyone could ever imagine.

Sean was talking to Tomas in their own language.

She put down the glass. 'Where is Luke?'

Sean smiled. 'Luke is just fine,' he repeated. 'No need to worry about him. He's having a splendid time playing in the garden. He loves the animals, it's a child's paradise out there.'

Pointing to her glass, he said, 'Drink it now, while it's still fresh.'

*   *   *

When Kate opened her eyes, it was dark outside. She was stretched out on the sofa where she had been sitting when she fell asleep. The empty glass had gone. She felt confused, her reactions suggesting that the nectar drink had been drugged.

Beyond the window on the far horizon the tiny glow of lights indicated the town.

Luke! Where was he?

She heard a movement and saw he was sitting in an armchair wearing headphones, listening to music.

'Thank God,' she sobbed in relief and stumbled over towards him. She took his hands. 'I wondered where you were.'

He indicated the garden and, as he pointed, she noticed a plaster on his wrist. Taking hold of his hand, she said, 'Did you fall?'

No. He shrugged. The door opened and Sean came in.

'He didn't hurt himself. They merely took a sample of his blood at my orders.' So he hadn't believed her.

'Just to make sure it was right for me,' he said.

'Are you ill?'

He avoided her eyes. 'There are occasions when I need to have blood transfusions.'

The thought of using Luke's blood chilled her. That and the kind of doom in Sean's voice which told her that the dream was over and she was at the beginning of the worst nightmare she could ever have imagined.

CHAPTER TWENTY-THREE

Everyone is born homesick for heaven, the trick is finding the way back.

BARBARA WOOD, The Prophetess

Sean looked down at her. He was smiling. 'I do apologise for our nectar. It sometimes makes you sleepy, until you get used to it. I thought you'd like to know that the car's ready to take you back to Blackhawk whenever you like . . .'

Kate looking quickly at Luke, watched the elation fade on his face. He was so disappointed, he was having a lovely time.

Their emotions had registered with Sean. He sat down opposite them.

'Kate—may I call you that? You don't mind? How would you both like to stay—just until tomorrow. We have so much to talk about,' he laughed, 'and we're practically related, you know.'

She had to decide quickly, but before she could get her thoughts into order, Luke said, 'Please, Mum, please.'

Kate's eyes filled with tears as he put his arms around her.

'You've got your voice back, darling,' she said hugging him delightedly, unable to believe her ears. 'This is wonderful!'

Across her head Tomas spoke to Sean.

'Tomas says he's been talking non-stop out there.' Sean smiled. 'That's our first miracle of the day. Who knows what the next may be?'

Suddenly Kate's fears, her sense of danger evaporated and her heart overflowed with love for Sean and Luke, ashamed that she had been letting her imagination run away with her. No father would harm his own son. Sean did look quite ill though, he always seized every opportunity of sitting down, as if he was exhausted. Perhaps he was suffering from one of the many medical conditions where blood transfusions were necessary.

'You'll stay?' he said. 'Good. Tomas—'

Words she didn't understand indicated that rooms were to be prepared.

'Just for one night. Now that's settled, let's have dinner. Out there on the terrace, I think.'

The view was magnificent as beyond the cliff garden the sunset turned the rocks to crimson and the first evening star appeared.

The candlelit table was as romantic a setting as Kate's dreams could possibly have invented. And the reality was so much better, for Luke had never had a place in such fantasies. Now there was a sense of family as Luke was encouraged by Sean to talk about the animals he had seen.

'The fishpond's great and that fantastic room upstairs with all the television cameras screening the grounds. And, Mum, the greatest Internet you've ever seen,' he added wistfully.

Sean smiled and poured more wine. 'It was the Internet that brought us together. Some of my clever Atalos—and there are some with quite extraordinary powers—have mastered the secrets of what they call the World Wide Web. It's all quite beyond me. I never was any good at figures, left it to accountants to deal with my contracts. Never read a word of them, just took the money and ran.'

'That machine is great,' said Luke not wishing the conversation to be diverted. 'They've got into science and medical channels—'

Warming to the theme Luke pronounced on the superb quality of weird-sounding stations, to be gently interrupted by Sean who laughed and said, 'Hold on, hold on! Your poor mother is baffled and so am I.' Then turning to Kate, 'Well, I suppose it's all more fun than the eternal hospital dramas on TV.'

'They're great too,' said Luke reverently. 'I'm going to be a scientist. Or a doctor. I haven't made up my mind yet whether I want to travel in outer space or to save lives.'

Sean smiled indulgently. 'Does your mother know the conditions of the prize you won?'

Luke looked across at Kate. 'I tried to explain it all to her but she was more interested in what I had won than how I did it,' he sounded faintly disappointed in this lack of grown-up interest.

Kate laughed. 'Come along, Luke. All I knew was that it was some sort of health quiz and if there were too many correct answers the winner would be decided by a draw.'

'Have you any idea how many got it right?' When Kate shook her head, Sean said softly, 'There were hundreds of right answers, from all over the world.'

Kate turned to Luke and said proudly, 'You're even more clever than I thought, darling. And lucky too, having your name pulled out of the hat.'

Sean shook his head. 'Not quite. Mr Wilderbrand's deciding factor was who had the rarest blood group. A lot didn't even know what their group was but Luke did know his, and he won. It's an excellent way of tracking down one's blood relatives.'

But the true significance of Sean's remarks and the reason for this strange competition were taking another sinister form in Kate's mind.

Luke, having finished off the dessert by a second helping, began to yawn and Sean, smiling across at Kate, signalled to the young Indian who had served them.

'Bed perhaps, young man. You've had a long day,' he said

Luke didn't argue, yawning again, he kissed his mother goodnight. And Kate bit back tears, touched by the sight of him shaking hands so solemnly with his new-found father.

'Shall we walk?' As Sean escorted her through the dusky gardens the once red rocks were ghosts in the moonglow.

'You are lucky to live in such a lovely place,' said Kate.

'Am I? Yes, perhaps you're right. It has a kind of magic, and sometimes I want to believe what they told me about my rescue after the plane crash, that I am their lost Atala—his reincarnation, his second chance to put right the past.'

He sighed heavily and looked at her. 'Sometimes I'm no longer sure who or what I am. It's as if—as if I'm being directed, stage-managed by some powerful influence outside myself.'

Again he paused. 'I know I'm not making much sense. What about you? We both share some of Atala's genes. What were your parents like?'

'I never knew them, they died when I was a baby. I was brought up by my step-grandmother and, according to her, I had a very odd mother and grandmother.'

When she described Florence and Jetta's passion for collecting pretty stones and rocks Sean interrupted, 'Don't you see the connection? They carried the Talisman, the spirit of the red rocks and they were both, even as children, trying desperately to get back.'

When she looked doubtful, he went on,

'Don't you see, Kate? It makes sense.'

'I suppose so,' Kate frowned. 'My mother did paintings of strange landscapes, sort of abstract, according to Gran, weird shaped rocks and skies—'

'And she had never seen Arizona, had she?' Sean interrupted eagerly.

'No, never.' The significance of Gran's story slowly dawned on Kate. 'She also said they both talked to themselves, in what she called a daft secret language that nobody could make head nor tail of.'

Sean stopped, rested against one of the shaded seats. He seemed breathless. 'Navajo,' he whispered. 'Or Atalos–Anasazi. That's what they were talking. This is wonderful.'

As they walked on, slower now, he said, 'At least you know about your early life. As for me, this deal with Atala, whatever they call it—was the first supernatural experience I've had.'

'But if you are Atala—and that just isn't logical—where have you been for the past hundred years?'

'God knows. I have no memories before the orphanage. A complete blank, nothing about parents who had either died, or were too poor and with too many kids already, abandoning me. That happened a lot—still does. Besides, as none of the other kids I ran around with had anyone either, we were all fairly cynical about family life. I'd never heard of Barrie's Lost Boys until I was in show business. I must say, it had a certain amount of appeal.'

'*Peter Pan* is Luke's favourite. We go every time it's on stage or at the cinema. He even tried to fly once. From the bed end—with disastrous consequences. He sprained his ankle.'

Sean laughed. 'Poor lad. What about you, Kate, with all those odd ancestors you must have had some fairly weird psychic experiences?'

'Not really. Just what Gran called "stepping off the time cycle". *Déjà vu.* Everyone has that at sometime or other. I had nothing strange until I came here. A couple of times I seemed to be the minister's daughter.'

'Atala's Janet?'

'Yes,' Kate replied reluctantly. 'And I think I saw Atala.' She explained how she'd seen him on the terrace, his hands pressed against the window. She didn't add that his eyes were Luke's, and also Sean Doe's.

'Well, that certainly wasn't me,' he said. 'But it is strange, as if he was trying to tell you something. Could be he was trying to get us to meet?'

Suddenly short of breath, he took her arm. 'Let's sit down here.'

This was the third time he had rested since they walked in the gardens and the darkness only partly concealed how tired and drained he looked.

'I think I'll turn in shortly. You must excuse

the habits of a recluse. I'm not used to entertaining exciting guests and having fascinating dinner parties any more. You don't mind? There's television in your room and I'm sent all the latest novels from Phoenix. Take your pick.'

As they went inside the house and climbed the stairs, he said, 'We've put Luke in with you. He might wake up and be scared in a strange house.'

His words implanted in Kate's mind the disappointing certainty that with Luke in her room there was no possibility of Sean visiting her. He held out his hand.

'Goodnight, Kate. Sleep well.' And as he turned away. 'Thank you for coming—and for bringing me Luke.'

Kate awoke once during the night to a reality better than any dream. Sean was alive, he was here in the same house.

She buried her face in the cool pillow, longing to hold him in her arms, her body aching to be near him.

*   *   *

When she opened her eyes next morning Luke's bed was already empty. She heard voices below the window. Sean was breakfasting on the terrace.

She breathed deeply, throwing her arms wide to greet this beautiful tranquil morning.

At five thousand feet there was a slight breeze to temper the heat which would be considerable by midday.

At her approach, Sean looked up. His ravaged countenance suggested that he had slept poorly, his hastily donned dark glasses doubtless a throwback to the time when a pop star would not readily face his fans or his mirror after a heavy night.

Welcoming her as she came out to join him, he said, 'How are you this morning? Good. There are so many questions I thought of during the night. So much we have to talk about. First of all, tea, coffee? Help yourself, that's the rule.'

He regarded her across the table. 'You look wonderful. Did you sleep well?'

'I did. I feel so well in Arizona, better than I have ever felt anywhere else.'

'Is that so? Scotland is pretty fantastic too. What about Edinburgh? What about your life there? I'm curious,' he added buttering a slice of toast.

She told him about the guest house, about the Royal Mile, Holyrood Palace, Arthur's Seat and the extinct volcano in her front garden.

He listened absorbed. 'I toured there once, you know. Didn't have much time to see around. That would be before your time, I guess.'

'No, it wasn't. I was thirteen and it was during the Edinburgh Festival. My pocket

337

money wouldn't rise to a seat for the Usher Hall.'

He smiled wryly. 'That was too bad.'

She didn't add that she had walked back and forth outside the theatre hoping for his autograph but that they'd organised a quieter entrance. All she got was a glimpse of her idol wearing dark glasses in the back of a car, waiting at the traffic lights in Princes Street. Not much, but enough to keep her in dream fantasy material, walking on air for weeks. The intoxication of being in the same town, just yards away from him on the same street, breathing the same air.

'You lose your sense of touching earth, of belonging, when you live in cities,' he said. 'I always hated that—the crowds, the traffic— even if I loved the applause. To the Indian the land is sacred where your birthplace is. There are special prayers to be said, to the smallest plant, the rocks and sand, even the tiny ants. And all these sacred thoughts and prayers are there locked in the landscape. Every tree and rock and anthill has this prayer memory.

'They say that if you listen to the landscape you can hear what the spirits are saying. That's the fundamental difference between us and the white people who are never satisfied, eternally restless. They never stay in one place. They keep moving around, the landscape means nothing to them. They wouldn't dream of praying for ants, or for any small creatures. As

338

for rocks, and trees and mountains, they never give them a thought. They are just a background that might be useful to exploit. They see a river and build a dam, a factory follows, then cars and planes. They find uranium and decide to make a bomb.

'We believe that all this inventing is heading for trouble, inviting something terrible to happen, and that one day these inventions will get out of hand, turn round and destroy us.

'Our medicine men warned long ago that the white man's greatest ambition was to rival the Great Spirit by creating things in his own image. They didn't know about computers or the ultimate robot. To them it was just a prophecy, a warning that we now know is reality. Man's desperate bid to use inventions and machines that turn everything into something else, and an even wilder invention as they try desperately to overcome nature. But they've invented a world with an artificial mind they can no longer control, a mind that will survive by turning on its inventors.'

Kate noticed that as he spoke he had changed, shedding the last vestiges of the pop star the world remembered, his unconscious use of 'we' identifying himself with these lost Indians.

'This search for better technology will go on until man destroys himself. He can't stop this race now, for weapons of self-destruction, as well as for engineering the human genes so that man can outwit death itself. Such arrogance is breathtaking, if man can do it, then he will do it.

'Why should they care whether they are destroying the earth and killing its heart. We see this as the ultimate blasphemy. The earth that gave you birth, gave you its sacred flesh. It feeds you, gives you shelter, gives you animals and plants. We believe that the earth is the mother, the sky the father—'

Luke's excited laughter from the garden below them stemmed the tide, brought him back to awareness of Kate, silently listening.

'I'm sorry. I get carried away sometimes. It's all so damned important and yet no one seems to care, no one seems to see what is going to happen. Like this hole in the ozone layer, the ice-caps melting—'

He shook his head, apologised again and Kate knew that his philosophy was that of Redfeather and the Magic Men too.

*   *   *

In the days that followed there was no mention of her returning to Blackhawk.

She had only to ask of course, but Sean presumed rightly that she wanted to stay, that Luke was happy and grateful for his new surroundings.

Daily talks and slow walks in the garden became the pattern of Kate's existence. A brief

340

sojourn of happiness she prayed would never end. All she asked was that she should never wake up to the thundercloud, which she felt still lurked offstage, waiting to extinguish the sun.

CHAPTER TWENTY-FOUR

—how fortunate are you and i, whose home is timelessness: we who have wandered down from fragrant mountains of eternal now

to frolic in such mysteries as birth and death a day (or even maybe less)

e. e. cummings, *Selected Poems*

Before the cloudburst, the only shadow on Kate's horizon was Sean's constant weariness. He seemed to fight against perpetual tiredness, his great outbursts of animation came as they puzzled over the story of Atala and Janet, and the baby who they now believed was Kate's great-grandmother.

When he wasn't talking, how still and silent he was. Not once did he try to kiss her, not even the social cocktail party peck on the cheek when they said goodnight. And yet she never stopped hoping as each day brought them closer and made her parting from him more unthinkable.

341

On the third evening of her visit, she suddenly remembered Chay, whom she had thrust to the back of her mind. She must let him know where she was.

After dinner she said, 'I have to make a phone call to Blackhawk.'

Sean frowned and she added, 'A friend who doesn't know where I am. He'll be concerned. I haven't got his phone number.'

Sean looked relieved. 'If you give Tomas the message, he'll deal with it, put it through our fax machine.'

She wrote the brief message and she thought that his face clouded as he read it. 'Chay Bowman? He's a friend of yours?'

Kate smiled at the annoyance he was unable to hide. Could it be that he was jealous? 'We met when I arrived in Blackhawk. He has been very kind to us—'

She didn't feel like going into details, with no wish for that persistent image of Chay's disapproving face which refused to be banished entirely, echoes of his dire warnings destroying this lost world she had found so unexpectedly with Sean Doe.

*   *   *

She was awakened early next morning by Luke, who was getting out of bed, assisted by Tomas. She tried to ask him what was wrong but the words were too heavy to spill out of her

342

mouth. Her eyelids were leaden, refusing to stay open.

Presumably he was just going to the bathroom and thankfully she drifted back into sleep.

When she next awoke Luke was back in bed, one arm lying across the sheet. There was a plaster at the inside of his elbow, his arm below showed bruising.

She jumped out of bed. They had done something to Luke, and again she had been deliberately drugged with that last glass of wine, or the coffee.

Luke's eyes opened. He looked wan, depleted. 'It's all right, Mum. They took some of my blood, that's all. Just like a blood donor, like the grown-ups do. It didn't hurt at all.'

'You wait here, darling. I'm going to see Sean about this.'

'I'm coming too, Mum. I want my breakfast.'

Sean was having breakfast on the terrace as usual. Waiting until Luke had finished his bowl of cereal and departed to look at the fish, she confronted him about taking blood from Luke without consulting her first or getting her permission.

'A blood transfusion, Kate. That's all,' Sean interrupted gently. 'You wouldn't deprive me of something to keep me alive a little longer, would you?'

'What do you mean, a little longer?' she asked in a horrified whisper.

343

He regarded her steadily for a moment. 'I am dying.' There were no heroics. He knew that the time of pretence was past. 'Even blood transfusions are too late to save me now. My tissues and muscles are decaying, a kind of rapid aging, a slow dying. The only thing that can keep me alive now is a new heart.'

Letting the words sink in, he nodded towards the house. 'They think I am Atala. They want to believe that I can save their world. By giving me a new heart, but it's too late—'

'No!' she exclaimed as his brooding glance flickered towards Luke playing below the terrace. And she knew in that glance what he felt. Letting the words sink in, he nodded towards the house. 'They think I am Atala. They want to believe that I can save their world. By giving me a new heart, but it's too late—'

'No!' she exclaimed as his brooding glance flickered towards Luke playing below the terrace. And she knew in that glance what her mind had rejected.

There had been other killings like the ones she had heard about. Now she knew the truth. Sean Doe had been responsible. In his name, on his orders the Magic Men had kidnapped and murdered two young Indian boys. But in vain, she guessed, for whatever followed afterwards, their blood groups were wrong, their hearts would have been rejected.

But now, for the first time, their efforts would be successful. For Sean Doe and Luke had the same group. Whatever other ancestry they shared, whether they were descendants of Atala or not, no one could ever prove.

Sufficient to know that the man the Atalos regarded as their lost god had everything on the premises for one last attempt.

Somehow she found her voice. 'You gave orders to murder those Indian boys I heard about in Blackhawk.'

He shook his head. 'It was not my idea.'

'But you condoned it. How did you think they would be right for such a diabolic experiment?'

'Kate,' he took her hand. 'Kate, don't you understand. I have no rights here. I am a prisoner too. Someone to be experimented on.'

She ignored his plea for clemency. 'How did they get away with it?'

'One of the Magic Men is also the school doctor. He has access to blood samples, records and so forth. There is a helicopter on call, a hospital room rented long ago in Phoenix and kept in readiness for such delicate surgery when I need it, when a heart is available.'

Pausing he regarded her horrified expression. 'Money can buy so many things, Kate. Life and yes, even death.'

He smiled across at Luke, who had returned but was leaning over the balustrade playing with a tiny lizard and taking no interest in this grown-up conversation.

'They know the boy and I are the same group.'

'And that he is your son.'

'No, Kate, only we know that. I approved of the blood transfusion, but nothing else will happen to him. I cannot condone a life, even my own, extended by another human's murder. I gave strict orders that it was never to happen again, after they took the first boy two years ago. I tried to make amends by donating a substantial sum of money to the foster-parents.'

He paused, took a deep breath. 'My orders were ignored. The two brothers—another disaster. Then they brought me a child prostitute—a rentboy. I'd have nothing to do with that. I'd been there myself once,' he added bitterly.

'Then inevitably there was a weak link in their chain. The man, a Mexican responsible for the kidnappings, died—in a faked car accident—because he wanted money or he would tell all.'

'What would happen if they found out that Luke is your son?' Kate asked, dreading what the answer must be.

'They have two options. Of setting the transplant operation in motion, or of letting me die and making Luke their god. It's all part of their magic, don't you understand? They don't think like you do.'

As he spoke Kate was remembering Luke's strange powers of resurrection, the blood and genes he had inherited were strong, not only from his father but from the child who had been Atala's daughter.

'I have very little time left, weeks rather than months. I want the boy to live, not as a captive god, for that is what I am, captive to a mad dream. They will never let him go if they suspect the truth.'

He shrugged. 'What have I to lose? The quality of my life is over now. I am glad I have met my son and I can go in peace, with my body—or Atala's body—destroyed beyond hope of resurrection.

'As for you, Kate.' Smiling, he leaned over and took her hands. 'You have grown very dear to me. Nothing in these past years here has equalled the few days we have had together. I may be fooling myself but I felt sometimes that it was mutual. Is it?' he asked gently.

'Yes.'

'Thank you.' He smiled. 'For me it is like being reborn, but sad, too, knowing how much I have lost that I can never have again.'

He laughed lightly. 'If only we could reverse time, I would marry that innocent young girl I seduced in the Savoy.'

He regarded her intently as she held her breath, willing him to say the words. But he shook his head. 'No, not now. It's too late—for both of us—'

'Sean,' she protested.

'No, Kate, no. I have nothing to offer as a husband. All I could promise is that you would be a penniless widow in a very short time. That surprises you, doesn't it? The millionaire recluse in the House of Anasazi Fire. The money I once had has long since disappeared. As I told you, I am no good at figures, if the money had been more carefully invested I would not now be facing bankruptcy. But the magic powers of my Indians don't extend to being good book-keepers. Every day sees a growing mountain of bills and court summonses.'

She listened, horrified, as he continued. 'If I survive much longer it will be to go to prison. My only consolation is that death will pay off my creditors, that I will be past prosecution and scandal long before the first police car rolls up the hill.

'I have made provision for my Indians. Willed that the house be turned over to the state. They'll recoup some of their losses, I dare say, by turning it into an expensive resort hotel. Ironic, isn't it? As for my people here they must return to life outside with the provision I have made for them; they won't starve, although they may well continue their quest for the Talisman, their search for another redeemer.'

*   *   *

At the end of Kate's account of her meeting with Sean Doe, Chay picked up the telephone on the table. He dialled his office where Rita confirmed what Kate had told him.

348

The real Mr Wilderbrand had died long ago

He turned to Kate and asked gently. 'Well, are you ready to go now?'

She shook her head. 'I'm not coming with you, Chay. I'll—we'll stay here with him until—until—as long as it takes and he doesn't need me any more.'

He knew he could never make her change her mind. 'What will you do then?' At her tragic expression, he took her hand. 'Will you come to me?'

It was a crazy question. Knowing she did not love him, perhaps now she would never love him made no difference. He remembered reading somewhere that in every relationship there is one who kisses, one who is kissed; one who loves, one who is loved. Like Matt Hepple who had loved Janet Glencaird.

'We could make a life together,' he said desperately.

At last she smiled, touching his cheek.

'Maybe, Chay, maybe.'

And she kissed him.

*   *   *

Chay drove back to Blackhawk and prepared to wait, trying to live as normally as possible, taking on clients, attending to his business, as all the while his eyes turned constantly in the direction of the House of Anasazi Fire where his hopes for a future grew more and more remote.

As he watched and waited, so Rita's eyes turned constantly towards him, while her own hopes for a life with him also dwindled. Whatever happened in the House of Anasazi Fire, she knew now that he was lost to her.

There were no winners in their sad story, and she had merely speeded up the ending by informing the cops in Phoenix of the true identity of the fake millionaire.

*   *   *

When the police cars rolled up the steep canyon road leading to the House of Anasazi Fire, they had to move aside to allow another car to pass. A young woman with long fair hair and a boy aged about twelve were being driven back towards Blackhawk Creek.

Still far distant from the house, they smelt burning petrol. As they increased speed and, cursing, negotiated the tortuous road through the canyon and along the drive, they were met at the front door by a servant who informed them that Viejo was dead.

Early that morning, he had thrown himself from the cliff that according to legend was the site of the Temple of the Sun God.

The eerie sound of Indian drums echoed through the quiet afternoon. An old servant pointed to a funeral pyre in the garden far below. They were already burning his remains.

'Those were our master's orders,' Tomas

said, his eyes red with weeping. 'His last wishes.'

*   *   *

Kate sat in the car with her arm around Luke, trying to obliterate that last terrible scene. The servants rushing to the balustrade overlooking the cliff garden at dawn. Sean's sick and broken body, as he had planned, destroyed beyond the possibility of resurrection. In death he became one with Atala. His spirit, his beliefs and hopes were the talisman, the mirror for another redeemer's coming.

Some day she would tell Luke who had slept through this terrible drama, either by accident, or deliberate stage management with drugged chocolate. Tomas had carried him out to the car still asleep, before returning to light the funeral pyre.

All she had now were her last minutes together with Sean before he retired for the night.

Taking her hands he had said, 'I want you to leave Blackhawk Creek, go back to Edinburgh. Let our son have the chance to grow up like any other youngster, but one who has the chance to bring some good back into this sad world.

'He has the gift of healing, he will use his powers well. There must be others like himself, and he will find them. Before it is too late,

351

together they will bring help and hope to the world and healing to our poor wounded earth.'

For only the second time in their lives, he had taken her in his arms and kissed her.

'I love you, Kate. Forever yours.'